Life is Better with You

Shannon Paige

For Dino.

You exceed any book boyfriend I could ever write.

Contents

Chapter One

Aspen

"Did you know gargoyle erotica is a thing?" I ask Luke, my friend and colleague, from where I'm lounging at my office desk. He actively shudders but doesn't turn around.

"Why do you know that?"

"Because it's Christmas and I'm procrastinating." I hoist my feet onto the desk, the weight of my Doc Martens making my screen shake. "There are whole subgenres of monster romance novellas."

Luke, his brown hair curling into his forehead and his shirt uncreased even on a Friday, swivels his chair and grimaces at me. "You know, normal people procrastinate by scrolling social media."

"*You* procrastinate by finding more Warhammer figurines for your desk," I say, waving a hand at where he has a select few standing to attention by his mouse. They change every so often, so I can only guess how many he has at home. "So who is the weirdo in this situation?"

"You," he says immediately. "Or did you miss the part where you said *gargoyle erotica*?"

I shrug. "Maybe it would broaden your horizons."

"I really don't think my horizons need broadening," he retorts playfully.

I gesture at him and his starched shirt and tie and sharply creased pants. He's a classic good boy, and I like to tease him about it. Last year, my first Christmas at PAYDAY, I got him an Excel mug that reads *Freak in the Sheets* because I knew it would make him blush.

What I didn't expect was for him to use it religiously every day. He's owned it, even if his ears still turn red when someone reads the mug's inscription.

He is *definitely* not the kind of person who would encounter monster porn in the wild, which is why it's my moral duty to make him aware.

"Get back to work," Luke says, glancing behind me. "Kai's coming."

Kai, or Malakai for full, is our boss and one of Luke's best friends. I roll my eyes. "You can't just use Kai to—"

"To what?" Kai asks from behind me.

I spin my chair to glare up at him. And up. Kai has the sort of build you expect from Captain America. Except he's Polynesian and resembles some sort of Samoan god come to earth.

"Unfair. You snuck up on me."

"Are you slacking?" he asks, eyes narrowing.

My screen dims, and I knock my mouse to bring it back to life. "No."

"Liar." He leans comfortably against my desk, oblivious to the way Amy, one of our in-house designers, is glaring at me. "Which means I don't feel bad asking for this."

"For what?"

"A project."

I groan. "It's Christmas."

"Think of it as a chance to expand your repertoire." He grins, white teeth flashing. "We're looking to expand PAYDAY into Asia, starting with China. Which means you, my great cybersecurity guru, have a bit of research to do."

I groan, dropping my forehead against the desk with a *clunk*. PAY-DAY, Malakai's baby, is a new payment system, similar to Venmo but more secure and with fewer consumer fees. We've been expanding a lot recently, and whenever we expand into a new country, there are a whole bunch of new laws I need to take into account when updating the app's security.

And China? Yeah. Their cybersecurity laws are on a whole other level.

"I wish I'd gotten you for Secret Santa," I grumble, my voice muffled against the desk. "I'd have gotten you a T-shirt saying World's Worst Boss."

"I'd have worn it with pride." He claps me on the shoulder and disappears into his office, leaving me to sulk.

Some Friday evenings, I teach coding classes at a high school downtown, aiming to encourage more young women into STEM. My goal is to make it more commonplace for women to have jobs like mine and to be viewed as experts *even though* they possess breasts and a set of ovaries. Revolutionary, I know.

Right now, though, I'm positive it's a mistake to promote working in STEM. No one should do it. It's a terrible job. The worst.

I raise my head and make my eyes as big and pleading as possible, but Luke ignores me, pretending to search for an error in his code when I know it was working two seconds ago.

"No," he says, not even glancing at me.

"Not even if I threaten you with gargoyle erotica?" I scroll back through the Buzzfeed article I had been looking at. "This thing has links."

"I can wear headphones."

"You *could* help me with the mammoth amount of work Kai has just thrown at me."

"It's your job. I don't even work in security." An excellent point. I hate it.

I huff a breath and fold my arms. "It's not the security part that's the ballache; it's the research." Pitching my skills against would-be hackers is where I thrive. Looking at our systems from the outside and trying to crack a way inside—that's the exciting part. It's a beautiful puzzle to assemble, all those pieces slotting together not-quite-perfectly.

Firewalls I can do. The challenges that arise from machine learning and artificial intelligence tools are *interesting*.

But researching foreign cybersecurity regulations that I'll have to magically navigate while simultaneously protecting us from an increasing number of cyber adversaries as PAYDAY gains prominence on a global scale?

Really, really not my thing.

I check the clock. Only half an hour before the office closes early for a Secret Santa gift exchange and karaoke party at El Tio's Cantina. Definitely not enough time to achieve anything. Although Luke, overachiever that he is, is still focused on his code like his life depends on it.

I roll toward his desk, the office carpet quieting my movements enough that I can slide right up to him. "Hey," I whisper in his ear. He jumps, knees jolting against his desk and knocking over one of his little figurines, some kind of alien warrior. He's meticulously painted each one, and he once confessed that it's something he does when he's feeling stressed. It's calming, apparently.

Sounds like the kind of thing that would have me starting a fire so I could burn both the figurine and the paint, but whatever floats his boat.

He rescues the mini warrior and inspects it, then glares at me. "Aspen, are you allergic to working?"

I smile sweetly at him. "Want to get a coffee?"

"How many have you had today?"

"Who's counting? *Grandma*." I roll my eyes but a playful grin escapes.

"It's Granny to you, thank you. And it's way too late in the afternoon for me. Maybe you should go to therapy to come to terms with your crippling caffeine addiction."

"Says the man who starches *and* color-coordinates his shirts and socks."

"Monster porn," he says, grimacing. "I never thought I'd hear *that* coming out of my mouth."

"It was incredible," I clasp my hands in a praying gesture. "Please say it one more time. I want to feel the power of corruption."

"Weirdo," he says, but he's smiling now.

"I refer back to the shirts."

He prods my side, and I double over, swiping at him.

"Get back to work," he says. "And I mean actual work, not looking up obscure erotica."

"Teacher's pet." I ruffle his hair, grinning as he immediately fixes it, and roll myself back to my desk. And sigh. It's not that I *don't* want to work. I love work—usually. Even when Kai gives me dumb research assignments.

But tomorrow, I'm flying out to New Jersey to see my mom, and I've been on edge all day. The last time I stayed with her (on the couch, mind you, because the guest room is filled with junk she doesn't want to clear out), we ended up having a fight so bad, I still wake up feeling both frustrated and guilty.

That was last Christmas. I don't have faith that this Christmas will be any better. My stomach is in knots at the thought of going back to that dingy house and playing nice for a whole week. But she reached out and invited me, so she's trying, in a way. I guess I can try too.

I pull up Michael Franti on my phone and stick my earbuds in, letting his upbeat voice fill my head and my heart. Then, with a sigh, I go to fetch another coffee.

**

El Tio's Cantina is possibly one of my favorite places in the world. Once, long ago, it was a hot spot and had mariachi bands perform on the weekends, but the years haven't been kind, and now it survives mainly on the weekday corporate lunch crowd. The stage is now set up with karaoke to entice patrons. Cheesy as it is, we like it. In fact, one of our favorite games, which we invented during a team-building event we had last year, is karaoke roulette. Kai bought a tabletop wheel and customized it with different musical genres, and whatever category the wheel lands on, you have to perform. And instead of a book listing the available karaoke songs, there's a repurposed advent calendar hung on the wall with the corresponding categories pinned to the pockets. Inside each pocket are a bunch of songs written on popsicle sticks. The singer has to pick blind.

The roulette wheel keeps our karaoke game fresh.

Paired with tacos that used to be one dollar before inflation, and five-dollar margaritas, it makes for the perfect evening. The team has been coming here every Tuesday for the past two years I've been at PAYDAY, and probably the three years the company existed before then, and it's one of my favorite traditions. Only beaten by my monthly wine-and-s'mores nights I have with my three best friends, where we talk about men and sex and the impending doom of a failing economy and existential dread. It's fabulous.

I wipe the grease from my fingers with a napkin as Kai stands on a chair and waves his arms to get everyone's attention. The time has come. The Secret Santa gift exchange.

This year, like last year, I got Luke. That should be fine, but I'm oddly nervous. The better you know someone, the harder it is to buy them gifts, as a general rule, unless they're family or lovers. Or, like my besties, you've known them forever. Luke is too close for me to give him something humorous this year, but he's not family. Not my boyfriend. Something sentimental or customized seems like too much.

My gaze lands on a huge-ass gift basket, neatly wrapped. There's a twenty-dollar limit, so it's probably filled with flavored popcorn or something.

I gnaw on the loose skin at the side of my nail, chewing it anxiously as Kai makes the same announcement he made last year: "Let's unwrap!"

Rick from finance dives in, grabbing a wrapped box and reading, "To Dan." Dan, a ruddy-faced guy from the sales department, waves his hand, and we all pass the gift along.

"Aspen!" someone calls, and next, "Luke!"

My nerves are back in full force as Rick passes Luke his poorly wrapped gift, and I almost don't notice as the basket is placed in front of me. I see now it has *Caffeine Addict* in swirling letters across the front, and there's a cute little pink bow -the same color as my hair- wrapped against the side.

This is ... weirdly thoughtful. Inside are a couple small bags of coffee beans with a typed note that reads, "These are my favorite brand." I take them out and turn them over. Ethiopian and—

My coffee inspection is interrupted when I notice an envelope tucked at the bottom. Frowning, I pick it up. It's totally blank, so I rip it open.

Michael Franti VIP concert tickets spill out onto the table in front of me. Two tickets. Black and white, the words blurring as I stare at them, my hand coming to cup my mouth. The sound that escapes me can only be heard by dogs and bats.

My hands are shaking. I think I'm having a heart attack.

These tickets are *at least* one hundred dollars for the pair of them. I've been wanting them *forever* but never persuaded myself to splurge on myself.

And they came inside a freaking gift basket?

Definitely having a heart attack. Am I breathing? I don't think I'm breathing.

"Who did this?" I wheeze, though I'm pretty sure I know. I've totally lost my cool, but I don't care as everyone looks from my face, which is probably as pink as my hair, to the tickets. "Oh my God." I look to Luke, the likely suspect, but he won't meet my gaze. Something on the floor has suddenly attracted his attention.

"Breathe, Aspen," Kai says. Amy pats my back. I'm choking.

This is a gift. From someone who *knows* me. I didn't think I'd get it from a bunch of guys who think smelling each other's farts is some kind of wit, but here we are.

My childhood dream of seeing Michael Franti in concert is finally about to come true.

Chapter Two

Luke

The gift basket was a gamble. Not because I didn't think she'd like it—I knew she would—but if she suspects it was from me, it would basically be a declaration of my feelings, and I'm not sure either one of us is ready for that.

It's not that she hasn't figured out I at least *had* a crush on her. But something unspoken, water under the bridge, is very different from a *declaration*. Especially as that's not in the cards for us now. We're good friends. We're good *as* friends. And yes, part of me wants more, but I've never wanted it enough to disrupt what we already have. Friendships have a longer shelf life in Aspen's life than boyfriends.

She squeals, holding up the tickets and kissing them, and Dan looks at me pointedly. He originally had Aspen for his Secret Santa, but when I heard him talking about it, I asked him to swap and swore him to secrecy.

She won't know, but this is the goodbye present I couldn't work up the courage to give her in real life.

Rick nudges me. "You haven't opened yours."

"Oh. Right." I slice the paper neatly up the middle and spread it wide. It looks like it's been wrapped in a car wreck. Way too much scotch tape and two mismatched sheets of wrapping paper stuck together. One has Santa Claus on it, and the other is a deep navy scattered with stars.

Already, I have an idea of who wrapped it.

Theoretically, any number of the guys could've done a job this bad. When Rick wanted to get an apology gift for his wife, he brought everything in and asked me to wrap it, joking that the sight of his wrapping would've made her more mad.

But to use two wildly unmatching scraps of wrapping paper and three tons of scotch tape? Has to be Aspen.

The T-shirt that falls into my lap confirms it. Aspen was the only one to even notice I sometimes wear eighties rocker tees on casual Fridays, and I don't think there's anyone else in the office who would get me a Led Zeppelin T-shirt, either. Except maybe Kai, but his idea of fashion doesn't exactly encompass band tees. He's all about high-end fashion and designer labels.

I glance up, looking for her at the other end of the table, and find she's watching me a little too carefully. When we make eye contact, she just grins and turns away.

That's Aspen. Not subtle, but undeniably cool about it.

I grab another taco and head across to the spare seat beside her, sliding the plate in front of her. "Thought you looked hungry."

"Thanks." Her eyes are doing that dazed, gleaming thing again, and it's hard to look away. "Can you believe this? Michael freaking *Franti*."

"You're a fan, right?"

She nudges me. "You *know* I'm a fan. The entire office knows I'm a fan." Her eyes narrow. "Was it you?"

I hold up my hands. "You can't defy the sacred laws of Secret Santa by asking."

"Dork." She chuckles and looks away again, picking up the taco and licking at the grease along the bottom. That shouldn't be hot, but somehow it is, and I force myself to look away before my brain can get too carried away.

Some parts of me have never gotten the memo that Aspen and I are *just* friends. Especially when she does things like this and makes me want things it doesn't seem she's interested in giving.

Kai twirls the chair beside me, sitting on it so his elbows are resting on the seat back. He offers me one of the beers in his hand. "Congratulations," he says, nodding at Aspen.

"Thanks!" She beams.

Of everyone in the office, Kai is the only one who knows the insane crush I've been carrying around for this girl.

Actually, he's the only person I've directly told about it. Mostly because two years ago, after Aspen joined the office, I turned down a promotion that included a transfer to California so I could stick around and see what might happen.

Much good that did me.

Aspen excuses herself to head to the bathroom, tickets now tucked safely into her black ripped jeans. I take a swig of beer. Then another.

"She liked it," Kai observes.

"I don't know what you're talking about." I am suddenly immersed in peeling the label off my beer bottle.

"Only you would be so lovesick you dropped a hundred dollars over the limit so you could see that smile on her face." He nods after her. "Was it worth it?"

"Yeah. Worth seeing it one more time before I head out." A grimace escapes my otherwise neutral facade, but I tuck it back under.

Kai nods thoughtfully, running a hand through his shoulder-length brown hair. He's taken it out of its usual knot, and Amy's stare catches on his Maori tattoos just poking below his rolled sleeves. Everyone stares at Kai like that. I should probably hate him for it, but I don't.

"Got everything situated and ready for your job transfer?" he asks. "I appreciate you doing this for the company. For me, especially."

I shrug. "I'm grateful for the opportunity. Thanks for offering it to me."

"That wasn't because I like you," he teases, nudging me. "And I'm not sending you out to San Jose because I like you. You're the only one I trust to do this."

I take another pull of my beer. "I know."

"You told everyone yet?" By everyone, he means Aspen. I've no idea if it's cowardice or stupidity, but I've been keeping my mouth shut about this whole thing. Aspen is my closest friend in the office, and I don't want to see her face when she hears I'm leaving.

This transfer is a great experience. A promotion. A new start. A *change* from where I've been feeling like I'm stuck in a rut. But when I look at her, I'm tempted to throw it all in the bag and stay just so I can continue being in her life.

That, more than anything, tells me I need to go. This isn't healthy.

Plus, I'm going at Kai's request, helping set up his office expansion in California, and it wouldn't be fair to him to back out.

We watch as Aspen heads back to the table, head aloft and so happy, it looks like she might cry.

Yeah, definitely worth it, and the best farewell gift I could think of.

She turns that grin on me. "Do you like your present, Luke?"

"It's great!" I don't have to feign my enthusiasm. Kai claps me on the back and heads off to terrorize some poor soul. "Whoever got it for me knows me pretty well, I think."

Her deep-blue eyes fix on me, and she chews her lip. "You think?"

"For sure." I smile back, hoping it reassures her that I like her gift.

Kai holds up his present, which is—surprise, surprise—a mug. He reads the inscription, "I'd like you better if you paid me more," and everyone roars with laughter. Aspen wipes her eyes and nudges my shoulder.

"I think Rick got that for him," she whispers, nodding to where Rick is sitting and looking pleased with himself.

"Did it look like it was wrapped by someone who only used their feet?" I whisper back. "Because if so, it was definitely his."

"I don't think it looked *that* bad."

"That's only because your wrapping skills are worse." I lean in and add, "I love it," before swiping the last of her taco off her plate and heading back to the bar. I walk past Amy, who has just unwrapped her gift, a pack of pens sporting demotivational quotes such as "it's never too late to fail" and "shit-show supervisor."

"I'm a designer," she complains to no one in particular. "I don't even *use* paper anymore."

I grin, thinking of all the memories I've made with this team over the past five years. I'm going to miss them.

***

By the time karaoke comes around, I'm three beers down. Half the office is drunk, and by the time the doors open to admit our partners and friends, we're well on our way to being raucous.

Aspen's three friends come in. I've seen them before, and Aspen talks about them the way she doesn't talk about many people—all big smiles and starry eyes and a loud, happy voice.

At the office, she's one of the guys, but with her friends, it's like she can finally relax.

I do my best not to watch her as she perches by the bar, legs kicking, big Doc Martens knocking into the old wood, and throws her head back to laugh.

"You should tell her," Kai half sings from behind me.

I don't break my gaze. "Or I could have another beer."

One of Aspen's friends—I think her name's Lina—throws Kai an admiring glance and whispers something to Aspen, who frowns, looks at Kai, and shrugs.

That's just Aspen all over. If she's even noticed any of us, she doesn't show it. Maybe she thinks we're all some kind of androgynous robots, built for our jobs and nothing else. Best friends, but not *guys*. At least, not the kind that she usually dates.

Definitely time for another beer.

"Your turn," Rick says, bringing over the roulette wheel. "Spin."

I flick the wheel and watch as it slowly comes to a stop on "90s Boy Bands." Here we go. I grab one of the popsicle sticks from the repurposed advent calendar and get the classic *I Want It That Way*. Aspen is busy enough with her friends that she hasn't noticed the roulette has been set up.

I climb onto the stage and grab the mic, the metal cool and heavy in my hands. By the bar, Aspen's finally stopped kicking her shoes and is looking in my direction. The music pulses around me as I start singing. I grew up on a steady diet of eighties music and classic rock bands, so this isn't quite my preferred genre, but I give it my all. Including some boy band dance moves for good measure. When my siblings and I were kids, we used to put on performances for our parents, and I've been singing for these guys ever since I first joined the company. This is familiar.

When I'm done, I give a sarcastic bow, and Aspen whoops. Rick brings her the wheel, thrusting it in her face. Her friends laugh and cheer her on as she spins. I step down from the stage, watching the colors, because I know what they all mean. Red, green, yellow, blue, purple, pink—each holding a different fate. Up to and including rainbow for Pandora's Box, which is a wildcard category. Anything and everything, from Josh Groban's version of "You Lift Me Up" to Madonna's "Like a Virgin," is a potential song. Everyone low-key fears getting it, but it's made for some of the best, funniest moments in the cantina's history.

But she lands on red. Epic duets.

I already know who she's going to point at before she does. "You," she says, finger directed straight at me. "Don't think you're getting off that easy." She pulls a popsicle stick from the calendar and reads it aloud for the whole room to hear. "'Just Give Me A Reason,'" she calls. "By Pink, featuring Nate Reuss."

Better than it could've been, I suppose. Last time, Kai got "Macarena," and credit to him, he killed it.

Aspen pretends like she doesn't want to get up onstage, but there's something about this kind of atmosphere that unleashes the rock star in us all, and she's no exception. Maybe she's even more into it than the rest of us—her family's background is in music, her voice is incredible, and she's definitely a bit of a diva.

That was something I didn't know about until we came here and I lured her onto the stage with the promise of free drinks for the rest of the month. Before that, she said she never wanted to perform. Maybe because she was new, or maybe because she doesn't like so many eyes on her. She hasn't said anything about it to me, but there's a birthmark across one side of her face, like spilled wine on a tablecloth, that she touches when she seems uncomfortable or self-conscious.

But I love it. It's so perfectly her, so utterly Aspen, that I couldn't imagine her without it. Wouldn't want to.

I hold out my hand and she takes it, letting me help her onstage. The lights dim, the music comes on, and the lyrics play across the screen opposite us. Aspen holds the mic to her face and croons the opening lines into it, her smoky voice perfect for the song, for the hidden hurt in it.

I almost forget to come in on my verse. When the chorus hits and we sing together in harmony, it feels like we were made for this. The rest of the world falls away as we sing, eyes on each other, giving the lyrics no more than a glance. The song wraps us in its glow, and I don't see anything else.

There's only Aspen. Only ever Aspen.

Times like this, I wish I hadn't decided to take the promotion. We could just stay like this, friends, close enough that I can see her smile—I can *make* her smile. She only gives a small piece of herself to her friends and coworkers, but it would be enough. The song ends, and she gives me a double high five. "Thanks, man," she says, giving me the grin she gives everyone. The feeling in my chest, the one only she gives me, loosens a bit.

No, I was right. Moving on was the right choice to make. I need to move on.

"Your fans await," I say, nodding at everyone cheering her on. For a second, she looks torn, but my phone buzzes in my pocket. I take it out and check the screen. JoJo, my sister.

Damn.

"You good?" she asks, frowning at me.

"Yeah, good. I've got to take this." I wave the phone at her, and she nods. Amy grabs Kai's arm from where he's talking to Aspen's friends, offering for him to spin the wheel next.

"Hey," I hear Amy say as I leave the room, her voice too high-pitched. "Our turn. I hope we get 'Classic Love Ballads.'"

In the corridor to the back of the karaoke room, I lean against a wall covered in peeling white paint. The bathrooms, with their blaring neon sign, are to my left, and to my right are the fire doors that lead into the alleyway.

This place is a dive.

But it's one of the things I'm going to miss the most when I move away.

"Hey," I say, pinching my nose as I answer the call. "What's up, Jo?"

"Why does anything have to be up for me to call?" I can practically hear the pout in her voice. "Maybe I just wanted to hear your voice."

"And did you?"

"Always." She laughs, throwing off the sulk. "But that's not why I'm calling. Did you know planning a wedding is one of the most stressful things on the *planet*?"

"You've told me six times now." I have a tally going. "This past week."

"*No.*"

"Yep. So, what's up?"

"No one ever talks about how much planning a wedding is."

"Actually, I'm pretty sure that's one of the number one things a bridezilla talks about."

She makes an offended noise. "*Rude.* It's not like you'd know any-thing about it. Unless you've got some news to share."

"Did Mom put you up to this?"

She huffs, and I rest my head against the wall. The beers have gotten to me, I think, because the world is very gently spinning. Kai is giving "Say Something" by Great Big World and Christina Aguilera a very half-hearted attempt, and Amy is hideously off-key. I wince.

"I was actually wondering if you've asked Aspen about the wedding yet," she says. "You know. As your plus one."

Asked Aspen. The world abruptly stops moving.

It was the stupidest lie I've ever told. Although, at the time, I didn't think it was a lie. Just a *wish* that Aspen would one day wake up and realize maybe we could have something great together.

Only, Mom took my harmless little wish and made it canon, and now my entire family thinks I've been dating Aspen since last summer.

Once I move, I'm going to have to create a fake breakup story. I'm in too deep to roll it back now.

"*And,*" JoJo adds, "Mom wants to know if you ever invited Aspen to Christmas like she asked you to months ago. You never gave us an answer."

Oh, hi, Aspen. Fun fact, my parents think we're dating, so would you mind visiting for a week to convince them that I'm not a sad loser who literally picked fabricating a girlfriend rather than confess that the one woman I want—you—has friend-zoned me?

I push off the wall and dig a hand through my hair. "Look, I don't want to discuss Aspen with you, okay? Just because we're dating doesn't mean she's any of your business."

"I'll get Mom," JoJo says, and at the same time, I hear a quiet "What?" from behind me.

I turn slowly, and there, obviously, is Aspen herself.

Chapter Three

Aspen

Luke's face flushes bright red. It's not exactly unusual—another reason I got him the Freak in the Sheets mug is because he's adorably awkward and blushes whenever I bring up sex. Except this isn't harmless teasing. He was talking about us *dating*.

It's not that I haven't thought about it. When we first met, before we became friends, before anything, I thought about it for a hot second. But then, I locked the thought so deep down, it hasn't resurfaced in over a year. Luke doesn't do casual flings. I don't do long-term relationships. I love my job too much to risk jeopardizing the dynamics. Case closed.

"Aspen." His tone is resigned, like *of course* he should've known I'd be there. He hits the end button and lowers the phone, holding his other hand out to me so I won't bolt. Which—fair. This is the kind of awkward situation I don't like to be in.

"You said dating," I say.

"Yeah, I know. But it's not what you think."

"We're not dating."

"I know we're not." He sends a quick look behind us, where Kai has pulled Lina onto the stage. She's been making all sorts of eyes at him, and either he's finally noticed or he's decided to be interested. Either option works for me. Kai's a good guy, even if he's a bit of a playboy, and Lina knows what she's doing.

Go get 'im, girl.

But that doesn't explain what's happening right here.

Luke's brown hair is standing up, and he drags another hand through it as he looks at me. Maybe I've had too much to drink. That's what you're supposed to do at work Christmas parties, and it would definitely account for what I overheard.

Except no. I definitely heard him say *dating*.

"Not here," he says, taking my wrist and tugging me toward the hallway. "Outside."

I trail after him, wishing I'd thought to wear something more substantial besides my black jeans and cream lace blouse. I left my cardigan inside. The air is cold when we step outside, and the last of the evening's light just touches the tops of the buildings around us.

He sucks in a breath and shrugs off his lightweight jacket, wrapping it around my shoulders. "Sorry," he says. "I know it's cold."

"Stop procrastinating and just tell me what's going on." I huddle in his jacket. It smells like him, all musky cologne and spicy warmth and that hint of pine.

"Okay, so." He clears his throat, obviously flustered, and I just stare at him. "You know my mom's been on my case, trying to set me up on all those blind dates."

I nod, because he's told me about them during our daily lunches in the breakroom, annoyed and frustrated with his mom's machinations. The kindergarten teacher his mom insists would be perfect for him has come up more than once, but for some reason, he's never been interested in pursuing her.

I guess that's not surprising, seeing as his *mom* is the mastermind.

"And now, JoJo's getting married," he says, and I nod again. JoJo's fiancé is being deployed soon, so the wedding got moved up. "And they've been asking me about my plus one and trying to set me up, so—because we hang out all the time—I said I was dating you, just to get them off my back." The flush on his cheeks deepens. "And . . . You know how I've mentioned Brittany."

Over the past two years, Luke has been amazingly close-mouthed about his dating history, but one drunken night at the cantina, he did briefly explain his long, tortuous relationship with his ex, which only ended a couple years ago.

"Yeah, the bitch."

"Right. And JoJo's best friend."

The pieces fall into place in my head. Finally. "So, she's going to be at the wedding."

"Yeah. Brittany's going to be at the wedding. *And* she's been hinting to JoJo that she's newly single again and could be my plus one. I can't have her trying to worm her way back into my life. I needed a concrete way to shut the idea down."

"So, you told them you were dating me," I say. It makes sense, even though my stomach feels weird. Kind of . . . uncertain. Like it's not sure whether to flip or to drop.

"I panicked. I'm sorry." He runs another hand through his hair, and it flops back across his forehead. I've told him a million times to get a haircut, though actually, I kind of like it like this. A fraction too long. A hint of disarray in his otherwise perfectly manicured image. "Don't worry; I've said you're busy over Christmas and you can't come to the wedding. They *know* that; they're just . . . on my back about having a date. And Brittany breaking up with her boyfriend has complicated matters even more." His sigh is deep, like it's coming right from his leather shoes. "According to Mom, 'Christmas is about family, being surrounded by the people you love.'" He mimics a high-pitched voice. "I think we're destined for a fake breakup pretty soon. I'll just ignore Brittany's flirtations, I guess."

The phrase *Christmas is about family* turns me inside out, and I'm suddenly nauseated, thinking about my own mom. *She* doesn't exactly do family time. She does boyfriend time, and sometimes I'm around too.

Sometimes I'm not. She pretends she cares, or even notices, but most of the time, I'm just not as important to her as whoever she's currently screwing.

Even though they're all assholes.

I bet Luke's family is nice. They'll sit around a big table and all eat breakfast together and maybe say grace before a meal. All his little nephews will wear starched collars just like him, and they'll all be lawyers someday when they grow up.

I dig my fingers into my pockets so I don't give myself away. This is a good, fun night, and I got Michael Franti tickets. The last thing anyone needs is a breakdown.

"Bad timing for a breakup," I say, trying to keep my voice light. "Can't you just say I have plans?"

"I've told Mom that. A half dozen times already. But although Brit isn't the only one I've dated, I guess several years of dating on and off makes people think it's a habit. An eventuality that we'll end up together permanently at some point." His laugh is hollow. "Which is not the case. We're done. *Done* done."

I give a half smile at his frustration. "If they think you're with me, they probably won't expect some dramatic get-back-together with Brittany, would they? When's the wedding? I'm pretty sure we can last that long."

"Ten days."

"We can *definitely* make it until after the wedding," I say, teasing him in his obvious discomfort. "And that way, your mom won't be tempted to force you into sharing your plus one with a nice girl she met from church. What's the latest one?"

"A librarian," he groans.

"I don't mind if you use me as your fake girlfriend to ward off the church-going librarians and elementary school teachers, the sluts. I'll be the ace in your pocket. Your shield to ward off Brittany advances." A thought occurs to me. "And hey, maybe you can pretend we had a blowup fight over the fact I didn't attend the wedding with you, and that can be your reason for ending things."

His posture relaxes a little as he contemplates that plan. "A nice, clean break would make it more believable. And Mom would definitely applaud breaking up with someone over that."

"Exactly. So it's cool. No need to pretend like I caught you out here dealing to minors." I grin up at him, and he gives a small smile back. "Anyway, it's pretend, right? No big deal."

Luke nods, the shadows across his face hiding his expression. "Yeah," he says gently. "It's just pretend."

"Great." A new song starts up, and I gesture back at the doors and the warmth of the cantina. "I should probably head back to the girls before I freeze. Here, thanks for lending me your jacket." I wiggle out of the sleeves, and push it back into his outstretched arms, and I'm suddenly absurdly cold without it. Without waiting for him to say anything, although I don't know there's much more to say, I head back inside to where my friends are singing and drinking.

Well, two of them are.

My three besties are what I call the "love dwarves": Horny, Happy, and Grumpy. Annabelle is Grumpy, despite the fact she's dressed to kill tonight. Her hair is in its natural afro; she's wearing black leather pants that highlight her long, long legs; and her red strapless top brings out the duskiness of her skin.

Gorgeous, but if ever a girl was the "mom friend," Annabelle's it. She had a heart-wrenching breakup five years ago, and she's never recovered. One day, hopefully, she'll find the right guy to sweep her off her feet, but even that probably won't stop her fussing over us.

Charlie, or Happy, is sitting beside Annabelle. Her auburn hair cascades down her back, freckles sprinkled across her porcelain skin, and she's wearing her signature bright smile. Her denim miniskirt shows off her prosthetic leg with the kind of confidence I aspire to have. Tonight, she's stepped out of her usual cowgirl clothing, ditching her hat and boots for a more feminine look. Sometimes I tease her for looking too like Jessie from *Toy Story*, but right now, she could be a model.

Lina is Horny, self-described, and she's already making moves on Kai, glossy dark hair falling over her tan face as she smiles at him. God, she's pretty. I have the three best friends a girl could ask for, and thinking about it makes my iron heart clang a little in my chest. Having them for roommates our freshman year at University of Utah was a blessing, and I'm grateful we've all found our way back to living in the Salt Lake Valley so we can hang out often.

"Girl, you look like you need two more of these," Lina says when I rejoin them, setting a margarita in front of me. Charlie glances behind me to where Luke is walking back inside, arms folded across his chest as he watches an approximate rendition of "I Will Always Love You" by Whitney Houston. Classic, but not when it's being mauled like that.

"What happened?" Charlie asks.

I down half my margarita in one large gulp, coughing as it threatens to go up my nose. Charlie raises her eyebrows, and I do my best to organize my thoughts and feelings.

Really, I don't mind that Luke has told his parents that we're dating. It's just . . . a little weird. We've only just breached that initial "I know him well enough I can buy him presents" but not into the "we hang out together outside of work." Sure, Luke and I come to team karaoke nights and message all the time, almost exclusively in memes and TikTok videos, but I don't hang out socially with anyone from the office. There are very clear lines you have to draw when you work in certain departments.

As the only woman in mine, I need to make sure all the barriers are firmly in place so no one can give me that look and ask what sort of favors I've offered in exchange for my career advancements.

Sexist pigs.

"Aspen." Annabelle sighs and shakes her head. "I recognize that look. She's thinking about the patriarchy."

"Again?" Charlie sips her margarita and crosses her good leg over her prosthetic. "You know you're supposed to have fun at these events, right?"

I roll my eyes. "Shut up." Quickly, I fill them in about Luke and his phone call, the fact that he said I was his girlfriend to his parents, and I'm about to get to how I'm feeling about it when Rick interrupts.

"Hey, Aspen," he calls. As one of the "'most senior'" (read: oldest) members of the company, he likes to take charge where possible. "Sing something for us, will you?"

I groan and roll my eyes, but I secretly don't mind. There's a rush that comes with performing that I can't just shove aside. It has a certain vulnerability, because no matter what you're singing, you're putting part of yourself into it. For ages, I was afraid of that vulnerability. But I've learned that embracing it makes me more resilient.

"Knock 'em dead," Charlie says, giving me a slap on my ass as I head up to the stage. I purse my lips as I wrap my fingers around the mic stand.

The room is busier now, filling up with a bunch of regulars who have nothing to do with PAYDAY. Some of them whistle and heckle. Jerks.

"How about another classic Pink song? 'Raise your Glass' seems appropriate for tonight," I announce, ignoring the roulette wheel in favor of doing my own thing. "In celebration of one of the best Christmas parties we've had at PAYDAY."

"Hell yeah!" Lina calls from where she's now perched on Kai's lap. "Sing the shit out of that song, girl!"

I blow her a kiss. "Love you."

"Damn right you do."

At the back, Luke has another beer in his hand and is leaning against the wall. He's like me in that way sometimes. I mean, don't get me wrong, I'm not exactly your shy, reserved type, and he is absolutely your shy, reserved type. But both of us always hover around the edge of big groups like this. Never quite committing to being part of it.

"Right, right, turn off the light," I sing, and start to sway. This is one of my favorites she's done because it's such a crowd pleaser. I lose myself to it, sinking to the depths of my range and pushing up higher for the chorus. The crowd is with me, and I'm enjoying the energy they're giving me.

"What happened to your face?" a drunk, male voice yells from the crowd. "Boyfriend slap you a bit too hard?"

It's not the first time I've heard something like that. People see the birthmark on my face and have this disgusting compulsion to comment on it, like I'm somehow less of a human being because I don't look like everyone else. Like a patch of my skin resembling watercolor abstract art on the canvas of my cheek, a splotch of pigment that makeup can't easily cover, is a valid reason to treat me differently.

As a kid, I hated it so much, I wanted surgery. I experimented with makeup and hairstyles to see what would cover it. People like this meathead taught me to hate myself.

But I'm done with that shit.

I stop the music and lift my chin, but before I can say anything, Luke is already there, towering over him, one hand on his collar.

I blink.

"Say that again, asshole, and you'll find out what it's like to be punched in the face," he says, his voice calm but with this edge in it I've never heard before. His gaze flicks to me, then back to the guy, the tiniest hint of a smile curling the corners of his mouth. "And I bet that mark won't leave you as pretty as she is, either."

Meathead stares at Luke, mouth gaping unattractively. Bet he didn't think Mr. Prim-and-Proper had it in him.

Neither did I, but holy hell. I'm speechless.

Luke tilts his head at the guy, smile dropping. "I bet you've just had too much to drink, right? You didn't mean it."

Meathead's mouth opens and closes before he shakes his head. Slowly at first, then vehemently. "No, no, no. Didn't mean it. Your girl's very pretty. Pretty girl." His words all domino together, tumbling out of his mouth and into a pile by his feet, confirming that he is, in fact, drunk.

"She's not my girl, but she deserves an apology," Luke says, still in that low, dangerous voice that carries. I shouldn't be able to hear it. Then again, the bar's deathly quiet, all eyes on Meathead.

This sense of warmth, of love, comes over me. Because every single one of those eyes is looking at Meathead with the same expression: disgust. They're on my side.

Luke is on my side.

Holy shit.

Kai appears on Luke's other side, and Antonia, the cantina's owner, strides through the crowd. Together, they escort the drunk idiot out.

***

I run my fingers along the salted rim of my margarita glass, half listening to Charlie, Lina, and Annabelle rate the guys in the office from one to ten. Kai, for obvious reasons—mostly because if he and Jason Mamoa were in the same room, he'd probably win in the looks department—comes in first place, but they can't decide who comes next.

Charlie has a soft spot for Luke, while Annabelle is arguing in favor of Dan. Maybe she has a thing for age-gap romances I didn't know about. Neither of them make sense to me, but like I say, I'm only half listening. Every time I close my eyes, I see that guy yelling at me again. Not the first time it's happened. Won't be the last. And I had a ton of people on my side today. But it still stings. After all these years, it definitely shouldn't, but my birthmark separates me from other people. Makes me look less—less pretty, less feminine, less *normal*.

Sometimes, like now, when my tipsy has overflowed into drunk, I wonder if that's why my dad left. He took one look at my face and figured I wasn't worth sticking around for. Even my own father didn't think I was lovable.

Lesson learned.

On the sticky bar, my phone lights up with an incoming call. For a second, I just stare at it, my body tensing before my mind catches up.

Mom.

Shit.

I could just not answer. That's especially tempting considering I'm supposed to be having a good time, and Mom knows how to take a good time too far and spiral it into getting arrested for a DUI, but I can't ignore her. She's my mom.

Charlie glances over and nudges Lina, who stops talking. All three of my friends watch me with wary eyes as I pick up the phone and answer.

"Hello?"

"Hey, baby." Mom always calls me that. I think her theory is if she *sounds* affectionate, it replaces the real thing. "How you doing? You good?"

"Yeah, I—"

"You all ready for Christmas?"

The only thing I'm ready for is chronic back pain from carrying the weight of holding this family together. "Sure."

"That's great, honey!" She sounds genuinely delighted. "I've been clearing out the spare bedroom for you."

"It's okay. I don't mind sleeping on the floor."

"Don't be silly, baby. I wouldn't make my little girl sleep on the floor."

Apart from all the other times it was too much effort to clear out the spare room. It's barely even a room. There's a bed, I think, under all the piles of crap she's collected over the years. Most of it is band paraphernalia. But I've never slept on it.

"Honestly," I say. "It's fine."

"Tim said maybe you'd like to sleep on the bed this time."

I go cold all over. Or maybe I'm hot. My heart is pounding in my chest, thudding against my sternum so hard I think it might crack. Something's cracking. I'm digging my nails into my palm, cutting into the flesh. My knuckles are white.

"Tim," I repeat flatly.

"Oh, we got back together, baby." Mom sounds happier about that than about the idea of me coming home. "It was just a silly fight."

Tim is her scumbag, good-for-nothing boyfriend. They've been off and on again more times than I can count, and the few times I've been home when they're on again, he's been real handsy with me.

"You told me that you guys were done."

"I was just angry, honey." She uses the endearment like a blade, sharpening it and slicing through my defenses. "You know I get mad sometimes and say things I don't mean."

"I bailed you out of jail."

"It was just a DUI," she says soothingly, like the fact that she drove off and got a DUI after their last blow-up fight (the one that had them breaking up "for real this time") is no big deal. "Anyway, we can talk about it more when you get to Jersey."

I shake my head. Tears sting my eyes. "I told you last time, I'm not coming if Tim is there."

"Aspen." The only time Mom uses my name is when she's mad or trying to guilt-trip me. Or both. "Sweetie, think about this. It's Christmas. I want to spend the holiday with you."

"Then don't spend it with Tim. I told you what he did last time I was there."

"It was just a misunderstanding, honey."

"Squeezing my ass and telling me he'd like to see my tits is not a *misunderstanding*, Mom."

Charlie hisses something, and Annabelle puts a soothing hand on my arm. I rein in my temper before I scream something obscene down the phone or tell her that I never want to see her again.

Her boyfriend or me. Every time she makes this choice, it swings the same way.

"Does that mean you're canceling last-minute?" she demands. "Three days before Christmas?"

Charlie scowls and mouths something obscene at the phone. I grit my teeth. "I told you last time that I'm not spending another night with him in the house. You knew that. If you decided to ignore me, then this is on you, not me."

She huffs, but before she can say anything more, I end the call and let my head flop down on the bar with a dull thud.

"I can't believe she'd do this," I say, though really, I can. "Now I don't have anywhere to go for the holiday break. I'm fumigating my apartment for mice starting tomorrow afternoon."

"Shit," Lina mutters and orders another round of drinks.

Charlie slides her arm around me. "You got nowhere to go over Christmas?"

If it's a choice between visiting my mom or staying in a toxic apartment, I would choose the apartment every time. But that's not really a choice. And death by mouse fumigation doesn't sound like the way to go. "Apparently not."

"My extended family is flying in tomorrow, or I'd invite you to stay with us," Annabelle says. "But there's literally going to be no room. You know what they're like."

"And I'm staying with Annabelle," Lina says apologetically, ordering herself a new drink. "My family has gone back down to stay with relatives in Mexico to escape the cold. Do you have a friend's place here you could crash at?"

"You can crash at mine," Charlie says. "My roomie's heading out on Christmas Eve, so it would just be you. Jason, next door, is coming to feed the cats, but I can tell him you'll be there instead."

Maybe it's worth braving my cat allergy to spend Christmas with five felines who despise my existence and who make me itch everywhere. But enough allergy meds can help with that, right? I could stock up.

The thought is so depressing, I let out a moan.

"Or," Charlie says, and by the tone of her voice, I know I'm not going to like what she has to say. "*Or* you could join lovely Luke."

"He's my second top pick after Kai," Lina says. "And the way he stood up for you to that guy? Girl, that was *hot*."

The room is spinning. How many drinks have I had? "He's *Luke*."

"He's a good guy," Annabelle says authoritatively. "And he's cute, in that boy-next-door kind of way. Kind of like Jim from *The Office*."

"Oh my *God*," Charlie the romantic exclaims, clasping her hands together. "You could be his Pam!"

"Guys, focus." Anyway, I think he's better-looking than Jim, in a nerdy kind of way, with those piercing hazel eyes and soft smile. Not that I would *ever* tell the girls, or they'd start planning our wedding.

Charlie shakes me a little. "And you don't have to *do* anything. Just eat home-cooked food and give him a hug or two when his family's watching. Dance with him at the wedding. Help him save face and out of the arms of his ex. It's the perfect solution."

I lift my head in time to see Lina take another shot. She wipes her mouth and chimes in. "*Or* you could have a bunch of hot, casual sex with a himbo. I would."

"He's not a himbo. He's exactly the opposite, actually. And you're just horny, as usual." My words are already slurring together, but when she slides a shot to me, I take it. I'm going to need it for this conversation. "And Luke is a work friend. A colleague." This is an important point, so I hold up a finger. "*Work friend*. I don't tread in those dangerous waters. Besides, he's not really my type."

"If anything, that's a compliment. We barely survived your nean-derthal-dating phase," Annabelle says, and fine, she has a point. My taste in men is about as good as a blind woman's taste in art. But I've been on a hiatus for the past six months, and it's been great. No men. No drama.

Sure, no sex, but a girl has other options, and my vibrator has been handling the drought just fine.

"You should do it," Charlie says, taking my phone and squinting at it. "Call him up. Say you'll do the favor. Like a Christmas charitable contribution or some shit. He'll be so grateful, maybe he'll do all that stupid research for you."

"Make it part of the contract," Annabelle says.

It's my turn to squint. "Contract?"

"You always have to walk into these things with a contract." Annabelle finds a greasy napkin, and Lina produces a pen. The two of them bicker over what terms to put on the "contract" while I mouth *help me* to the bartender. He shakes his head with a smile and turns away, so I'm left to think over my choices: cat allergy or fake boyfriend.

How the hell has my life come to this?

Chapter Four

Luke

It's easy enough to leave. After Aspen's performance, and that asshole's interruption, the vibe of the evening is spoiled. I only stay long enough to see her friends gather around her with drinks and comforting words, then head outside and order an Uber to pick me up.

I didn't exactly have a plan for telling her about my job transfer tonight. Two years of friendship, and a crush on my part, are about to end, and I can't figure out how to properly say goodbye. Verbally or emotionally. The gift basket was a start, but while she suspects it was from me, she doesn't definitively know.

What does it matter what your family thinks? I'm never going to meet them. It's just pretend, right?

Even the frigid wind doesn't take the sting out of those words. Stupid, yes. I hadn't expected her to be over the moon about the idea of fake dating me. I hadn't even expected her to *know*. But she wasn't anything except surprised and confused and maybe a little weirded out.

Last sign I needed to extinguish the flame my heart's been carrying for her. No more. It ends tonight.

Maybe when I get back to work after the holiday break, I'll call in sick the last week before I move. Work from home. Kai won't mind.

The Uber pulls into my driveway, and I step out and let myself into my house, slipping off my shoes and leaving them by the door in the space left for them. I flick on lights as I go, grab a water bottle from the fridge, and sit in front of my PC. The purple and green lights gleam at me from under the desk, and as I switch it on, rainbows flash across my keyboard. The water in the cooling system sloshes, and the screen lights up.

With any luck, the guys will be on tonight, and I'll lose myself in a game or two. My semi-packed bags mock me from the bed.

Discord shows me Kai is already online, along with another of our old college friends, Chase, who's already playing *Phasmaphobia*. I'm more in the mood to shoot something—*Call of Duty*, maybe—but ghost hunting will do.

"Hey, man," Kai says when I join their voice chat. "Made it home safe?"

I twist the cap off my water bottle and chug half of it in one gulp. "Obviously."

"You guys spend too much time at work," Chase says.

"Just because we have colleagues we want to spend time with," Kai retorts, though I hear the smile in his voice. He's proud as hell of the culture he's created at PAYDAY. "And colleagues with hot friends."

"Lina?" I ask. "Thought you were going to take her home."

I can almost hear him shrug. "Aspen needed her more than I needed to get laid."

"How long's it been now?" Chase asks. "Three days?"

"Five, actually. It's been a real drought."

Chase snorts, and I join his game room, picking a map and checking the loadout. He's got the difficulty on insanity as default. Whatever. I just shrug and take another swig of water.

Honestly, I shouldn't be feeling so down about everything. Sure, I'm leaving and never gave this thing with Aspen a shot, but what was I expecting? I've seen some of the guys she's dated. Bike leathers, tattoos, potential criminal records.

Maybe not felons, but one guy was for sure the leader of a motor-cycle gang.

"What about you, Luke?" Kai asks. "I saw you guys headed toward the alley. Did you finally tell her?"

Chase laughs, immediately knowing who he means. "That he's been pining after her since forever? What do you think?"

"Actually, it's a little more complicated than that." Briefly, I run them through the conversation with my mom and what Aspen over-heard—and then what I told her.

When I'm done, Chase whistles. "Damn, dude. Sounds like a crazy night."

"Yeah. It was."

"You should've asked her to come along with you," Kai says. "Just be straightforward with Aspen. Ask her if she has plans and if she would mind coming with you to the wedding. To help you out as a friend."

"Yeah, like she'd *not* have plans. Also, that would undermine my decision to get over her and finally move on." I ready up in the game and cough pointedly. Chase loads us in, but once we're in the truck outside the school map, Kai starts the conversation again.

"Look, I know you haven't had the best experience with women, but you've liked her for years, and you're about to move away. What's the point in playing it safe? Shoot your shot, and if she turns you down, you don't ever have to see her again. And if she goes for it, you've just gotten yourself an awesome girlfriend, dude."

I select a thermometer, an EMF reader, and a torch. "I've had girlfriends before, you know."

"Yeah, but how many have you been *this* into?"

"You're a solid guy," Chase says. "She'd be stupid not to go for you."

"We're friends," I remind them both. "And if I don't screw this up by asking her out and getting rejected, we'll stay friends. That's more important."

"Maybe she just doesn't know you're interested," Kai muses.

I give a short laugh. "I'm pretty sure she knows. Or suspects, at least. I think. But like I said, we're friends."

"I have friends I fuck," Kai says. "That's a thing."

Aspen might have friends she sleeps with too, but they're not her friends for long. In the two years I've known her, she's never been involved with anyone for more than a few months. Even if she *did* want to date me, which she doesn't, it wouldn't end well.

"That's different," Chase says.

"Also, I'm leaving for San Jose in a few weeks," I remind them. "So that's a solid no on the dating front. *Or* the friends-with-benefits front, Kai."

He starts to say something when my phone goes off, distracting me, and the ghost finds us. We die.

"Game's bugged, I swear," Chase complains as we load back into the menu. "Ah, it was a Deogen. Would've found us, anyway."

I'm too busy staring at my phone to care about what ghost it was.

"Aspen's calling," I say.

Kai makes an exasperated sound. "So, answer it. And if you don't tell her you're in love with her, I swear—"

I slip my headphones off and accept the call. "Hey, Aspen."

Noise clatters in the background. Sounds like she's still at the bar. I put her on speaker so I can hear her better.

"Luke?" Her voice is slightly thick around my name.

"What's up?" I keep my tone light so she doesn't know that my heart is pounding out of my chest. Either she's hurt or she's calling about me telling my parents we were dating. Dread feels sticky in my throat, and I have to breathe around it.

"I have two choices," she slurs. "Cats or a fake boyfriend."

The dread congeals into confusion. She's *definitely* drunk. I release a long breath. "What?"

"I have a contract. Lina wrote up a contract. Do you agree?" There's a note of vulnerability in her voice that makes me want to wrap her in my arms and never let go.

"Aspen," I force myself to say, shoving the feeling down, "I don't know what you're talking about, and you're drunk." The last thing I need right now is her saying something she regrets, so I gently add, "Sleep on it. Take some time and think about what you're trying to tell me."

"I know what I'm trying to tell you." Her voice is impatient now, though still slurred. "I'll come and be your fake girlfriend and keep Brittany away if it means you'll give me somewhere to stay over Christmas." There's some chatter, someone prompting her in the background, and a giggle that definitely doesn't belong to Aspen. My breath is trapped at the top of my chest, and I feel dizzy.

She can't mean this.

Past Luke has been waiting for years to hear an offering like this from Aspen. This would have meant the world to him. But Present Luke, the person focused on his career advancement, intending to move out of state and get over his crush, is struggling with the Sophie's choice now presented to him.

"You help me with Kai's stupid research," she says. "And there are no cats."

"Cats?" I croak.

"At your house." She gives an impatient sigh. "And no sex."

My heart stops entirely. I hear its absence in my ears. "No . . . sex. Aspen, I—"

"It's you or the cats. If you have space. If you don't mind—shit." The vulnerability in her voice increases, widening into a gulf that I could fall into. "You do mind. I'm sorry, I shouldn't have asked—"

"Wait, wait. I wasn't saying I didn't want to—" I pinch my nose and take a breath. "Are you suggesting you join my family for the holidays as my fake girlfriend?"

"It was a stupid idea."

Honestly, yes, it is. There's no way it can go well, and the thought of having her there, having her so close *pretending* to be with me when she obviously doesn't feel the same way, is torture.

But if I tell her that it's a bad idea, she'll think it somehow reflects on *her*. Like she's somehow undesirable.

I think of the asshole from earlier, and my jaw clenches. "We just need to think this through," I tell her. "Don't you have Christmas plans?"

"Canceled," she says abruptly. "And I have a cat allergy. So, no options currently."

If she has nowhere to go, that changes things. I can't force her to be alone over Christmas, and I know my mom will accept her with open arms, no matter how last-minute it is.

I've worked with her for two years. In close confines. She's been within touching distance, or actually touching me, more times than I can count. I've been fine.

Well, not fine. But I've survived it. I can survive this, too, even though I'm not sure if it's more of a good deed or self-flagellation.

"Say yes," someone yells down the phone. "If you let her down now, I'll—"

"Shut up, Charlie," Aspen says. "Luke?"

Here goes nothing.

"Sure. Sure, I'd love to have you along. My family will be ecstatic to meet you. But I'm leaving tomorrow morning. Does that work for you?"

"We'll make sure she's packed," another voice yells. "And she'll text you her address."

I'm almost certain this is a fever dream. I grab sticky notes from my desk drawer and start scribbling a to-do list. If I'm taking Aspen home with me after all, that's going to change my plans. I'm going to have to—

Aspen with me. Pretending to be my girlfriend. Did Santa get my wish list a year too late? Or did I make the naughty list this time, and this fake-dating scheme is my punishment?

"You need to help me out with the China research," Aspen warns. "That's on the contract."

"Okay. Whatever you need."

"And I'll be there for the wedding. If you want. So you don't have to go alone. I'll be in charge of Operation Paws Off. No chance you're getting back with Brittany."

"Thanks? I think. I don't know if I'm more scared or curious." Definitely curious, and maybe a little turned on. This is going to be hell. "Drink some water, Aspen. I'll pick you up at ten tomorrow."

"Sounds—" There's a shriek, a clattering sound, and the call cuts off. I call back, fingers fumbling over the screen, but no one picks up. I reach across my desk to grab my wallet, but before I can head back to the cantina to make sure she's okay, a message comes through. *Fell off my chair, I'm ok.* Another message follows with her address.

Dazed, I slip my headset back on to find Kai yelling at me. Guess I forgot to mute my mic.

"Goddammit, dude, why the hell did you try to persuade her not to do this?"

"Um," I say. "I think I have to go."

"She's seriously pretending to be your girlfriend so she can spend Christmas with you?" Chase demands. "What the hell, man? You fall through a portal into a rom-com or something? Shit like this doesn't happen in real life."

"Shut up, Chase," Kai says. "Luke, dude, this is your moment. You have ten days. Make them count."

Ten days for me to fall out of love with Aspen for good. Or ten days to convince her to give me a shot. I feel like I'm on a precipice, and right now I don't know which way I'll fall. Or which way I want to.

"Any advice?"

"Get her naked," Chase says immediately.

"Idiot." Kai curses him out.

"Okay, fine," Chase says. "Get yourself naked. Once she sees the goods, she—"

"For God's sake." Kai groans. "How the hell did you get Marissa to marry you?"

"I'm just saying . . . sex helps."

I tune them out as I look over my to-do list that needs completing before picking up Aspen in the morning. "Look, I've really got to go. I'll keep you guys updated, okay?" Without waiting for them, I disconnect, alt/F4 the game, and unlock my phone again.

My clenched stomach unwinds. I didn't even realize it was knotted until I let out a sigh, deep from my diaphragm.

Aspen is coming home with me for Christmas.

This charade probably won't end well. It's going to eviscerate me with sneak peeks of what could've been if Aspen saw me in a different light, if the expiration date on our friendship wasn't just around the corner.

If I wasn't leaving.

The logical thing would be to call back and find a different solution, but I guess I'm a glutton for punishment, because all I can focus on is that for a week and a half, I can torture myself pretending she's mine.

I push up from my chair, pacing with a mixture of nervous energy and dread. One hand is raking through my hair while I think about the massive turn of events tonight; the other cradles my phone. I text my mom, hoping her phone is silenced and she'll get this message in the morning—too late to make me talk about it, but still early enough to prepare for an extra guest.

Hey, Mom, I type. *There's been a change of plans.*

Chapter Five

Aspen

I don't have a list of the worst times to meet a fake boyfriend's parents, but suffering from the hangover from hell, complete with unbrushed hair and teeth, seems like it would make it into the top five.

Luke picks up the bag I don't remember packing and throws it into the back of his Jeep, acting like it weighs nothing. I know for a fact it weighs several somethings. My noodle arms had to take quite a few breaks hauling it down the stairs to the front of the building.

"Morning," he says with a smile. He's irritatingly fresh. I *saw* him drinking with my own two eyes, but he's behaving as though ten in the morning is a perfectly reasonable time to be awake and functional.

I mumble something incoherent and clamber into the passenger seat, buckling myself in, then wiggling against the lump in my back pocket. When I pull it out, I see it's Lina's "contract" napkin. Embarrassment blooms, flushing my cheeks.

Someone smite me from this earth now. I want to disappear into the asphalt and embrace my new existence as a sewer rat.

"Here," Luke says, reaching past me and opening the glove box to pull out a bottle of ibuprofen. "And I got you a coffee. Thought you might need it."

"You're a fairy godmother." I accept the pills and take a sip of the coffee. "I barely had time to crawl out of bed this morning. Pretty sure this is the worst hangover in the history of the world."

Especially because it made me tell Luke I would *pretend to be his girlfriend* in exchange for food and board over Christmas.

How sad. How pathetic. He probably thinks I'm the biggest loser on this planet.

"How much did you have to drink?" he asks sympathetically, putting the car in gear and setting off. He drives a stick shift. I send a quick glance at the sure way his hands rest on the wheel.

I've never seen his mannerisms be so confident, so relaxed, so manly. Or maybe it's just because this early-morning light is drilling a shaft straight through my skull.

"Too much." I groan, closing my eyes and laying my head against the headrest. "I'm so sorry."

"What for?"

"All of it." The incriminating napkin lies on my thigh. "This is so embarrassing."

"More embarrassing than lying to your mom about a girlfriend because you hate blind dates and have a horrible ex?"

"Um." He has a point, I guess. "Are you embarrassed?"

He slides a glance at me, and the sunlight illuminating his face highlights green in his eyes. "Enormously," he says matter-of-factly. "I wanted to die when you overheard me."

"Then you know how I feel. Except mine is worse because I'm *also* hungover." I fold my arms, then decide that was a bad idea because my stomach is ready to eject itself all over his neat interior. "How did you manage that, by the way? Aren't you on the wrong side of thirty to be unaffected by alcohol?"

"I've been awake for a couple hours longer than you, and I've already had my coffee. You'll feel better soon."

"I hope so." As he pulls out onto the highway leading up Emigration Canyon, I give him a squinted once-over. And blink. This is not the Luke I know, the one with not a hair out of place, in a crisp, freshly ironed shirt. Today, he's decided to embrace his inner outdoorsman. He's wearing a buffalo plaid button-down, open, exposing a green Henley underneath, paired with jeans and a Carhartt jacket. A gray beanie flattens those cute curls to his head.

He looks extremely attractive. Like he's headed to a Patagonia catalog photo shoot. I've never noticed his broad shoulders before, or the line of his collarbones. The man has good collarbones. How is this the first time in two years that I've noticed? How has he been hiding it all this time?

I realize I'm gawking and turn back to face the front. *Pure thoughts, pure thoughts.*

The coffee is warm against my skin, even through the insulated cup, and I wrap my hands around it as we head northeast on the I-215, skirting around downtown Salt Lake City. Sunnyside Avenue is living up to its name, but the tree tips are frosted, and there's an icy tinge to the blue sky and the mountains in the background.

For the first time, the sight of the glaring light doesn't make my head explode.

"Thanks for the coffee," I say awkwardly. "I feel a little more human."

"You're welcome."

"The snow looks pretty, huh?" I hunch in my seat as we head up through the sweeping bends toward Park City. Snow is piled at the side of the road, gray with fumes and speckled mud, but higher up, draped across the mountains, it's fresh and beautiful.

Luke glances at me and turns the seat warmers on. "Yeah, it's one of my favorite things."

"The snow?"

"Sure. There's something so satisfying about hiking in the cold, isolated wilderness."

"That's such a Boy Scout thing to say." The coffee and ibuprofen really are working wonders. It's a miracle. I might as well pledge my eternal gratitude to the gods of Big Pharma.

Red dusts the top of Luke's cheekbones, and I cackle in delight. "Wait, you *were* a Boy Scout?"

He doesn't so much as look at me. "Why don't we talk about your terrible drinking habits instead?"

"No, no. I've got to hear this." I twist in my seat so I'm facing him, resting my cheek against the headrest. "Did you make fires? Put up your own tent? Can you use a compass?"

"What have I signed up for?" he mutters. Failing to keep his smirk hidden.

"I'm serious. Give me the details! I need to know."

"Why?"

"Reasons."

"Because you want to tease me about it?"

"Wait until the office hears about this," I say, grinning as I imagine their response. "No one's going to imagine that you go hiking. I bet everyone thinks you sort paperclips and sharpen pencils in your spare time."

He gives me a look of half disgust, half horror. "You'd compromise my reputation?"

"I know; it's a real shame. But someone's gotta do it." I giggle again, until the awkwardness of what we're doing hits me anew. My smile fades. "How long until we get there?"

"Another half hour. Maybe more in the snow. See that storm already started up ahead?"

"Is it going to get bad?"

"In the canyon, maybe. It often is this time of year."

He'd know, too. Because I know he visits home often, like a devoted son. The thought brings me a pang of guilt. Mom called me again last night, but I ignored it, letting her go to voicemail. Not that she bothered leaving a message after the tone—she wants to speak to me directly, to make me feel bad about the choices I've made and the boundaries I've put in place to protect myself.

Luke glances at me again and sucks his teeth. "Hey, Aspen," he says, his voice surprisingly gentle.

"We should talk about rules," I interrupt. "So we walk in there knowing our story."

"Right. Our story."

"If we're going to pull this off, we need to have an idea what we're doing. A backstory. It needs to be believable, otherwise no one's going to buy it." I tap my fingers against my thigh. "And we need, um, boundaries."

There's a silence that lasts just a second too long before he says, "Boundaries in what way?"

"We need to act like a couple, but . . ." I swallow. "We shouldn't blur the lines with too much physical intimacy."

"I wasn't trying to—"

"We can hold hands. People expect that. And hug. No kissing."

Luke's voice is perfectly steady. "My family is affectionate. We like to give hugs, and PDA happens occasionally. Is that something that makes you uncomfortable?"

My mom isn't exactly a hugger. Not with me, anyway. She never so much as kisses my cheek, and if we do hug, it's a quick, awkward thing. But of course Luke's family are huggers. I already knew that. Everything about him is my opposite—it's like someone took all the things I know and have experienced and flipped them around to make Luke.

"No," I say, though I don't know how much I mean it. "No, that's fine."

"They might expect us to kiss," he continues. "At least on the cheek. Is that something you'd mind?"

"No. It's fine." I stare at the napkin with the smudged rules Lina wrote out. *Sex* is written and underlined three times, followed by a question mark. I curl it into a ball so he can't see it. "Closed-mouth kissing only."

"If you're uncomfortable with any part of this, we can turn around and go back."

I wince. "No, we can't. They're fumigating my apartment."

"Oh."

"Yeah." I toy with the hem of my sweater and wait for him to ask, but he just focuses on the road. The snow is a lot deeper up here, and as the road gets steeper, I can feel the Jeep start to struggle. Road signs flash: *Chains required up ahead.*

"Give me a moment," he says, flicking the blinker and pulling off the road. "I just need to put chains on."

My eyes about bug out of my face. Who is this man, and where is the Luke I know from work? "You know how to put chains on tires?"

The look he throws me is of pure male smugness. "I got my Eagle Scout medal when I was fourteen," he informs me and shuts the door behind him, then walks around the back to get the chains from the trunk. I deliberate for all of five seconds—stay in the warmth or head outside to watch him work—and eventually choose hopping outside.

My feet sink into fresh snow with a crunch, and the wind is far icier than it seemed down in the city.

Luke is crouching, untangling the chains with ease. It's like he's not even trying. I can't even untangle my necklaces.

"Are you cold?" he asks without looking up. "You can wait in the car if you want. No need to stay out here with me."

The sweater is not cutting it. My eyes were barely open when I grabbed it to put on, and my coat is somewhere in the back seat. But I can't quite drag my eyes off of him, because hot damn. He's juxtaposing those handsome facial features with the kind of brawn that girls dream of.

Girls except me, I mean. I don't dream of brawn or anything even approaching Luke, because I know better. Nice guys get hurt, and I don't hurt nice guys. It's a good rule to live by.

He fits the chains easily and tightens them, then hops back in the Jeep and rolls forward to loosen them again. I hug myself as I watch, fingers going numb.

"Eagle Scout, huh?" I say when he's done and we're back in the Jeep. He sets the heat to blasting. "Did they teach you to put on snow chains?"

"Nah. That was my dad."

"Nice to have a dad around to teach you stuff like that." I'm all robotic again as I realize I'm about to meet him, and I don't know how to act around a father figure. "I barely remember my own dad," I blurt out. Luke doesn't flinch at my awkward confession, so I continue. "One of my few memories of him, perhaps one of my favorites, was taking a car ride like this. A road trip into the mountains, singing at the top of our lungs to a new Reggae-style rap song that some rising artist had released earlier that year. That's where my love of Michael Franti started, actually. Singing 'Soulshine,' driving up the canyon with my dad smiling back at me. He had a toothy grin and warm eyes that crinkled at the edges. I felt so happy and special. Staying connected to Franti's music somehow keeps that feeling alive in me." I've shared too much, and embarrassment floods my cheeks. I don't usually verbal vomit all over a guy, especially on the first day, but it's easy to talk to Luke. To share with him a rare memory of a loving father and me as an adoring daughter; one of the few straws I can still grasp and remember what it felt like to be loved by him.

"Sounds like a great memory. I'm glad you have it." Luke's voice is honey and sunshine. Empathy and understanding. He's always been a good listener when I've needed one, and he never makes me regret that I've confided in him.

A swift shot of anxiety courses through my veins. My brain is caught in a loop now, thinking about what an impulsive and idiotic decision I'm making. Posing as Luke's girlfriend, basically a fraud, all so I can get a roof over my head and a nice, home-cooked meal.

And to help out my friend. I need to focus on that.

"Um, so what's our story? Our fake story. So we don't blow our cover."

"We met at work," he says. "Got together after a night at the cantina after you heard me sing and realized I have the best voice you've ever heard."

I slap his arm, unable to stop myself from laughing. "Isn't it the other way around? You fell for me and my charm?"

"Fine. But only because you *do* have a better voice than me."

There are so many things I could bring up, but instead, I'm back to attacking the hem of my sweater. My fingers are less numb now, and I wrap them in the soft material. Annabelle got it for me one time when she noticed I didn't have any sweaters, and I wear it everywhere. It's cream and soft and unbelievably cozy.

"Hey," he says, voice soft. There's a moment of hesitation, and he glances at me. "You don't have to answer this if it makes you uncomfortable, but why did you do this? I mean, what happened to make this your best option?"

"It's a long story. Kind of boring, kind of tragic. We don't have to worry about that now."

To distract myself, and him, I open the glove box and notice what I hadn't before. "Ooh, Skittles. Want some?"

He holds out a hand with a smile that curls at the corners and warms his eyes into more of that moss green I noticed before. I have to force my heart back into its box.

So what if he has beautiful eyes? So *nothing*.

I am not here to get all cutesy with a guy who shows signs of being open to something real and lasting. I don't do long term. Aspen Shaw, daughter of Tina-the-serial-dater, doesn't *do* permanent things, and she certainly doesn't do nice guys like Luke.

Ever.

Not even if they get me Skittles.

I desperately hold on to that thought as we eat up the miles to meet his parents for the first time. As his fake girlfriend.

Heaven help me. What have I gotten myself into?

Chapter Six

Luke

The journey takes longer than I think either of us expected, but by the time we pull up to my family's ranch, it's clear Aspen's recovered from the worst of her hangover. At least, if the way her mouth drops open when she sees the homestead is anything to go by.

I try to see it through fresh eyes. I grew up here, playing in the barn with the animals we raised and climbing up into the rafters even when Mom told me not to. I rode horseback all over our thousand-acre cattle ranch and explored the mountains with my brothers, Matthew and Mark.

"There are so many trees," Aspen says as I pull up to the main house. The house, built in the eighties when my parents moved back into the area and added on to the existing structure, looks more like a modern log cabin mini-mansion. I kill the engine, and we sit in the ticking silence. It's no longer snowing, but snow coats everything, and I wonder if she brought everything she'll need.

Park City is close if I need to run out and get anything. Or she can borrow one of my hoodies.

The thought sends heat pulsing through me, and I banish it. Self-preservation demands I keep my mind on a short leash, which means there's no way she can wear any of my clothes. That's not the route to friendly, platonic behavior.

I clear my throat, though it's too late to purify my mind.

She flips down the visor and stares at her reflection, her eyes widening in open horror. "Oh my God. I can't meet your parents looking like this."

"You look fine." A bit messy, sure, but the red creases in her cheek from sleeping on something rumpled have faded.

"I look like the wicked witch that lives in the woods," she says, fingers digging under her eyes. "How have you not been swallowed in the shadows under my eyes?"

"I didn't even notice them."

"Impossible. They're voids. Larger than my eyes."

"Aspen." I take her hands, dragging them down from her face. The feel of her skin against mine sends a bolt of electricity through me, but I don't let it show as I meet her eyes.

I force a breath through the constriction in my chest.

"You look great," I tell her.

Her breathing is a little too shallow. Her pulse feels quick under my fingers as I wrap them around her wrists, trying to ground her.

"How do you think they'll react to my face?" she whispers.

I want to ease her concerns. More than I've ever wanted anything in my life, which is saying something, because I've wanted Aspen as long as I can remember knowing her. It's an itch, an urge, a need—something I thought I'd stamped out, but embers flare up in unexpected moments like this.

I don't know how to ease her fears without my affection for her leaking out, so I just squeeze her hands. She doesn't pull away, and that sends a thrill of victory through me.

Stop reading too much into it before you get carried away, dumbass.

"They'll think you're beautiful, because you are. Now, let's go. They're probably wondering what we're doing." I release her, and she practically jumps from the car, landing in the snow with a soft crunch and an even softer "Ooh."

This is it. We're about to meet my parents. My palms are sweating. I'm going to simultaneously be showing my family my "fake" feelings for Aspen while hiding the true nature of those feelings *from* her. My head already aches from the mental gymnastics.

In the car, Aspen and I finalized our fake relationship details. We've been together since last summer, we're not living together, I haven't met her mom. Just in case my mom asks—because let's face it, my mom will ask. I love her, but she has this way of putting her nose in everyone's business.

She'll say it's out of love, and she believes it, but it's out of bottomless curiosity, and nothing will ever cure her.

I grab our bags from the trunk and sling them over my shoulder. My oldest brother Matthew and his husband Kwan are already here, judging by the red hatchback in the driveway, which means their twins are running around here somewhere, along with Mark's kids, Oliver and Millie.

There's a good chance Aspen will be overwhelmed by the size and volume of my family.

I take her hand, sliding my fingers through hers. She stiffens for a second, and I stop walking so she can get used to the contact. "Before we go in, just so you know, it'll be a full house."

"A full house," she repeats. "Everyone I saw in the Christmas card photo awhile back?"

Two years ago, around Thanksgiving, I sent my obligatory Christmas letter, including an embarrassing ugly sweater family photo, to a college friend who used to live in the apartment Aspen had just moved into. When she tried to return to sender, we got to talking, and I learned she was a coder looking for a job and would be a perfect fit at PAYDAY. We've been friends ever since. She's known about my family for a long time, but I guess she never considered she'd meet them one day.

Me? I used to hope for it. Now, I wish I could avoid it.

They're going to love her. I bet my mom will be mentally planning our wedding before we get to attend JoJo's in a few days. It's going to make our fake breakup that much harder for them to accept. And me.

I try to force the collateral damage to the back of my mind. It's a problem for another day.

"Yeah," I say. "Everyone. But they're all going to love you."

Aspen's sharp intake of air is noticeable. She tugs at my hand. "This was a mistake. I'll brave the fumigation."

"If you were going to back out, you should have done it back in Salt Lake." Not releasing my grip, I drag her to the front door. "Just relax."

"How am I going to remember all their names?" Aspen whispers.

"How well do you know the New Testament?" I tease. "My siblings are named in the same sequence as the Bible. Matthew, Mark, Luke, and JoJo. Or, as we like to call her, Jo. My mom couldn't get on board calling her only daughter Johnnie."

Aspen makes a face. "Were you raised in a cult, or—"

"Depends who you ask." At her shock, I grin. "It was more of an accident than anything else. My parents, Peter and Ruth, started dating after meeting at church, and they thought it was funny that they both had biblical names. They saw it as a sign and got married. They named Matthew after Mom's dad, who passed away from cancer. I guess by the time Mark came along, they just continued the theme."

"As you do." Aspen grins, clearly enjoying every morsel of information about my family history.

"Then, obviously, Matthew wanted to keep the tradition alive, because what more normal thing could any well-adjusted man want, so he named his adopted twins Jonah and Noah. Three generations of biblical representation on our family tree. Are you frightened yet?"

Aspen laughs. "Should I be?"

"Only by the sheer number of family members you're about to meet." I take pity on her and squeeze her hand. "Just kidding. They're great, really. Just, when you're meeting them, think 'Bible,' and it'll help you remember their names."

"And their spouses and their children." Aspen counts off her fingers. "We're only here ten days. Will that be enough time?"

"Almost certainly not," I say and push open the front door into the warm smell of baking. Mom's probably in the kitchen, and judging by the chatter, so is everyone else.

The eight-year-old twins, Jonah and Noah, zoom past us, almost knocking Aspen off her feet. Oliver follows after, laughing, and thankfully doesn't bump Aspen even further off balance.

"Hey," I call after them. "Watch it."

"Sorry, Uncle Luke." I'm not sure which twin says it. I can tell them apart, but only when they're side by side and facing me, or when I know which clothes they picked out that morning. Thank the stars they don't wear matching clothes. Their dads are way too cool for that.

"Luke?" Mom calls from the kitchen. She heads out, wiping her hands on a towel, and beams when she sees us both. "And Aspen. It's so nice to finally meet you, honey. I'm Ruth."

Aspen's hand is sweaty in mine, but she manages a weak smile. "Hi, Ruth. You have a lovely house."

"Oh, you haven't seen anything yet." Mom comes for a hug, kissing me on the cheek, and does the same to Aspen. When she pulls back, she gives Aspen a wide smile. "You're even prettier than Luke said.

Come on, we're all in the kitchen." She turns to go but stumbles on something small and yellow in her path. "Those boys," she mutters, swiping the Lego from the ground.

"They like leaving traps for grown-ups," I explain to Aspen as we head down the hallway to the kitchen. The space is dominated by a huge table, where Matthew, Mark, and Kwan are sitting close together, chatting and laughing. Dad is already pouring two drinks, and five-year-old Millie is scribble-drawing at a small table in the corner. Mom and Rebecca, Mark's wife, are bustling between the countertop and the stove, pots and dishes clattering as they work.

It's busy. It's way too loud. But there's music going in the background, and it smells like cinnamon and home. My shoulders relax. Even Aspen gives a tiny smile.

"Luke's home," Mom announces unnecessarily. "And he's brought Aspen with him."

Rebecca waddles toward us, apron tied around her very pregnant stomach. Mark follows, and soon my entire family is surrounding Aspen with smiles and hugs and too many introductions.

"We've been dying to meet you," Matthew says. Kwan smiles and nods. It's taken a while for them to be relaxed and open here, but now they lean against each other, content in the chaos.

"Okay," I say, steering Rebecca away. "Give her space so she can breathe."

"It's so nice to meet you all," Aspen says. "I think I've got a handle on a few of your names, but if I forget them, I'm so sorry."

"That's fine," Matthew says cheerfully. "Just remember me as the favorite brother, and you'll be fine."

I grab one of the candied walnuts on the table and throw it at him. "I think you mean *I'm* the favorite brother."

"To Aspen, maybe."

"Boys." Mom swats us both with a kitchen towel and smiles at Aspen. "I'm sorry about these two. The oldest and the youngest boy. They were born bickering."

Aspen looks so small in the midst of my large and overwhelming family that I instinctively want to pull her into my arms. A bad instinct I need to repress if I'm going to have any chance of surviving this week.

Holding her would also violate the boundaries she was very clear about. Boundaries will keep us both safe and our friendship intact.

I clear my throat and force myself to focus on making her feel more relaxed here. So, attention off her. "Where's JoJo and Andre?" I ask.

"Oh, I think they're in the barn," Mom says. "She's changing her mind for the umpteenth time about where the lights should go. I've just left them to it."

"And Granny Mae?" Of everyone, I think Aspen will like Granny the best.

"Oh, you know her, she's probably out in the stable looking after the horses." Mom's face creases as she smiles, but I don't miss that she's looking tired. Having JoJo get married here probably isn't the easiest thing in the world. Jo knows what she wants—or so she thinks. Before she changes her mind another fifteen times.

"You can meet them in a bit," Rebecca says. "It's due to snow later, so that'll drive Granny in. Probably." She gives Mark a soft, sweet smile, and he softens right back.

Matthew and Kwan have a tender-but-teasing relationship, but Mark's relationship with Rebecca is all sugar. The last thing I'd have expected from a grouchy, no-nonsense cowboy.

"You should get settled," Mom says. "You'll be tired after that driving, and lunch is soon. Peter, could you show them to their cabin?"

"Cabin?" Aspen's voice comes out an octave higher than normal.

"We thought you'd want a break from all the chaos," Rebecca says, patting Aspen on the arm. I'm tempted to intervene, but there's nothing that can be done at this point. This has clearly been discussed in advance. "Jo and Andre are in Granny's cabin, and you're in the cabin side of the duplex."

Aspen sneaks a glance at me, but I keep my face blank.

I remember when Rebecca and Mark refurbished the cabins a few years ago. The duplex is a smaller studio cabin that shares a wall with a large, six-person bunkhouse. This used to be housing for the ranch manager and the ranch hands.

The manager's cabin, notably, only has one bed.

Shit.

Well, obviously, she'll have to take the bed, and I'll squeeze onto the couch. No way am I going to share a bed with her and risk her figuring out how much I want her. And it would *definitely* not help with the whole not-pining-after-her-anymore thing.

"'Granny's in the bunkhouse, and Brittany and the other bridesmaids will bunk with her." Mom's voice is careful, and everyone looks at me.

I want to groan and roll my eyes. It's been over for two years now. *Two*. Do they seriously think I haven't learned my lesson with Brittany, who ditched me by cheating? Even now, when I brought a girlfriend home?

A *fake* girlfriend. But they don't know that.

Aspen senses the weird tension, and her delicate hand slips back into mine. "The duplex sounds great," she says.

"Great" is pushing it, but it's better than her sharing with Granny and Brittany. Granny never liked Brittany, and Brit . . . Well, she's my ex-fiancée. I don't want Aspen having to navigate sharing a room with my ex.

Dad smiles at us both. "Do you want to head to the cabin so you can unpack and get sorted? Lunch is in half an hour."

"Sure," I say for us both. "That would be great."

Conversation starts up behind us as we head back outside, but before we reach the door, Oliver appears again. He's ten and has Down syndrome, and he's the sweetest kid alive.

"This is Oliver," Dad says as my eldest nephew stops in front of us. "Mark and Rebecca's oldest."

Aspen smiles down at him and holds out her hand. "Hi, Oliver. It's nice to meet you."

His smile is so wide, it swallows the rest of his face, and he taps his cheek, mirroring where her birthmark is. "You have a different face too," he says so happily, it's obvious he means it as a good thing. "You're special like me."

"Oh." For a second, Aspen just blinks down at him, and I worry he's said the wrong thing. But then, her smile widens to match his. "That's right. We are special, aren't we? Do you like it?"

Oliver reaches up a curious finger and gently traces the edges of her wine-stain birthmark, feeling the uneven skin.

"It's a pretty color," he says, his assessment complete.

Her cheeks go red, and I could hug him.

"I think your mom wants you in the kitchen," Dad says, patting Oliver on the shoulder. He runs off, his steps light and seemingly unbothered by what feels very much like a significant moment.

Now, on to the next significant task: repressing all sexual desire in a room alone with Aspen that only has one bed.

I mentally try to calculate the odds of winning that battle. The percentage is low.

Chapter Seven

Aspen

I understand the look on Luke's face as soon as we walk into the cabin. The interior is gorgeous—just as beautiful as I've already come to expect from this place. Stone fireplace, rugs on the hand-scraped wooden floor, oversized art hanging on the walls, big windows looking out across a snowy wilderness with breathtaking mountain views.

Rustic. Infinitely classy.

Indisputably set up for a couple. The king bed dominates the room.

One bed. Singular.

Granted, it's huge. The bedspread alone could wrap me up in a cocoon several times over. We could have a pillow fort in the middle and still have room to sleep on either side.

But that doesn't change the fact that we're expected to share.

Luke waits for his dad to leave us alone, making a joke about unpacking and settling in, before turning to me.

"I'm so sorry," he says, and I believe him. "I had no idea they were going to put us in here."

Sunlight gleams through the frosted windows. If I was going to rent a place like this for a week, it would cost me a whole month of my salary.

We can do this, I decide. And if nothing else, I have this weird urge to smooth the anguish and discomfort from his face.

"This is fine," I say, perching on the edge of the bed. Just as I predicted, the mattress is deliciously soft. "Stop looking like you dropped me in a tank full of flesh-eating piranha."

"All piranha are flesh-eating," he says absently, dropping my bag beside me and heading to the sofa. While I'm sure it's soft and very expensive, there's no way his lanky ass is going to fit on there.

"What are you doing?" I stand up and walk toward him.

He raises an eyebrow. "What do you think I'm doing? I'm taking the sofa."

"Your six-foot-plus body won't fit on the sofa. Your back will kill you."

"I'm in my thirties, not my *eighties*. And for the record, I'm six-three."

"Wait." I take hold of his arm and drag him back. "If either of us is going to take the sofa, it should be me."

He tugs the beanie off his head and shakes out his floppy hair. Too long. It hangs over his forehead, just brushing his eyebrows. I've been dying to give him a haircut for months. "I'm not letting you take the sofa, Aspen. I'm the one who's put you in this position."

I eye the bed again. You could fit a family of five on that thing. "We can share the bed," I say, and his head jerks up to meet my gaze. "It's enormous. And, I mean, I trust you not to take advantage."

"I wouldn't." His cheekbones flush, and he holds out both hands defensively. "I would never."

He's weirdly adorable when he's flustered. We've teased each other before, obviously, but it's never been quite like this. I should probably stop—it wouldn't be fair to either of us. I've already got to get through this Christmas-and-wedding situation. Finding different ways to make Luke blush wouldn't be a sensible or profitable use of my time.

Although it might be a fun distraction for when his family gets too overwhelming.

Just so he doesn't get any ideas about crippling himself, I pick up his bag and haul it to the bed next to mine.

"There," I tell him. "Problem solved."

He eyes me suspiciously, but he eventually shrugs and drops the issue. "We should unpack if we're going to be here for the next week and a half."

I start to say I don't usually bother unpacking—spend enough time traveling when you're a kid, and you learn to live out of your suitcase pretty fast—but I stop myself. Luke is a nice boy from a nice family, and he doesn't need to know quite how semi nomadic and unstable my upbringing was.

"I'll take this drawer over here," he says. "You can have the closet."

I don't think I brought enough stuff to fill a closet. Honestly, I don't know exactly *what* I brought. I took the three dwarves home with me last night, I remember, and while I was picking out a dress to wear to the wedding, they were packing everything else I needed.

If Annabelle was there, though, I'm confident I'll at least have some warm clothes and a toothbrush.

As Luke opens his suitcase and removes his perfectly folded clothes, I take a deep breath and unzip.

And choke back a scream.

Right on top, in full view, is a set of lacy red lingerie I bought to wear for an old boyfriend once, when I was feeling sexy. We broke up before I ever had a chance to wow him with it, and Lina has never let me forget.

Shit.

I snatch them up before Luke can get a good look, only to see a condom box perched on top of my clothes.

I make some kind of strangled choking noise and grab them, and Luke turns, getting a full view of me standing in front of my suitcase, my hands full of condoms and lingerie. My cheeks are sizzling and ready for bacon and a fried egg.

Kill me now.

He stares for a fraction too long, gaze flicking from everything in my hands to my face. And back again. He looks utterly lost for words and shifts uncomfortably.

I've made him uncomfortable. Dear sweet baby Jesus, I could *murder* my friends right about now.

"My friends were drunk," I blurt. "I'm so sorry. I'll just—" I open the nearest nightstand drawer and shove them in. When I look back at my suitcase, I see the edge of a frilly bra sticking out.

Luke, the gentleman that he is, has turned away.

"It's okay," he says, voice a fraction strained. "I'm sorry. I won't look."

"I'm going to rip them limb from limb." I smother my mortification in a thick fleece pullover, probably packed by Annabelle. "I hope you're ready to lie to the cops with my alibi, because no one will ever find their bodies."

"Aspen." The strain in his voice has turned to amusement. If he relaxes, I know he's going to wheeze with laughter. "It's fine. You don't need to murder anyone."

"They've already murdered my dignity," I mutter.

"Bold of you to think there was any of that left."

"Rude!"

He really does laugh then, and it's a rich, warm sound that makes my stomach forget it's supposed to be suspended motionless in my torso. I throw a shoe at him as an outlet for my nervous energy. This morning is the only time we've spent together outside of work or work-related activities, and I'm curious to see what will happen.

***

We're a little early when we return for lunch, so Luke gives me a quick tour of the house. It's enormous, and even with all his family here visiting, at no point does it feel cramped.

"Mark and Rebecca live here full time, running the cattle ranch," he explains as we peek into a kids' playroom. Millie is there, and when she sees us, she releases something from her hands. *A cat*, I realize as it sprints past us, tail upright. She smiles with an expression of surprisingly wicked delight.

Cats.

"I didn't know you had cats," I say, pressing a hand to my nose. Am I itching? Knowing me, I'll be fine until I'm sitting down to eat, and then I'll start sneezing everywhere.

"Millie," Luke says, starting forward, then stopping and glancing back at me. "You know you're not supposed to take the barn cats inside."

Millie blinks adorable blue eyes at him and twirls what looks like a string of Mardi Gras beads around her neck. "He was lonely."

I don't know much about cats, but that particular feline monster looked more traumatized than lonely.

"No more cats inside the house," Luke says, holding up a warning finger. "If I see another one, I'll have to tell Granny Mae."

I've already got questions about Granny Mae, who is apparently still out in the barn with the horses in this weather, despite being in her eighties. She sounds like a character.

Luke pats my arm as we leave the room. I'm already scratching my arms, though I don't know if that's because of allergies or overthinking.

"It's okay," he says. "I brought allergy meds."

"Wait, you did?"

"You said something about cats on the phone last night, and I figured you were allergic, so I brought some just in case you ended up coming into close contact with the barn cats." He says it like it's nothing, like going out of his way to buy *me* allergy meds when he could have just told me to bring some myself, is no big deal.

"Hey, Luke." I'm flushing already. "Um. Thanks."

"For what?"

"For being considerate."

He looks at me for a long moment before shrugging. "Isn't that what fake boyfriends do? Come on, I think I heard Granny come in."

When we get downstairs, I discover my suspicions are correct. Granny Mae *is* a character. She's tall still, despite her clearly advanced age, and although her fingers are twisted with rheumatism, she's deft with them. She's wearing a button-up western shirt over wrangler jeans, with a handkerchief scarf rolled up and tied around her neck. A Stetson cowboy hat is hanging from the coat hook, and she's still wearing her cowboy boots.

Her silver hair has a tint of purple. The gleam in her eye and the set of her jaw leaves no doubt that she's a force to be reckoned with. And for the first time in my life, I fall in love at first sight.

The twins are dancing in front of her, Oliver is trying to show her a picture he's drawn, and everything is chaos. When she glances up and sees us, however, she clears everyone around her away with such efficiency, it's almost terrifying.

"Luke," she says, giving him a brisk nod. He grins, and the open affection warms my heart in a way I really wasn't expecting. It makes me feel raw, somehow. Exposed.

Then, Granny Mae's gaze swings to me, and I have just enough time to wonder if she'll like what she sees before she gives me an unexpected hug. She smells like hay and leather and Bengay muscle rub, and for some reason, it makes my eyes sting. When she pulls back, she pats me on the cheek.

"I like your style," she tells me, pointing to my pixie haircut. "Funny how decades ago, young people used to make fun of old lady hair colors, but now it's all the rage."

I touch my hair gingerly. Annabelle dyed it for me a week ago, transitioning from hot pink to cotton candy, and I thank my lucky stars we spontaneously decided to tone down the color just before meeting Luke's family.

"It's nice to meet you," I say.

"I've heard a lot about you." She sniffs. "Is that homemade crock-pot soup I smell?" Without waiting for an answer, she leads us into the kitchen. Luke takes my hand as we go, the smooth slide of his fingers between mine feeling both confident and natural. I'm getting used to the feel of my hand in his. It anchors me as we embark on this dating charade.

Two tables have been pushed together, taking up almost all the space in the large dining room. Rebecca, whose pregnant belly is straining at the material of her stretchy cotton dress, is having her shoulders massaged by Mark.

For the first time, I imagine Luke's hands on me like that, working out the knots and tension that have laid undisturbed in my shoulders.

Beside them are Matthew and Kwan. On our drive up, Luke mentioned they've been married around ten years now and adopted the twins at birth. From everything Luke's said about them, they're the best dads anyone could ask for.

Sitting next to them is JoJo. She's a stunner in a casual gray dress that accentuates her generous curves, her long, dark hair tumbling down her back. Her fiancé, Andre, has a military bearing and the haircut to match.

I cling to the warmth in Luke's tone as he talks to his family. Here, he's so relaxed. At the cantina, around our work friends, he's relaxed, too, but it's different. That's his professional space with his professional friends.

This is his home, and it's as though he's expanded to fit the space. All the parts of him I never knew about before have unfolded, and I have to keep my eyes wide, or I'll miss bits I've never seen before.

His brothers tease him about the times he got stuck up trees, when he went climbing in the barn rafters and fell and broke his leg. JoJo teases him for his love of fantasy series and computer games—he used to take his Nintendo to bed with him when he was little and play it under the covers.

Luke's parents bustle around, making sure everyone has drinks. The ranch might be managed by Rebecca and Mark now, but it's clear that it's still the older generation's home.

The sense of love and community emanating from them all fills my soul with yearning for this level of belonging. While they're asking me gentle questions about my life, no one is, for even a second, suspecting I'm a fraud, but I am tense. My legs bounce under the table, and I play with the small hoop in the side of my ear, below my barbell cartilage piercing.

Beside me, Luke reaches across and places his left hand on my knee. I freeze, my tapping legs stilling, and I think he's going to respond to my instinctive flinch and draw his hand away. But he doesn't move.

Warmth from his skin seeps through my jeans and into my bones, and I can't think past the contact.

I agreed to casual touching as part of our rules. Holding hands, the occasional hug, closed-mouth kisses. They're all part of the deal. And this is casual.

At least, he probably thinks it's casual. While I'm struck dumb, cemented into my chair by awareness that feels like a spotlight, he continues to eat and exchange jokes with his family.

"So, Aspen, why did you decide to come here for Christmas?" Ruth suddenly asks, startling me out of my daze. She's leaning across the table like hearing my answer is the most important thing in the world. "You're welcome, of course, but Luke told us you were busy."

Luke doesn't break conversation with Matthew, but his thumb rubs my knee soothingly, and that gives me the strength to answer.

"Last-minute change of plans," I say, forcing lightness into my voice like helium. Luke's fingers tighten, pressing into my jeans and grounding me. Ruth smiles politely, like she senses the truth behind that statement, like she can see through my breeziness and read every one of my scars like printed words on a page. The weight of her attention digs into me, and I shift uncomfortably, not sure what else to say. I look around at Luke's family, all engrossed in conversation—engrossed in each other—and feel thoroughly out of place. I've had my doubts about this whole thing from the start, but now, for the first time, I'm wondering if coming here was a terrible mistake.

Chapter Eight

Luke

U nder my hand, Aspen's muscles have all locked up, although she's kept her expression relaxed enough.

We haven't spoken about her reasons for taking me up on this whole fake-dating thing, apart from her apartment being fumigated. She said something about a tragic backstory, but it's clearly not something she wants to talk about.

Mom, reading Aspen's discomfort better than anyone else ever could, starts talking about something else. And slowly, slowly, Aspen relaxes.

Once she does, I remove the hand on her leg before I get too used to how good it feels. While she eats, I do my best to focus on Kwan's stories about some of the houses he's had to showcase to potential buyers. Usually, I love Kwan's stories. As a real estate agent, he's got some great ones. But right now, my mind keeps drifting back to the warmth of Aspen's leg under my hand. The way her muscles relaxed once I gently squeezed. I didn't ever want to let go, and that's exactly why I needed to.

When everyone's finished eating, Matthew and Mark jump up with me to do the dishes before Mom can, and we start clearing the table. Rebecca waddles off to the bathroom, and the twins find Aspen.

"Oh no," Matthew mutters. "They're going to ask her about Star Wars."

I haven't seen them in a few months. Last time, they were into dinosaurs. The time before that, it was Batman.

"You're Aspen," says one of the twins, maybe Jonah.

"That's right," she says.

"Luke's girlfriend."

She glances at me quickly, blushing when she realizes I'm looking. This is probably the moment I should look away, or even take a new plate to dry, but I can't stop watching.

"Yeah, that's right," she says.

Noah's eyes are dinner plates. "Whoa," he breathes. "Did you draw with a marker on your face? I got in trouble when I did that to my brother before."

"That's enough," Kwan intervenes, but Aspen shakes her head with a smile that loosens something in my chest.

"It's fine. This is just something I was born with, see?" She touches it lightly. My fingers tingle with the urge to do the same. In an alternate universe, one where I didn't piss away my chance to show her how I felt about her, I'd have kissed every inch of it and told her how beautiful she is until maybe she began to believe it. But I didn't, so I can't.

"Oh, okay." Jonah shrugs, no longer interested in her face. "I like your hair."

"I like it too," Noah says, not to be outdone. "Aspen, do you like Star Wars?"

Matthew heaves a sigh. "There it is. You might want to rescue her."

Before I can even put the plate down, Aspen is speaking again. "I sure do," she says. "Ashoka Tano is one of my favorite Jedis."

Jonah and Noah squeal with excitement, and Oliver, who's been watching Aspen with undisguised adoration—probably close to how

I'm looking right now—beams at her. "May the force be with you," he says.

As solemnly as though she's in church, she replies, "And also with you."

"She's good with the kids," Mark says as he hands me a glass. "Nice to see you so happy."

"First time I've heard a full sentence from you in years," Matthew teases, "and you waste it on him?"

Mark shrugs. "Good he's brought a girl home. Mom was worried."

"Mom's *always* worried," Matthew says, rolling his eyes. "She was worried when JoJo met Andre and they got engaged within a year, but look at them. They're so in love, they can't see straight."

Obviously, Matthew has a higher tolerance for JoJo's brand of loved-up, because when I turn and see Andre's tongue down her throat, my nose wrinkles. "Gross."

Mark nods in agreement, handing me another plate.

"Oh, come on," Matthew says, rolling his eyes. "Like you weren't the same when you met Rebecca."

"Not around other people."

I cup my hand around my mouth and call out, "Get a room!" JoJo breaks away, flushing, and Andre grins like he single-handedly captured the moon.

"As for you," Matthew says, handing me a pile of precariously stacked plates, "I've seen the way you look at Aspen; like a love sick puppy."

"No, I don't," I say automatically.

"Yes, you do, bud. It's fine. We've all been there."

Pretend, it's all pretend. I've just been really good at pretending and convincing my family that I'm into her, when all I *actually* want to do is move on and crush my feelings into smithereens.

Mark glances at me, then at Aspen, and sighs. "Shut up," he tells Matthew.

"What?"

"Read the room."

Matthew snorts. "I'll have you know I'm an expert at reading the room, and especially at reading the emotional responses of—"

Mark flicks dishwater at him the same time I snap him with the tea towel, and he howls with way less dignity than a thirty-six-year-old should have. Mark grins, Kwan throws his head back and laughs, and a glance at Aspen tells me she hasn't heard any of this. She gives me a shy smile, and I can't help smiling back.

The loosely formed plan I came here with, the plan to get over Aspen once and for all, feels like a house of cards, ready to fall with the slightest pressure.

It's only been one day of hanging out with her, and already my feelings are percolating, like a teakettle above a flame. When I accepted the job transfer, I pulled my emotions back from boiling to a simmer. Last week, I would've said they were tepid at best.

Now they're rising, and there's not a damn thing I can do about it.

In a few weeks, when I won't see her daily, my feelings should subside over time. At least, that's what I'm banking on. But looking at her now, sitting in my mom's kitchen and talking to Oliver like she's a part of the family—that's an image that no amount of time is going to be able to scrub from my mind. She fits in so naturally. I'm an idiot for not making it happen sooner.

The desire to keep her here is like an ache in my chest. Back when I was with Brittany, I used to think I knew what love was, but that was infatuation. I was so taken up by the idea that someone as pretty and popular as Brittany could want to be with someone like me that I lost all sense of myself.

Aspen makes me feel understood. Like she sees me.

The T-shirt she gave me is evidence of that.

Matthew nudges me, and when I glance over, he makes goo-goo eyes at me. I toss the towel in his face.

***

The afternoon passes in a blur. Mark, Andre, and I build a wooden hexagon arch for the wedding while Aspen and JoJo hang strings of lights on faux Christmas trees clustered throughout the barn. Jo wants a "winter wonderland" theme, and so far, she's getting exactly what she asked for.

Matthew and Mom are busy setting up the photo collage of JoJo and Andre. Matthew's got a real eye for this sort of thing; Mom picks out the pictures she wants, and he arranges it.

And, on the enormous speaker, soft rock is playing. Sting, currently. Mom sings along under her breath, and Matthew sings along louder. Aspen raises her head from where she's working, balanced on top of a stepladder.

"I've met Sting," she says suddenly, and I blink at her. "Nice guy."

"You've met Sting?" Matthew gapes at her. "No way."

Kwan and Dad come out with hot cocoa—with a little Baileys in Dad's, if I know him—and Kwan does an exaggerated take. "You know *Sting*?"

"I used to travel with my mom on tour when I was a kid. She was a backup singer for a lot of musicians back then." Aspen is seemingly unconscious of the attention she's attracting. "We met a bunch of different artists. He was super nice, though. Even sang a duet with me during sound check once." She shrugs, suddenly noticing the way everyone is staring at her, and she flushes. "It was at some fancy hotel in Austin, I think. He was doing the US leg of his tour, and Mom was one of his backup singers at the time." She shrugs again, and it's adorable the way her nose scrunches under everyone's scrutiny.

I don't know much about her mom. She doesn't talk about her family all that much, and especially not her childhood. But this is an insight.

Touring. Stopping off at hotels and meeting famous artists like it's nothing.

Matthew fires off a bunch of questions, and we all stop working to have the hot cocoa. Aspen sips as she answers Matthew, nose and cheeks flushing from the warmth of her drink, and I learn for the first time that she's also met Whitesnake and Chicago.

Mom nearly faints when she hears that. Chicago is her *favorite*. She has all their albums. I've lost track of the number of times she's referred to Bill Champlin as her "hall pass."

"Hot?" Aspen says in response to Mom's question. Her nose does that adorable wrinkling thing again. "I mean, not when I met him. Maybe he was when he was younger."

"There you go," Dad says to me with a wink. "No competition."

"Oh, hush," Mom says, slapping his arm.

I roll my sleeves up, warm despite the chill, and Aspen's eyes trace along my arms. When I raise my eyebrows at her, she blushes and glances away, hands wrapped around her steaming mug.

That was odd.

"All right," Mom says when Mark, the last to polish off his drink, is finished. "Back to work. I want the barn ready tomorrow so we don't have to do anything over Christmas."

"Yes, ma'am," Matthew says with a wink, dodging her good-natured swat. I take the wood Mark measured and start sawing. Sawdust coats the slick ground, and I lose myself in the physicality of it. Back at my house in the city, I regularly work out at the gym with Kai, but it's not like the good, honest work of the ranch.

As the light fades, we get the arch assembled in the barn, and Dad gets a fire going in the massive firepit and lays out the ingredients for s'mores. The kids, who've been running around all afternoon, have finally tired themselves out and head inside for some Christmas cartoons until the adults are ready to roast marshmallows.

Aspen rejoins me, and I slide an arm over her shoulder, pulling her into my body. It's what people expect—or, at least, that's the excuse I give myself.

"There aren't enough seats for everyone," Kwan says as he drags garden chairs and logs out to the firepit. "Jo and Andre, Luke and Aspen, you'll have to share."

At the other side of the fire, Rebecca is already perched on Mark's lap, and her head is tilted back, eyes closed as he massages her shoulders again. Her belly sticks out so far, I'm amazed she's found a comfortable position to sit in. She's due to pop any second, but here she is, still running the ranch alongside him. Nothing Mark says can stop her.

Andre sits and opens his arms, and JoJo snuggles up to him.

Which just leaves Aspen, who looks as though someone just told her to swallow a frog whole. And honestly, physical touch is the last thing I need after a day of bopping down thoughts of her like a Whac-A-Mole game that never ends.

"It's fine," I say, starting to get up. If only one of us is getting the chair, it's going to be her.

"Hey, don't get up," she says, pushing at my shoulders. Carefully, like she's afraid of hurting me, she lowers herself right onto the edge of my knees. "It's fine, see?"

She's barely sitting on me. Her tiptoes are taking the majority of her weight, and she's leaning forward, probably so she doesn't inconvenience me. I have to fight the urge to wrap my arm around her waist and pull her against my chest like a real boyfriend would.

"So," JoJo says from where she's curled up on Andre. It's taken all day, but she's finally relaxed. Which means she's about to say something she shouldn't. "How did you finally persuade her to date you?"

Chapter Nine

Aspen

Underneath me, Luke catches his breath. His hand instinctively comes to land on my hip, holding me in place like he's afraid I'm going to run or tip over.

"Babe," Andre says, nudging his bride-to-be. He's a sweet guy, short but amazingly buff. If I wasn't so distracted by Luke's adept use of power tools, I might have been tempted to ogle him.

As it is, my attention has been well and truly caught by the man whose fingers are currently digging into my hip.

When he speaks, though, his voice is easy. "Shut up, Jo."

JoJo looks at me directly. "It's such a relief," she tells me. "I'm not sure I could handle another round of my best friend dating my brother."

Luke coughs, and Matthew leans over to thump him on the back. I've come to like Matthew a *lot* in the short time I've known him, and he gives me a wink as he sits back.

"I've gone on dates since Brit and I broke up," Luke says defensively. "And can I just remind you that we've been broken up for over two years. It's over for real this time."

This is why I'm here. To convince his family, Brittany, and maybe even himself that their relationship is dead and won't be resurrected again.

I take this topic of conversation as a cue and lean back until I'm resting against his chest. "Tell me more about this infamous Brittany," I casually request, hoping my tone conceals my curiosity.

Who *was* this woman if Luke still might be hung up on her?

Luke shifts under me, subtly moving so his weight is better positioned for me, and his hand creeps around my waist. There are several layers of clothing separating us, but I can still feel the contact like it's burning into me.

"I've mentioned her," he says, tone irritated. "We were together in college."

"You guys got *engaged*," JoJo says. Her head lolls against Andre's shoulder. "It was serious. That's why you guys kept getting back together over and over."

Luke's sigh brushes past my hair, and when I glance at him, his expression is apologetic. "Please ignore my insensitive, idiot family," he says, eyes locking with mine. The flecks of green have disappeared in the darkness, swallowed by the firelight and shadows.

This isn't the man who's sat opposite me in that poorly air-conditioned office for two years. I don't know who he is.

All of a sudden, I feel defensive over the razzing Luke's family is giving him. So what if he made a mistake? We *all* make mistakes over our exes, and this is why Luke pretended to be dating me—so his family would lay off him about it.

I relax into his arms and place a hand on his cheek. His jaw flexes. His grip on me tightens.

"We all have pasts," I say, my voice as sultry as I can make it. "I'm more interested in your future."

His eyes are wide, their colors dark. Kissing him on the mouth seems like a step too far, so I reach up to peck him on the cheek, quick and chaste. When I lean back, there's a tiny smile playing on his lips.

"S'mores," Granny Mae says briskly as she joins us, breaking the moment, the children trailing behind her. She has a bunch of marshmallows on sticks, and the twins clamor for her to do theirs first. When everyone's settled, Millie climbing on Ruth's knee for a cuddle and Oliver grinning over at me, Granny Mae looks around.

"Why this silly silence?" she asks. "What's going on?"

"Jo's putting her foot in her mouth again," Matthew says.

JoJo sticks her tongue out at him. "I am not."

"You are, babe," Andre says apologetically, pressing a kiss to her temple. "But that's okay."

Granny harrumphs and waves away the chair Peter is already bringing her. "I'm all right, dear," she tells him. "If I sit down now, my hip might never let me get back up."

She's amazingly straight-backed as she stands, gilded by the flames. The twins get their marshmallows as Granny looks across at Luke and me, taking in our coziness. For a flicker of a moment, I wonder whether it's because she disapproves. Does she wish that Luke was with someone else?

Maybe she preferred Brittany.

Granny clicks her tongue as she stares at us and the now-awkward way we're sitting. "Did I interrupt something?" she asks wryly, raising an eyebrow. Oliver tugs on her arm, and she relents, putting his marshmallow into the flames and turning it every so often until it's the perfect amount of crispy. My mouth waters at the idea of biting into one, the sweet gooey center melting on my tongue.

"We're just being respectful," Luke says.

Matthew snorts. "Coward," he mutters under his breath.

Ruth glares at them both. "Behave, you two. Anyone would think you were brought up in a barn."

Matthew nudges Luke, nodding to the barn, and they both snicker. Luke's chest bobs under me, and I'm bumped along with his mirth.

It's cute. Sweet. I relax a little more against him.

Granny looks directly at me, something suspicious in her gaze. I get the sense she's making a quiet tally of every awkward and unconvincing thing Luke and I do. Is it possible she doesn't believe this is real?

No. Surely not.

Maybe?

I mean, we haven't exactly been all lovey-dovey the way JoJo and Andre have been. Is that what she expects?

"Don't hold back on my account," Granny says, and it sounds like a challenge. "You can kiss your man around us, honey." The emphasis she puts on *your man* makes it sound like she doesn't think he is. "Go on, now. Don't be shy. Life's too short to hold back expressing how you feel." She holds my gaze, as if daring me, and it makes me feel like I have to. But my body locks up at the demand, my mouth dry. This is every level of awkward—there are the seven levels of hell, and then there's this. Kissing with an audience. Kissing Luke for the first time with his whole family watching expectantly.

With Granny watching, probably waiting for it to be weird and awkward and look like a first kiss. There's no winning this.

"Young love," Ruth says with a sigh, like we're sixteen again.

Hesitantly, I glance up at Luke. His gaze is on my mouth, and for a dizzying, heart-lurching second, it stays here. Then he looks at me, and I read an apology in his knitted brows and shadowed eyes.

We don't have to do this, he tells me silently. But his fingers are holding on to my waist, his arm is a steel band around me, and I know, somehow, that if I run, he's going to catch me, if only to apologize for putting me in this situation. It's a strange feeling.

But I need to convince his family. To be a good friend and get them off his back. That's the thought that prompts me to lay a hand firmly on his chest, fingers splayed, and give him my best impression of a coquettish smile. My palms are sweating. I lean forward, and he ducks his head, one large palm cupping my head. To make sure I don't get the angle wrong, I suppose, because it's totally possible I'll mess this up. I haven't kissed anyone in several months.

And now there's Luke and his lips meeting mine, and all thoughts racing in my head go quiet.

As kisses go, it barely qualifies. It starts off more like a suggestion of a kiss. The *promise* of a kiss. His hand is still cupping my head, but there's no pressure there, even though it probably looks like there is. It probably looks like this kiss is a lot more passionate and intense than reality, given our body language and the way we're leaning into each other.

I count to three, and just before I lean back, his mouth moves, lips capturing mine and drawing them in. We linger. A hint of a nibble, and his breath catches as we pull apart.

Something warm and liquid erupts in my belly, and my hands tighten on his coat, nails digging in, fingers curling.

"Granny," Millie whines. "I want you to do my s'mores."

Everyone laughs. I break away, knowing I'm blushing head to toe. Luke's eyes open, and he looks almost dazed. He blinks, and his lips curve into a slow smile.

I avert my gaze. After everything, looking at his lips is a step too far. I don't want to think about the kiss or about how Luke is a good kisser. A *very* good kisser, if this sampling is any indication.

He presses his mouth against my ear, and my stomach enacts a complex gymnastic routine. Everyone else has moved on already, talking about the upcoming wedding and various plans. I vaguely hear Ruth talking about food, and Peter offers Andre a sympathetic wince as the voices rise in the cold winter air.

"I'm sorry," Luke murmurs, breath hot against my skin. I have to remind myself to breathe. "They don't know when to stop."

"No, it's fine." Am I overly chipper? I don't think I've ever heard my voice in this octave before. "Totally fine. We knew we'd have to do this."

"I know, but it doesn't make them pressuring you into doing it okay."

I glance across at Granny Mae. She's busy toasting more marshmallows—she's the queen of s'mores, apparently—but when she looks up, she gives us an approving nod. Like we passed some kind of test.

Weird. The thought sits warm in my chest, though. Like the approval of these people *matters* to me.

The conversation drifts past me. Granny Mae is at the center, tugging at people's threads, knowing everything with the kind of look in her eyes that suggests she sees more than she's letting on. She's the proud matriarch, and this is her family.

And I . . . like it. Luke's lap is comfortable, and I find myself sinking against him as Matthew teases his siblings relentlessly, taking the comebacks in good humor, and Mark is pretending not to hover around his pregnant wife. He wrangles the kids so she doesn't have to get up. He doesn't say much, but you can tell there's a heart of gold under that gruff exterior. You can see it every time he looks at Rebecca and their children.

It's so radically different from anything I've ever known. I keep pinching myself, half expecting to find it's a dream. When I wake, they'll be as dysfunctional as my family, with the arguing and the fake tears and the guilt trips.

But I don't wake, and if it's a show, it lasts flawlessly until everyone heads off to sleep.

And we go to the one bed I'm about to share with Luke.

There's a weird awareness now whenever I look at him, so I don't. I hurry to the sofa, grab the back cushions, and make a barrier down the middle of the mattress. There's still plenty of space on either side, just like I suspected there would be.

My idiot friends—probably Lina, let's be honest—packed the sexiest pajamas she could, so when I emerge from the bathroom, it's in a pair of tiny silken shorts that barely cover my ass and a black camisole with lace trimming that covers my boobs—just.

"Don't look," I call as I inch around the door. "Close your eyes."

"Okay," comes the response. "Eyes are closed."

I make a mad dash for the bed, cursing my friends and promising them a vile and violent death by my hands. Luke, true to his word, has his eyes closed, and I squirm under the covers, making sure they fully cover me before saying, "Okay. I'm decent."

Luke opens his eyes and looks down past the cushion barrier at me. Even sitting in bed, he's absurdly tall. "You don't have to be embarrassed."

"I do when you can practically see my ass hanging out in these things."

He blinks, and his face turns oddly blank. "Oh."

"Yep." I roll over so I'm facing the window and its long curtains that fall all the way to the wooden floor. The only light is a golden glow from his nightstand. Even the lamps have tassels. This place is so fancy, it makes me feel like some kind of cockroach. "I'm saving us both, trust me."

Luke clears his throat. "Why did you bring them?"

"My friends packed for me because I was too drunk. I guess it's Lina's idea of a joke." Or a hint. But with our kiss still hanging in the air, bringing up sex seems like the worst idea right now. I close my eyes, hoping to force the memory back into the little box it belongs in.

"A joke." Luke's voice is strangled.

"I know. I'm going to kill them when I get back."

He doesn't say anything, but I'm guessing he's thinking about the lingerie. The condoms. Hopefully he doesn't think *I* planted them.

I groan and bury my face in the pillow. The most important thing is that I keep control over my emotions. No feelings. Not even when he's lying in the same bed as me, not even when he treats me better than any man I've ever known.

Simple. Uncomplicated. *Friends*. If either of us cross that line, we'll lose what we have, and I care about our friendship and work relationship too much to mess that up.

Even if sometimes, maybe, even when I don't admit it to myself, the rebel in me wants to see what's on the other side of that line.

***

I wake to the sound of a rooster crowing. My consciousness tunes it in gradually, like a radio sliding into a station, and I yawn, blinking away the fuzz from the night's sleep.

Then I freeze. There is an arm around my middle. The cushions I placed between us are teetering off the foot of the bed, and Luke is pressed up against my backside.

No, I realize with a rush of mortification that may never go away. It's not that Luke is crammed against my backside; it's that I've wiggled my way back into him. The expanse of bed ahead of me stretches almost as far as my embarrassment.

His low, steady breaths tell me he's still asleep, though. Which is something. I don't think I could endure this if he was awake. After all the fuss I made about the barrier and my stupid pajamas, and now here I am, pressed into his arms.

It's actually kind of . . . nice. I haven't been held in a long time, and his skin is warm against mine. Plus, he smells good. This whole room smells like him, like musk and pine and spices.

What I *should* do is move before he wakes up so he never knows that I single-handedly destroyed my pillow barrier to get close to him.

What I actually do is lean back against him, letting his warmth soak into me. His breath dances across my ear, and I can feel his long, slow heartbeat. He unconsciously pulls me even closer, and my butt comes into contact with his crotch.

And the long, thick ridge through his pajama pants.

I freeze. My breath punches out of me.

This isn't my first time waking up with a guy. I *know* morning wood is a thing. Even when they wake up alone or with someone they aren't attracted to.

But like the kissing, I just hadn't thought of Luke as someone who . . . well, gets aroused. Is attracted to people. Has normal sexual urges. I've never allowed my brain to go there because that is a dangerous train of thought and leads to a place I'm not prepared to go.

Or, at least, *hadn't* been. Because now that we're here, I realize Luke doesn't fit the asexual robot box I put him in, along with my other male coworkers. Now, I know how rugged, capable, and manly he is.

And yes, he's hot. Kissing him yesterday was very *pleasant*. Being wrapped in his arms is extremely nice.

Having his erection pressing against me isn't exactly a burden, either. It sends hot prickles of something across my skin. The sensation of being wanted.

Ridiculous, really. Because he's *asleep*. Someone needs to remind my awakening libido of that.

It's just because I haven't had any in six months. Lina was right: that *is* too long to be going without sex. I'm just horny and seeing things that don't exist.

But this exists. This *definitely* exists.

Luke stirs, fingers tensing against my side and his breath stuttering, and I slide out from under his arm. Time to go. And maybe I can reconstruct the pillow wall before he fully wakes up.

Chapter Ten

Luke

I pretend to be asleep just long enough for Aspen to close the door behind her, then roll on my back and stare at the ceiling. My hard-on shows absolutely no signs of going away.

There's no reason it would, seeing as Aspen was rubbing her ass all over it. Waking to her in my arms was simultaneously the best and worst experience of my life so far. Best because having her there felt like every dream I've had finally came true.

Worst because my dick, which I've been constantly schooling into submission around Aspen, thought it should make an appearance, and there's no way she didn't feel it. That's probably why she left so suddenly.

I just can't get the way she softened into me out of my head. Like she loved what she felt. How *I* felt. Maybe she just hadn't noticed my morning predicament.

Though if she did and she liked it . . .

Don't go there.

I've been torturing myself with what-ifs for years, and just because she's in closer proximity doesn't mean she's going to change her mind about the way she sees me.

Stop the slow march to insanity, Luke. She's not into you. We are moving on.

I grab a cushion, one of the ones that's been relegated to the bottom of the bed, and set it on my lap as I check my phone. A bunch of texts from Kai and Chase asking how it's going. Chase's advice is, again, to get her naked. To quote him exactly, *get her in a hot tub*. Kai's advice is to flex. *What's the point of going to the gym five times a week if you don't have any gains to show for it?* is his phrasing.

So that's a nada on the useful advice.

My phone lights up with a call from JoJo, and I welcome the distraction.

"Hey," I say, stifling a yawn. By the look of the light outside the curtains, it's still pretty early. Not that the rooster seems to agree. Noisy as always. "What's up?"

"Mom needs help with the cinnamon rolls for breakfast," she says immediately. "Mark's insisting Rebecca take her weight off her feet, and you know what Matthew's like in the kitchen."

I sure do. Matthew's the only man I've known who can make burning food into an art.

"I thought Aspen could help. Mom would love getting to know her better," she continues.

Aspen, pink hair smoothed and a robe wrapped around her waist, enters the room, and she looks relieved to see me on the phone.

"Did I hear you mention my name?" Aspen asks, rifling through her bag for clothes.

"Mark wants your help in the barn." There's a smile in Jo's voice. "Andre and I have last-minute wedding errands today, so I want to make sure Mom's got all the help she needs."

I rub my eyes and avert my gaze from Aspen as she bends over. *Focus.* "Sure, okay."

"Great. Also, I like Aspen a lot. She's sweet."

"Yeah, I know."

"And it's obvious she adores you."

I lean back against the headboard. "Right."

"I mean it," she insists. "I know you say you guys aren't super serious, but she's so into you." She squeals. "I see another wedding in the future!"

"And that's my cue to put the phone down. Bye, Jo."

"No, wait, don't hang up. I—"

I end the call and flop my phone back on the bed. The irony is so painful, it's like a knife to the chest. JoJo is so loved up, she sees love everywhere.

Aspen doesn't seem to notice my mood. She picks up her phone and clicks her tongue in irritation.

"Dead," she says. "Didn't charge last night I guess."

"Try my cable?" I hold it out and she plugs her phone in, the charging icon appearing on the screen. "You can leave it here if you want."

"I'll have to." With another frustrated sigh, she perches on the edge of the bed and looks at me. Just looks, eyes curious like she's searching for something she's not entirely sure she'll find.

"Jo's asked if you'd be up for making cinnamon rolls with my mom," I say to break the silence. "I figured you wouldn't mind."

"Well, sugar and bread *are* two of my favorite food groups," she says, lifting one shoulder. Her gaze still doesn't break mine. Then, she nods decisively. "New rule. No sex."

I almost choke. The image of her body curved under me, all those flimsy layers pushed aside . . .

Quadratic equations. Python. C++.

I clear my face of all expression. "I thought no sex was already a rule."

"What I'm saying is no sex is *the* rule." Patiently, she waits for me to catch on. "As in, the only rule."

Finally, I understand. All her other rules limiting touching, limiting kissing, limiting the ways in which we can be a couple, gone.

I swallow, mouth dry. Two days in, and we've made more progress than two years of being co-workers.

Maybe there's a chance . . .

"Why?" I ask, pushing the thought aside.

"Because Granny looked suspicious last night. Like maybe she doesn't believe it's real," she says. "So, we need to step up our game. Act more like a couple. Act like it's not weird when we touch each other."

She really shouldn't be using those words if she doesn't want me to get the wrong idea.

"You look dazed," she informs me.

"I am dazed. This is a lot of new information and options. I just need to process."

"I don't mind," she says, and maybe it's my imagination, but it looks like she blushes. "I was thinking about it, and I don't . . . mind behaving like a girlfriend. I trust you. You're a good guy. You won't hurt me."

This is the opportunity I'd been waiting for during all that time as colleagues. And it's happening now. The timing could not be worse.

But maybe it's still worth giving it a shot, just like Kai said. If she's willing, if she trusts me, if she doesn't mind acting like a true girlfriend, then maybe I have a chance at opening her eyes to the possibility of making it real.

It's not like I have any realistic chance at escaping this arrangement with my heart intact. Might as well throw everything I have into making her want me back.

I give her a long, slow smile. "Think you can keep up?"

"Is that a dare, Simmons?"

"Is that a yes?"

Her blush deepens—not my imagination, then—but she holds my gaze. Aspen is never one to back down from a dare.

I lean in. "I won't make it easy," I murmur. "I'll treat you like a queen. By the time these ten days are up, you won't be able to resist me." To prove my point, I open the nightstand drawer on my side and whip out the allergy meds, and she bursts out laughing.

"You know what?" she says as she accepts them. "Maybe I won't."

***

Aspen

The kitchen is warm and already full of the delicious scent of frying bacon when Luke and I walk in. His hand is around mine, fingers linked through, and he tugs me across to where his mom is in front of the stove.

"That smells amazing," he says, inhaling. "Do you want some, sweetheart?"

I jolt. Shock and fire shoot through my veins like lightning, and it's all I can do to nod.

I've had my fair share of boyfriends. Lina used to laugh at me for dating around so much, especially when the sex was mediocre, but it was nice to have someone who wanted me. Who would buy me dinner and smoke a joint with me and tell me I have the best body he's ever seen. Even if it was just for a casual fling.

None of those guys ever called me "sweetheart." A couple called me "baby." Some called me "Ass" for short because they thought it was hilarious.

Not Luke. He just came straight out with *sweetheart* like it was nothing. Natural. The same way he put his hand on my knee yesterday.

And I, clearly in a fit of madness, gave him the green light to do whatever he likes.

"Your dad wants you in the barn," Ruth says, handing Luke a plate of bacon. "Can you take that to him?"

"Sure. I'm looking forward to returning later to the smell of the cinnamon rolls." Luke kisses my temple in passing, another casual gesture that leaves me breathless, and heads out of the room with his bacon, leaving me with his mom.

His mom. Alone.

I can't help comparing her to *my* mom. Ruth is older, maybe by about ten years, and her face is creased to match her smile lines. They're permanently embedded in her face, but it's a pleasant kind of aging.

My mom's face shows signs of a hard life. Puffy from too much alcohol, lined from tanning beds, hair chemically damaged. She's pretty—I'll always think my mom is pretty—but she looks tired, always hiding under a layer of makeup so thick I could dig it off with a spoon.

Ruth is the epitome of sweet and motherly. There are no hard edges, no air of simmering resentment, of toxic need. When she smiles at me, she makes me feel more welcome than my own mother ever does.

The thought burns in the pit of my stomach.

"Before we get started, why don't you have some breakfast?" she says, passing me some bacon. "Do you want eggs?"

"No, no, this is fine. Thank you."

She ushers me to the table, and I eat as several family members come and go. The twins are playing some imaginary game of Star Wars, judging by the sound effects they make every time their sticks clack together. Oliver is following them around, wearing a superhero cape, and Ruth shoos all three children out. Through the window, I see Millie chasing chickens around with single-minded focus, not seeming to notice the gently falling snow.

And there's Luke, also not seeming to mind the snow: he's stripped off his coat and sweater and is wearing a tight cotton T-shirt. Mark is throwing wood into a pile by his feet, and Luke is wielding an axe, splitting each log effortlessly. His T-shirt clings to his pecs, his abs—holy shit, Luke has *abs*—and I get an HD rendition of the way the muscles in his arms and broad shoulders work in unison with each swing of the axe. It's freezing out there, but he looks like he's working up a sweat. And it's so damn enjoyable to watch.

He looks *amazing,* actually. Full lumberjack hot, and where the hell did those *arms* come from?

I look away, blinking, in time for a ruffle-haired Matthew to wander into the kitchen, still in his pajamas. He gives me a bleary good morning and curses his luck in having twins (even though I'm pretty sure he was the one who wanted them) before retreating.

Rebecca sinks into the seat opposite me just as I'm finishing up, and she gives me a wry smile. "I love being pregnant, but these final days are the absolute worst. My feet are too swollen to wear anything except crocs and Mark's boots." She groans, massaging the small of her back. "I'm a beached whale. Mark has to help me out of the bath."

"Well, you're older now, and each pregnancy takes its toll on your body. I'm glad my childbearing years are over," Ruth says, expertly kneading dough while we eat.

Rebecca chuckles tiredly. "Don't rub it in."

I feel like an intruder in the family dynamic.

After kneading the dough for a few more minutes, Ruth goes into sergeant-major mode. She gives me short, not unfriendly instructions, and soon my fingers are coated in flour and cinnamon.

And that's when Granny marches in, already in her cowboy hat and boots. "Mmm, cinnamon rolls," she says. "You know how to make an old lady happy."

"Been out with the horses already?" Rebecca asks. "You can take a day off, you know. Mark's got it."

"Sure, Mark's got the touch, but if I get into the habit of staying in bed all day, I'll lose my youth." She winks at me, and I suppress a giggle.

Ruth rolls her eyes and gets out a rolling pin. I sprinkle some flour on the counter.

"Sorry about JoJo last night," Ruth says. "She doesn't have a filter when she's had a few drinks."

Granny snorts. "She just feels guilty about Brittany, that's all."

"Really?" I ask before I can help myself. "Why?"

"Oh, they went to school together," Ruth says quickly, before Granny can say anything, like she knows Granny's about to come out with something wild. Honestly, I'd like to know what that would be. "That's how Luke met her, actually. Through Jo."

"It was always going to end in disaster," Granny says. "She didn't have true grit."

"Now, that's not fair," Ruth says, but Granny shakes her head. I've stopped what I'm doing, absorbing everything. There's a strange tension here, a sense that this is an issue the women have disagreed over for a long time. A wound that they keep having to pick open again.

"Don't tell me it's not fair when she treated our Luke the way she did," Granny Mae says and cuts a look at me. "Did he tell you the whole story?"

"That's enough, Mae," Ruth says.

"No, no, Aspen should know the truth." Granny leans over to the fruit bowl and picks up an apple. "They were together for a while. She came here sometimes. Hot one moment, cold the next. Whatever suited her. And when they ended . . ." She sucks at her teeth. "You know she cheated on him?"

"This isn't our story to tell Granny," Rebecca says from the table. She's handing a cup of juice to Millie, who's run inside for a snack. "And it's been over for a long time."

"He never got over her betrayal," Granny pronounces. It's like the clang of a gavel. A verdict. "Lost his trust in women because of it."

"They were both too young to be making such big decisions." Ruth's voice is placating, shooting me a worried glance, like she's scared I'm going to take offense to this, to assume that Luke has too much baggage for me to handle. "They got engaged as soon as he graduated school. It was too early. Too much."

Granny huffs. "Once a cheater, always a cheater."

"Now, that's not fair," Rebecca says patiently. "It was a long time ago. Why don't we drop it? This conversation can't be comfortable for Aspen."

Granny looks me dead in the eyes. "You know, you're the first girl he's brought home in all that time."

The weight of that responsibility, the pressure of their expectations, settles on me like lead. I have to swallow past it.

"He's dated since then," Rebecca says, wiping mushy banana off Millie's hands while she tries to escape from the table. "And he's been focusing on his career."

"Sorry, Aspen," Ruth says pointedly. "We didn't mean to bombard you with all this Brittany talk."

"Oh, it's fine," I say, trying to sound offhand. "What does she do?"

Granny snorts. "She's an influencer, if you can believe that."

"So am I," Rebecca says. To me, she adds, "I have a homestead momma account, and it does fairly well, especially my sourdough bread videos. Sometimes, Brittany and I collaborate, or we promote each other, though her following is a lot bigger."

I can't imagine it, Luke with a content creator. He's practically allergic to social media. I've seen rocks that are more alive than his Instagram account.

Maybe that's because of her.

My cheeks flush as I look down at the tray of rolls I've been making. Outside again, Millie shrieks with delight, and I can hear the steady tones of Peter, Mark, and Luke talking while they do their chores. It feels as though things are falling into place. I understand Luke on a deeper level now.

I know what it's like to get your fingers burned.

Granny pats my shoulder and grips it firmly. "You're good for him, honey. He's himself around you, and I can't tell you how important that is."

You're good for him.

I've never felt less good for anyone in my life. Luke is kind, he's such a good person, so genuine and honest, and we're here lying to his family. They believe we're something we're not, and guilt eats away at my chest, winding up my throat to burn like acid in my mouth.

You're good for him.

I wish, so much it almost hurts, that I could tell her the truth.

Chapter Eleven

Luke

A spen giggles as we unfold the wrapping paper and collect the scissors and scotch tape from where Rebecca and the twins left them. It's evening, the sun is setting behind the mountains, and Aspen's been drinking all day. She started with mimosas while baking with Mom, and when Dad started making Christmas mules, she was more than happy to polish off several of those, too. I swapped her last one out for water.

"You okay with the scissors?" I ask. I'm a bit buzzed too, but Aspen looks like she's borderline drunk. Not as bad as I've seen her get at the cantina sometimes, but enough that I don't want to risk her chopping off a finger.

Although, having seen the quality of her gift wrapping firsthand, I don't think that's got anything to do with the alcohol.

Aspen sits cross-legged in front of me. "I'm great. So good."

"You sure?" When I first came in from the yard, she had gone back to being standoffish with me, though the alcohol loosened her up as the hours went by. When dinner came around, she was relaxed enough that she leaned into me and even pressed a kiss to my shoulder.

It's dangerously familiar and intimate. Close enough to genuine, I can almost touch it.

"I'm sure." She laughs again. "I'm so bad at this."

"I know."

"What?"

"You think I haven't noticed how bad you are at wrapping?" I fold down a corner. "I remember Rick's birthday present."

"Mugs are hard to wrap."

"You made it into a triangle. Which, by the way, should be a physical impossibility."

She laughs again, deep and rich. A real belly laugh. "Maybe I should've asked you to do it. You actually know what you're doing. Do you do this every year?"

"When JoJo and I were younger, we used to team up and wrap everyone's presents together. She does what you're doing now."

"Cute. My mom and I just use gift bags."

She doesn't mention her dad. I know from her story on the drive up that he's not in the picture, and when her expression shifts from playful to wistful, I don't dare ask.

If I could, I'd erase that look in her eyes. Wipe it away, promise her anything she needs so long as she'll smile again.

"You have a nice family," she says quietly.

"They're a bit much sometimes. You can say it."

"No, it's nice." Her eyes seem too big for her face when she looks up at me. "You're nice."

I swallow and clear my throat, trying not to grin at her and failing. "You're drunk."

"And you're buff." She prods my arm. "Flex. There, see? You have *muscles*." She says it reverently, like they're the Holy Grail, and damn, I guess I should've worn short sleeves at work more often.

Her hand doesn't move from my arm, fingers curled around my bicep, but her expression falls again.

"Luke," she says, quiet and vulnerable, "do you think we're doing the right thing? Lying to your family?"

"Where's this coming from?"

"I mean, your family thinks I'm *good* for you." She makes a dismissive noise, like she can't believe she's good for anyone, and I want to shake her, to tell her all the ways she's made me better without even knowing it.

Made me try harder, want things I've never aspired to before. Made me push out of my comfort zone and discover new things. How much she inspires me with her strength, with her resilience and determination. Her volunteer work teaching underserved girls free coding classes is admirable.

Seeing her work, seeing her code with that intensity and precision, catching errors I wouldn't have noticed if I'd read it a thousand times, has made me stay up late reading and researching, just to keep my skills sharp so I don't get left behind.

I guess that's why Kai gave me the opportunity to go to San Jose and head up an important project. Indirectly because of *her*, because of who she's unknowingly pushed me to become. And she has no idea.

"It's fine for me," she continues. "I mean, I'm not going to see any of them again after. But what about you?"

"What about me?"

"Won't they ask questions? Talk about me the same way they talk about Brittany?" Her eyes plead with me, so filled with guilt it hurts, and my chest aches with how much I want to hold her. "Your family isn't like my mom. We don't talk to each other like you guys do; she doesn't get involved in my life the same way ..." More sadness, pouring out of her. It eats away at me and seems to burn away her drunkenness. "It's Christmas Eve, and I haven't even spoken to her."

"Then you should." I check my phone for the time. It's seven. The kids are probably sprinkling oatmeal as "reindeer food" in the yard right now before bed. It's always an early night for them on Christmas so we have time to fill their stockings and make it look like Santa's been here.

No one will miss her if she heads off for a bit.

"Call her now," I say. "I can finish up here." And while I'm worried about her, talking about her mom is easier than talking about our deal and the ending she has in mind for us.

Easier for me, anyway.

Aspen looks down at her hands and the tape she's still holding. "You sure? There's still so much left to wrap."

"I'm sure. Go back to our cabin. I'll find you when I'm done."

With one last glance at me, peering with narrowed eyes like she's peeling the meaning from my words and seeing if they match, she pushes to her feet and leaves the room.

***

Aspen

I find my phone charging where I left it what feels like a thousand years ago—this morning when Luke and I discussed ramping up the physicality of our fake dating.

Now, it's believable. Luke is playing the part of the ideal boyfriend, and I'm the girl his parents think he's going to end up with, but in a shocking turn of events, won't. I can see it in their eyes, this hope, this certainty that our pretense is the *real deal*.

And Luke seems so nonchalant about it. Content to be putting on this show for them. How did Luke act around Brittany when she was his fiancée?

My gut tightens at the thought of Brittany. An influencer. She's probably beautiful. Blonde, perfectly manicured, with push-up bras and false lashes and—

I catch my thoughts before they can drive off the bridge into a lake of bitterness. Even if she *is* all those things, what does that matter?

What *matters* is that she cheated on Luke. I can't forgive her for that. And it has *nothing* to do with what she looks like.

I snatch my phone, unlocking it and staring at the missed calls. Five missed calls, all from Mom. They were all made in a ten-minute period about two hours ago.

My chest constricts, my lungs temporarily stilled, and I redial, pressing the phone to my ear so hard it hurts as I listen to it ring. And ring. And ring.

Voicemail.

Shit.

My hands shake as I call her again. And again. Eventually, on my fourth try, she picks up.

"Hey, baby," she says, and by the way her words slur, she's drunk. There's a rasp I recognize as well, the one I heard all too often after Dad left. Misery. "Merry Christmas . . . Eve?"

"Mom." I perch on the end of the bed, conflicted about everything in this beautiful paradise. I spent the day baking with someone else's mom, spending time with someone else's family, and I liked it. Even though it meant I wasn't spending time with my own mom. "What happened?"

She pauses a beat too long. "Nothing happened."

"Don't give me that." Sometimes, when we talk, I feel like the parent. I've been the responsible one since I was eight years old—too young to be sensible, to wipe away my mom's tears. The child inside me died the day my dad left. "Something's going on. You don't call me like that out of the blue for nothing."

"Maybe I just wanted to speak to my baby girl on Christmas Eve." Her voice sharpens, misery rusted, yet cutting. I feel it slice through my skin, digging into my heart. "Even if my baby girl doesn't want to speak to me."

"I was busy. Didn't have my phone on me." Excuses won't cut it, so I change tactics. "Can we FaceTime?"

"No!" The answer is too fast, and I suck in a breath.

"Why not?"

"Because I look like a mess."

"Why are you drinking?" It's the most hypocritical thing to say when I can feel the buzz of a day's worth of drinking in my veins, but she's way more gone than I am. And I don't do this daily. "Is Tim there?"

This time, her pause is longer, stretching the silence until I can't bear it.

"No," she says finally.

"Mom, what happened?"

"It's not a big deal."

"Then why isn't Tim with you on Christmas Eve?"

"Look, it's fine," she says, but I can hear the resignation in her voice. The sadness. And that little edge of defensiveness. "We just got into an argument, that's all."

If I close my eyes, I can see Tim's face. He's a nasty drunk, and he never knows when to stop. My voice is low when I ask, "What did he do?"

"It was my fault, baby. I said the wrong thing."

"Mom." I want to yell, to scream, but if I do that, she might hang up, and I need to know. "Tell me. What did he do?"

"He just . . ." She takes a deep breath. "We got into a fight. The neighbors called the police, and they took him away to calm down."

I close my eyes, feeling hot tears track down my face. I know what she's not saying. That bastard hit her. He fucking *hit* her, and she's defending him like he's not a piece of shit. Like she deserved it.

Luke's family appears to have it all figured out, but that's not normal. Probably not realistic either. *This* is what relationships devolve into if you're not careful. If you let your guard down, if you trust, if you believe they're right for you, they inevitably let you down.

Mom has believed in every one of her scumbag boyfriends, and look where it's gotten her. A black eye, probably. Maybe a split lip. Bruises all over her body.

I'm itching with anger, and I punch my pillow even as I bite back a scream, all the profanities I want to unleash on her. That won't help, and I need to help. I need to be there for her. That's my job.

"I'm coming home," I tell her, sniffing and wiping my nose. "I don't know how, but I'll get there. I'm coming."

"He'll be released by the time you can get here," she says, but I know it's because she doesn't want me to see her bruises. Like not seeing them would make me any less determined to kick the *shit* out of Tim.

"You need to press charges."

"He loves me."

"That isn't love!" I yell, and I know I've gone too far. The line disconnects.

I hurl my phone across the room, grab a pillow, and scream.

Chapter Twelve

Luke

There are clothes everywhere. Aspen is stuffing toiletries into her bag with grim-faced determination, jaw clenched and tears streaming. She sniffs defiantly, scrubbing the back of her hand across her cheek, and glances up at me as soon as I enter the room.

"Aspen, what happened?" I run through all the things that could be wrong. *Her mom is hurt. Her mom's in trouble. They had a fight. Was there an accident? Is she leaving?*

Crap. It's Christmas Eve, and although it's not actively snowing right now, it's been snowing on and off all day. The roads are going to be a nightmare, and I'm not fit to drive. No one here is. Especially not Aspen.

She looks at me through red-rimmed eyes. "I need to go home. To New Jersey."

"New Jersey?" There's no way I can be hearing this properly. I catch her hands, stilling her for a second. "You want to go to *New Jersey, tonight?*"

"It's where my mom lives."

"Tell me what happened." I brush the tears from her face, and because I can't help myself, I run my thumbs across her cheeks, her face cradled in my hands. "Talk to me."

Aspen averts her eyes, and I can almost feel the anger in her. It fizzes. I guess it's always been there, under the surface. I've seen it sometimes, though it's more like bitterness that comes out when she talks about the future. About *happily ever after* being a myth. It's clear she doesn't believe in it, and that's one of the things I want to change her mind about.

Right now, though, I just need her to tell me what's wrong.

"It's my mom," she mumbles. "And her shitbag boyfriend. They got into an argument, and he hit her. He *hit* her. I knew he was a piece of shit, but *this*." She shakes her head, chin wobbling, more of those tears breaking free and rolling down her face. They splatter against her chest. "The neighbors called the cops and he's in jail overnight, so she's alone and he *hurt* her."

"Hey, hey." I pull her closer, sliding my arms around her and resting my cheek against her bubblegum hair. When she sighs, it's like all the air in her body is being expelled at once, and she rests her forehead against my collarbone. Her arms lock loosely around my waist, and her chest heaves.

"I can't believe he would do this to her. That she stays with him."

"Is he the reason you changed your mind about going home?"

Her arms tighten reflexively. "He tried to feel me up a couple years back. Cornered me and told me Mom never had to know."

She shudders, and I hold her closer. The same anger I sensed in her rises in me, and I have to force it back.

Calm. For Aspen's sake.

"She never believed me, not really, and I've just avoided seeing her whenever he's around."

I have to choose my words carefully. "What would you achieve going back there now?"

"I can't leave her to his mercy. Because—" Her voice cracks, and I feel her tears soak through my sweater. "What sort of daughter am I if I leave her there?"

"Does she want him back?"

"She doesn't understand how bad he is."

"Listen to me." I lean back and meet her eyes so she knows how serious I am. "If you want me to drive you to the airport tomorrow, I will. If you decide you want to go there, I'll help you arrange it. Hell, I'll come with you." There's no way I want her walking into something like that alone. "But just take a moment, Aspen. Breathe. Think about what you want to get from this." I run my hand up her spine, and she shivers from the contact, pressing herself more firmly against me. When was the last time someone just held her? Comforted *her* instead of the other way around?

"I don't know what to do," she mumbles, voice muffled against me. "She doesn't want to hear it, but he's *hurting* her."

What if he hurts you, too? "I know. But listen, is that going to change if you're there?"

She sniffles. "No."

"I know you want to help your mom. And I get it. If my mom was in trouble, I would want to help out too." I trace small circles across her shoulder blades until she relaxes a little more. Inch by inch, muscle by muscle. "But it's okay to set boundaries and stick to them. It's not your responsibility to make sure her life goes the way you think it should. And if she's not going to listen to you . . ." I suck in a breath, worried I've gone too far, but she doesn't move. Just breathes. The warmth of her breath permeates through my sweater.

"It's like I'm the mom," she says at last. "And it's been like that for a long time."

"That must be hard." I start to guide her to the bed before leading her to the sofa instead. It's devoid of back cushions, but the seat is still soft, and there's space for her to curl up against me. She does, not even seeming to think about it as she tucks her knees up and over my lap, and I hold her in a semi-fetal position against my chest.

This isn't pretend.

"You don't have to be the mom," I tell her. "You don't have to be a parent."

"If I'm not, then who is?"

"She's a grown woman. Maybe she can figure it out this time." I wait a beat before adding, "I know boundaries are hard. And I know you want to help. I love that about you, the way you throw everything aside to look after people when you think they need you."

She braces her hand against my chest, pushing herself back so she can look at me. "I do?"

"You do. You're incredible, Aspen."

The corners of her mouth quirk. Not a smile, but approaching one. I stay where I am, knowing if I move and break the moment, she'll lose that smile. Maybe she'll even lose the vulnerability.

"You're a good listener, Simmons. You know that?"

"So I've been told. And you can talk to me, you know. Any time you like."

She hums and falls back against my chest. A small sign of trust from a woman who doesn't trust easily. My heart does a cartwheel.

"Last-minute Christmas flights out to New Jersey are probably enormously expensive, right?"

"Yeah, I'd think so. And we can't drive down the canyon until tomorrow either. Everyone's had too much to drink. There's probably no flights headed east this late at night anyway. But," I add, skimming my fingers along the back of her neck, "if you want to go after you've slept on it, I'll book us two tickets."

She shoots straight up. "Luke, you can't. It's Christmas."

"Sure, I can."

"Luke—"

"That's the deal. I'm not letting you go alone."

One hand rakes through her hair, and it's a beautiful, helpless gesture. "You're being ridiculous. You can't abandon your family to travel across the country on Christmas Day."

"Sure, I can," I repeat. "That's what fake boyfriends do."

Her eyes fill with tears again, and it's all I can do not to kiss away the anguish written across her face.

Baby steps. Don't want to scare her off.

"I've got something for you," I say instead, unfurling from the sofa and digging through the inner pocket of my suitcase until I find it. A small paper bag that shows its age—a year old now. I bought it last year for Secret Santa when I drew Aspen. Then, at the last minute, I chickened out and got her something else. Something more impersonal.

I kept the gift, though. Never sure why, just unable to throw it away.

When she decided to come here with me, I knew this would be the perfect time to finally give it to her.

I hand her the wrinkled bag. "I was going to wrap these and give them to you tomorrow, but I figured you might want to see them now."

Her expression creases into a frown. "You didn't need to get me anything."

"Just open it."

She does, shaky hands tugging at the tape holding the bag shut, then tipping the box onto her palm. Her confusion continues until she opens the box and sees the silver aspen-leaf earrings. There's a square piece of paper tucked in there too, and she picks it up, reading the sentiment printed on glossy cardstock. "'Aspens symbolize courage, determination, and overcoming fear. The leaves may tremble, but the tree does not break.'" Her voice cracks again, and she looks up at me with brimming eyes. "These are beautiful. And thoughtful. Thanks, Luke."

"Let's play hooky," I suggest, collecting the couch cushions and putting them back in place. "We can stay here the rest of the evening. I've got more Skittles, and we could watch a movie."

"Won't your parents be mad that we're missing the Christmas Eve festivities?"

"Nah." I wink, tucking her back into my side. "I bet Jo and Andre are doing the same thing. Except with fewer Skittles and way more sex."

She laughs, the sound barking unexpectedly from her, and she snuggles up against me, one arm slung around my waist. "I wouldn't mind staying here. With you."

I hope she doesn't hear the way my heart thuds at that. I switch on the TV, trying futilely to concentrate on whatever the hell we're going to watch, not the fact I'm cuddling the girl of my dreams and trying to figure out how to never let her go.

"I wouldn't mind that either," I tell her. "Actually, it sounds kind of . . . perfect."

Chapter Thirteen

Aspen

I don't usually wake up horny, but the instant I'm awake on Christmas morning, I'm aware of two things. Firstly, I'm sprawled gratuitously over Luke, his bare torso burning through my skimpy pajamas and a *definite* bulge at his crotch, nudging against my knee.

Don't look at it, don't look at it, don't look at it...

The second thing I notice is that *holy shit* am I turned on. My panties are wet. It's embarrassing, actually, how drenched I am, considering it's first thing in the morning.

And I'm in Luke's arms. Warm, safe, connected.

My body definitely wants him. Every single time I feel his hardness twitching against my knee, my entire body burns, the heat of a fire on cold skin. It's intense, so intense I'm throbbing with need. It's the kind of thing you read about but never experience.

Until, apparently, right this second.

My mouth is Sahara-level dry, and I've got the slightest hint of a hangover, but my body is still desperately telling me to straddle him, to feel the way he rests between my thighs, listen to the way he groans as I—

No. No, no, no. Pure thoughts, Aspen; pure thoughts.

Is my type actually lumberjacking tech nerds? Have I developed a complex where kindness and muscles, in sizable doses, kickstarts my libido?

I must have just had dirty dreams. It's been a while, after all.

Luke's arm curls around me as he shifts, and by the way his breathing fractures, I can tell he's woken up.

This time, there is absolutely no *way* I can play it off as him cuddling me. I am most definitely the initiator. He's pinned to the bed under me. I've trapped him with my *body*.

Mortification wars with my desire, and I'm momentarily speechless.

"Morning," he says sleepily, pressing a kiss to my forehead. He can't be fully awake yet, or he'd know that we don't need to play at being a couple when we're alone.

As I try to peel myself off of him, my shin bumps against him, and I can almost feel his attention shift to the contact. *Shit.*

I move back, and he releases me almost as fast. There's a flush, one I'm coming to recognize, burning at the top of his cheekbones. He's adorably flustered, and goddamn, how is it possible for him to be so attractive?

How the hell didn't I *notice* before? I must have been blind. Blinkered.

Luke's expression turns to one of concern, and I realize I'm still just staring at him, probably in abject horror. I squeeze my legs tightly together so there's no chance he'll get a glimpse of how I'm feeling. God, I'm not sure how to proceed.

This is embarrassing. Or it would be if I didn't already know he was hard. As it is, I'm consumed with the temptation to jump him.

Would he mind? He's a guy, right? He wouldn't mind if I suggested we do something . . . like jump on each other and have mindless, naughty, all-consuming sex. Just this once.

He clears his throat, his flush not leaving, and shifts to hide his crotch. "Are you okay?"

No. I've just discovered I want to have sex with you, and it's like discovering masturbation for the first time. It's a whole new world I never knew existed.

"Um." I try to focus on the issue at hand. Simple question. All I need to do is give a simple answer. "Yes. I'm fine."

"Are you sure?"

"Yeah, I—" *Rein in your libido, girl. This is not a friends-with-benefits situation.* Except he's right there, looking good enough to tempt me. Tousled hair a tiny bit too long, no shirt, still hazy with sleep. I can taste the possibilities. It's Christmas today. A day made for magic. Made for giving special gifts, like amazing orgasms, right? Not all gifts have to come wrapped . . .

And he held me yesterday while I cried. He's seen me at my worst, and he's still here, looking at me like I'm the only thing that exists for him—like the sun could've died and sunk the earth into darkness, and he would never have noticed.

He reaches forward and strokes my arm. When I don't pull away, he trails his fingers up my shoulder and cups my neck, and I lean in instinctively. My entire body flushes. I'm ready for this. *Ready.*

"Aspen," he whispers, bringing his forehead down to rest on mine. I don't even care that I haven't brushed my teeth. The only thing I can think about is the way our bodies are angled, the way his gaze drops meaningfully to my lips. He leans in, and his lips graze mine, testing my response. This is it; it's going to happen, and—

Banging on the door interrupts us. "Uncle Luke!" one of the twins calls. The doorknob rattles, and apparently we accidentally left it unlocked. I have just enough time to climb back under the covers before four small bodies pile in along with the snow and a burst of cold air that cools the flames on my skin.

"Uncle Luke!" Millie says. She's in her pajamas, but her pink puffer jacket is zipped up, and her wool hat has a crown on it. A Disney princess, probably. "It's Christmas. We have to do *presents*. Now."

"Hey, hey, what have we said about barging in on people like that?" Luke asks, quickly throwing his pillow over his lap as Millie launches herself toward him, and he catches her in midair. The twins climb onto the end of the bed and start bouncing, still wearing their shoes. Luke orders them off, and I can't help laughing as they totally trash the room in about ten seconds of small-human-tornado.

When they're gone, Luke grimaces apologetically at me. "I'm so sorry. I know they're a lot."

"You don't have to apologize." I climb off the bed, the interruption having given me enough space to get some perspective. If he truly wanted something with me, and didn't just get caught up in the moment, he'd have made a move sometime over the past *two years*. We probably both would've regretted such an impulsive decision. I just haven't performed a little self-care in a while, that's all. I don't usually go this long in between, so this has been too big a break for my lady bits.

He runs a hand along the back of his neck. "We should probably—"

"I need to call my mom, okay? Just to see how she's doing."

His hand drops to the covers. "Sure. Whatever you need. Just let me know if you want me to drive you anywhere."

"Don't worry about it." I give him the world's most awkward wave as I walk into the bathroom and dial my mom's number. She answers on the second ring.

"Hey, baby! Merry Christmas!"

I don't know how my mom's alcohol tolerance is this good, but she's always irritatingly fresh after a night of heavy drinking. Maybe because most nights are.

Hey, Mom. Merry Christmas."

"Guess who's here!"

Oh no.

But to my relief, it's not Tim's voice that comes down the speaker. It's Sherry from next door. Her husband left her and their three dogs last year, so I guess she didn't want to be alone over the holiday season either.

"Hey, cutie," Sherry says. She's in her forties and has the irresistible urge to mother everything she comes into contact with.

"Hey," I say, some of the tension leaving my shoulders. "I'm so glad you're spending Christmas with Mom."

"Well, I saw her alone last night, and I figured she needed some company." If she means it as a dig, it doesn't come across that way. Her voice is too light and happy, though there's a forced edge to it.

Christmas is a difficult time of year for a lot of people.

"And, of course, Tim was released this morning," Mom says. "He just got back, actually. Say hi, Tim."

Tim's voice comes onto the phone. "Hey, Aspen. Merry Christmas. How are you doing, baby girl?"

He knows I hate it when he calls me that. I tense, and Luke comes up behind me, his body warm and his arms comforting as they wrap around my waist. His cheek presses against my hair, his stubble catching against my temple. He doesn't say anything, just holds me. My tension melts away.

One day, I'll deal with that bastard. But Christmas isn't the moment.

"There, see?" Mom says, back on the line. "Everything's good."

"Good. I'm glad. You gonna be cooking Christmas dinner?"

"You know I am. And I opened your present, honey. You're so sweet." I booked her a session at a recording studio. A half day, which should be enough for a few songs. I know she still writes them sometimes, when she's in a good place.

"Did you like it?"

"Honey, I loved it." Her voice is full of genuine enthusiasm. "It's the sweetest gift I've ever had. Thanks. I love you."

I relax against Luke. This is about as good as a conversation gets with Mom, and the fact she's telling me she loves me means she's not holding any grudges about last night and everything I said. I close my eyes. "I love you too, Mom."

"Merry Christmas. Talk to you soon."

"Okay. Merry Christmas!" I end the call and just stand there for a moment, enjoying Luke's presence behind me. Steady and warm and caring. His hands are still locked around my waist, and his stubble grazes my jaw as he turns his head.

"That sounded like it went well," he murmurs near my ear.

"My mom's next-door neighbor is there. It's a Band-Aid, but at least it means Tim has to be on his best behavior for today." I sigh, my shoulders sagging. "I'm sorry my family is such a disaster."

"Don't be sorry."

"Your family seems so perfect, and mine's a mess."

"No one's family is perfect." Luke's shoulders shake with a half-suppressed laugh. "Once when Mark and I got into a fight-turned-wrestling-match, he tried to pin me down in the duck pond."

I laugh, leaning back into him. I never expected his hugs would feel this good. "He tried to drown you?"

"He was trying to *win*. Dad found us and dragged me back out. Mark was grounded for a *month*. He was on stall-mucking duty for weeks. You could hear his complaining from a mile away."

"Mark?" I can't imagine that stoic man attempting murder *or* complaining. "Really?"

"Yeah. When he grew up, he really grew up."

"Your mom must be proud of you all."

"She is, I think. But even she's had struggles to overcome. When Matthew came out . . ." Luke sighs against my bare neck, and I do my best not to feel it. Not that I succeed. "She found that hard. All her life, she was taught that it was a sin, you know, and she had to work against a whole doctrine of teaching. Her church at the time didn't support her embracing Matthew and his then-boyfriend. It was this whole thing."

"Wow. But everyone seemed so comfortable yesterday."

"They are now. But mistakes were made, feelings were hurt. Apologies and forgiveness. Believe me, no one escapes having trials." He turns me around to face him, his hazel eyes serious, hair falling over his forehead and obscuring his eyebrows. I think I'm in love with his eyelashes, so thick and dark. "What I'm trying to say is no family is perfect. Not even mine. And part of being family, I guess, is loving each other despite the cracks and flaws and all the stuff that goes on underneath."

My throat is thick, but in a good way this time. "Stop. You're going to make me tear up."

"I've got you." And he does. He hasn't released me from his embrace, and his soothing energy anchors me.

If there's anything the last couple days have taught me, it's that he really does have my back, whenever I need him to.

"Do you want to go to Jersey?" he asks.

I shake my head. Mom isn't about to get rid of Tim anytime soon, and Luke was right; me being there isn't going to change anything.

And if I'm fully honest with myself, I don't want to break this bubble Luke and I have created. I know we're not an actual couple, but I hadn't known how badly I needed to feel someone's arms around me, accepting me and all my flaws, taking care of me for once.

"Let's get dressed," I say. "It's Christmas, and I can't wait to spend it with you and your family."

Chapter Fourteen

Luke

Christmas karaoke isn't so much of a tradition as an unmissable opportunity.

"We need to check the sound system," I explain as Aspen and I duck into the barn, hand in hand. I'd be lying if I said today hasn't been the best Christmas in recent history. She's wearing the earrings I got her, and she's so damn cute, I can't stop looking. "And what better way than with karaoke?"

The kids are inside watching a Disney movie marathon. Millie got all dressed up in her new Elsa dress, and the boys are building new Lego sets. This is our moment.

"Sometimes we go sledding," I add, "but the storm makes that not an option today."

Aspen gazes around the barn, smiling. "No, no, Christmas karaoke should definitely be a thing."

"I agree," Matthew calls from where he's testing the mic. "One two, one two, testing, testing."

"He thinks he's the best singer out of all of us," I tell Aspen under my breath. He hears me anyway.

"That is untrue." He jabs a finger in my direction. "I *know* I'm the best singer."

Mark, standing nearby, cocks an eyebrow. "Really?"

"Fine. I'll share first place with you. But only because Barnyard Funk was destined for better things."

"Barnyard Funk?" Aspen asks.

I grab her arm. "Don't encourage them. They're the worst."

"I thought you'd *never* ask." Matthew fiddles with his phone, and Three Doors Down starts playing from the speaker. Mark takes his place beside him, both standing in front of the arch we put up yesterday, and they rock out. It's dramatic, over the top, and utterly cringeworthy.

"Don't watch," I tell Aspen, trying to block her eyes, but she's giggling. Matthew headbangs to the slow, depressing song while Mark holds the mic with both hands and does his best soulful eyes.

"I *love* this," she says, putting up hands and swaying. When they get to the chorus, she harmonizes, and . . .

Damn.

Damn.

I've heard her sing almost every week for two years, but there's a difference between hearing her in the cantina and hearing her in this barn, with its spacious interior and curved ceiling. Her voice was made for acoustics like this. It reminds me of smoky whiskey, with that perfect sexy rasp that gives way to sweetness when she slips into her head voice.

Matthew breaks off to yell, "Hell yeah!"

"Matthew Fraser Simmons," Mom says, pointing her finger at him. "Less of that language, thank you." Then, she turns to Aspen. "You have a beautiful voice, honey. Even better than Luke said."

Aspen shoots me a surprised glance, and I could have cursed Mom for giving that away. Aspen never needs to know how much I've talked about her to my parents. All the little things I've told them because I never thought my lie would come to life like this.

"Aspen," Matthew says, holding out a hand to her. "Sing with me."

"Hey, wait." I slide my fingers through hers. "I think it's time we took the stage together. What do you say, Shaw?"

She grins teasingly at me. "Okay, Simmons. Ready to show them how it's really done?"

Matthew crows at the dare but lets us take the makeshift stage. Aspen unhooks the mic from its stand and rocks back on her heels, getting a feel for the space.

"'Don't Stop Believin''?" I suggest. "It's a classic." And, crucially, it's one we've done before. Standing up together like this is familiar, and as she takes her place beside me, facing my family, I have to fight the thought that we should do this next year.

Every year.

It's a good thing I'm not trying to resist her anymore, because I'd be failing big-time.

The music starts, and she takes the first line, filling the room with her yearning, smoky voice. I take the next line, and we let loose, sharing the verses, belting the chorus. No way is Matthew going to outdo us here.

They need to hear how good Aspen is, and what better way than now, like this? She paces the stage, capturing the small audience's attention with her performance. During the break in lyrics, I grab her hand and we dance together, limbs loose, grinning at each other like idiots.

When I next look up, my mom and Granny are at the back, watching us with matching grins. Matthew is pretending to sulk at his inevitable defeat, but he's grinning too wide to really sell it.

"Victory," I crow when it's over. Without thinking, I wrap my arm around Aspen, and I pull her into my chest. She laughs, cheeks red, and looks up at me. There's no pulling away, no sense that this isn't as natural for her as it is for me.

No alcohol involved. Just us.

"JoJo?" Mark says, but she holds up her hands, shaking her head.

"No way I'm following that."

"And we have a winner," Dad says, coming up to raise both our hands into a victory stance like we've won some prize.

And yeah, I feel like I have.

Matthew groans, but when we head over, he grabs Aspen's hand and shakes it vigorously. "That was incredible," he tells her. "Not you," he adds, glancing at me.

Aspen beams. "I think we make a good team."

"But you'd make a better team with us," he says. "Right, Mark?"

"Hey." I pull Aspen into me possessively. "Stop trying to recruit my girlfriend into your sad band."

"It's not a sad band! We would've been successful if we'd ever had a gig. Right, Mark?"

Mark shrugs. The music's off, and he's back to being the Mark we all know and love, whose words are painstakingly dug from him with a trowel. "They were better."

Matthew throws his hands into the air and mutters, "Betrayer," but before he can take the stage again, JoJo puts on a country slow song playlist. The twanging guitars and soft southern voices are way too loud until she turns them down, and Garth Brooks croons at a far more reasonable volume.

"Andre still needs to practice," she says by explanation. "And so do you, Matthew."

He sticks his tongue out at her and goes off in search of Kwan. Mark, who is a surprisingly good dancer, leads Rebecca out onto the floor. They glide across the concrete in perfect rhythm, just like they are in everyday life. Mark leads his wife with quiet confidence. Rebecca, despite her burgeoning belly, is graceful and feminine in his arms. Their moves are second nature, and I'm in awe watching them so in sync. They communicate with just their eyes, and he leads her effortlessly. They have a true connection. I want that type of relationship in my life.

When I dated other women, I wanted what Mark had, and I thought maybe I'd found it once.

Now I know better.

Mom switches on the string lights so they twinkle down on us, and I hold out my hand to Aspen.

"Wanna dance?"

Aspen blinks a few times before looking up at me. "You expect me to . . . do that?"

"We'll have to at the wedding. Might as well practice now."

She mouths *the wedding* and *dancing*. "I don't think I can."

"You can." I'm certain about that point, at least. "All you have to do is follow my lead."

"And not step on your feet."

"Come here." I take her hips and position her so she's at a slight angle to me. "You ever danced a two-step before?"

She makes a face at me. "You really think my mom is the kind of woman who thought country dancing was an important life skill?"

"Noted. That's okay." I place one of her hands on my shoulder and take her other one in mine. "It's in a six count." With my other hand on the back of her shoulder, I guide her steps, counting as I do. "Look me in the eyes. Focus on the pressure of my hands," I tell her when she freezes. "Feel my signals."

"Oh my God. I've stepped on your feet, like, five times now."

"It's okay. Trust me to lead you."

Her mouth twists. "How do you know how to *do* this stuff? Do you know everything? Is that it?"

To one side, Dad pulls Mom onto the dance floor. Kwan and Matthew have joined as well, though they're more swaying in a circle than anything else. They lean in for a kiss right as Aspen nods at them.

"Can we do that instead?" At my reaction, she rolls her eyes. "*Swaying*, I mean."

"They're only doing that because Matthew can't dance."

"*I* can't dance."

"Anything worth doing takes practice." I try to twirl her out, and it kind of works. When I guide her back to me, I slow down our steps and pull her closer, hips to hips, my arms encircling her waist. Our bodies are touching at various points as we slowly sway in a circle. Aspen looks up at me, never breaking eye contact. There's nowhere I'd rather look.

"There," I murmur, giving in to temptation and nuzzling her neck. Her hair smells incredible—lavender and vanilla mixing with her natural scent. I don't know what it is about this woman, but everything about her is designed to appeal to my base senses. I've never been more caveman than when I'm around her. She's practically edible.

Nibbling on her earlobe would be too far. Too far. I remind myself of that as my lips graze her skin and her breath catches.

"Your stubble," she says breathlessly. "You haven't been shaving."

"Oh yeah?" I rub my jaw against the curve of her neck—close, so close—and she laughs, fingers digging into my shoulder and, if anything, pulling me closer. "How's that?"

In answer, she avoids me by pressing her face into my neck. Her breath is hot, and she winds her arms tighter around my neck. I slide mine lower down the small of her back, holding her pressed against me. Flush. Every line matching against every curve and dip, perfectly positioned against me. I knew we'd fit together. I just knew it.

"Just so you know," I whisper, so low she's definitely the only one who can hear me now. "This is the best Christmas I can remember. So, thank you."

***

Aspen

There is the very real possibility that my heart might explode out of my chest. Maybe I'll expire on the dance floor, and they'll have to sweep the gooey parts of me together so I don't make a mess for the wedding.

Luke Simmons can dance.

He can sing, he can dance, he can code. He can look good in flannel *and* a dress shirt. He's witty and adorable and hot and I've only just started noticing his physique. Like his strong, defined arms.

Which are currently around me.

Sigh.

"I mean it; it's been fantastic. Thanks for being here," he tells me against the sensitive spot below my ear. He keeps doing that, the slight rasp of his stubble sending shivers through me. Thrilling shivers. I am officially a lost cause. My body is lit up like a Christmas tree every place we touch—which, right now, is most of them.

When did his chest get so broad? And *hard*. The man has a beautiful body, and I'm pressed up against every delicious ridge and valley. Lucky me.

His hand moves lower on the small of my back, and I'm abruptly aware that he's inches away from my ass. Does he know that too? Is he as aware of the contact as I am?

Given that he's currently saying something to me, I have to guess that's an almighty no.

I wrench my mind into the present moment and away from the filthy thoughts it *wants* to drop into. His mom is here, for Heaven's sake.

"Sorry?"

There's a look on his face that I can't identify. "I asked if I could kiss you." He looks over my shoulder and wrinkles his nose. "Matthew is . . . wow, yeah, he's really acting it out. I think he wants us to kiss. Or he wants to make out with a frog. I can't tell which."

The snort I make is the least sexy sound I've got going for me, but the soft warmth in Luke's eyes makes me think he hasn't noticed. Or maybe he doesn't care.

I take a deep breath, filling my lungs for the moment when I inevitably won't be able to breathe. "You don't have to ask anymore."

The smile that spreads across his face is like dancing firelight, and tongues of flame lick up my body as he leans down and presses his lips against mine.

The last time we did this, I couldn't count it as a kiss. But this right here—yeah, *this* is a kiss. His mouth is warm, lips moving with relaxed certainty, and his hand slides up my spine as I tilt my face up to his. Maybe too eager, too wanting, but a huff of air escapes him, and he opens my mouth.

This kiss is an exploration. We're learning each other. The way our lips slot together, the feel of his tongue against mine, the way his breath catches, the press of his fingers when he reaches the back of my neck.

I wonder if all the other girls he's kissed have had long hair he can wrap his fingers around. All that silky texture for him to want.

I've never had that. My mom cut my hair when I was five, after I begged and begged and begged her to, because Sinead O'Conner had hers cut short too.

But if he cares that my hair is short, he doesn't show any sign of it, because his fingers are playing in the short lengths at the base of my neckline. Luke's tongue slides against mine again, stroking with quiet assurance, and I'm all parts melted. My knees want to give way. I've never been that kind of girl before, one where her knees abandon all structural integrity just because she receives a good kiss, but Luke Simmons is *doing* something to me.

Is this for real?

I mean, I know it's not supposed to be real. I know this "relationship" was built one hundred percent on a false premise, but I can't figure out if what I'm feeling right now, if the way he's kissing me, the way I'm kissing him back, is real. If this means something to him, or if he's just putting on a show because we have an audience.

The lines have blurred. We've smudged the chalk, let the tide wash the marks in the sand, erased the pencil marks. All that's left is this undeniable sense in my mind that there *were* lines. Once. There used to be very solid lines that every press of his hands, every movement of his lips, has swept aside.

I wrap my arms around his neck, hold tight, and hope the same tide doesn't wash me away.

Chapter Fifteen

Aspen

I wake with a smile on my face, my dreams having revolved around Luke, wrapped in his arms, dancing and kissing like it's our new hobby. Rolling over, I pat his side of the bed, reaching for his arm. "Hey," I mumble, still thick with sleep. If I was at home, I wouldn't even consider moving for another fifteen minutes, but I want to tell Luke about the dream I had.

My hand encounters nothing but tangled sheets.

No Luke.

My eyes fly open, and I scan his side of the bed. Empty. He's gone, and the cold bed indicates he left a while ago.

I sit up, running my hand through my hair. There's a feeling of wrongness about this that pushes away the warmth that was in my gut just seconds before.

He should be here. In the bed. With me.

We've only been in this new routine a matter of days, and already that's what I've come to expect. What I've come to *want*.

I take a deep breath in through my nose, then exhale slowly and try to center myself. Waking up alone isn't exactly something I'm unfamiliar with. Most mornings, I'm alone. Even when I was dating,

I didn't usually invite the guys to stay over. It was casual sex, then a prompt goodbye. Until next time. Sleepovers suggest permanence.

I should be glad he's not here. I need a chance to recalibrate and get back to my normal pattern of reality.

But the fact is, I'm not glad. And the moment I leave this place, we'll go back to how things were. I'll go back to my life, he'll go back to his, and we'll intersect at the office just like we usually did. Maybe have a few more inside jokes. Maybe we'll both remember this fondly.

Reality creeps forward like rolling mist, and I have a feeling it's going to obscure everything. My stomach twists, and there's a sour taste on my tongue.

Disappointment.

Maybe my single life, the one I'm going back to, isn't better than risking companionship after all.

The door opens, and Luke walks in. He's already fully dressed, toeing off his hiking boots and carrying a steaming mug toward me.

"I brought you coffee," he says, sitting on the edge of the bed and handing it to me. His hand pauses as he studies my face. "Are you okay?"

"Yes." I smile and fidget with the gold chain around my neck, chasing away that feeling of being abandoned and forgotten. He got me coffee. "So great. This is amazing."

For a moment, I think he's going to push, but he just nods, eyes never leaving mine, and proffers the mug. "I put a tiny bit of maple syrup in it, just the way you like it."

"You did?" I take a sip, and the bitterness of the coffee is offset by that sweet profile. It's different from sugar, a richer flavor without being overpowering. And he put just a dash in.

How does this man know me so well?

"I've seen you do it at work," he says, answering my unasked question. "You bring that tiny bottle in with you."

"That's because the kitchen doesn't stock maple syrup, but . . ." I trail off, staring at him. "I can't believe you went out and got this for me. It's what, twenty degrees out there?"

He shrugs. "Maybe even ten. I didn't check the temperature."

"This is so sweet. Thank you." I take a sip and close my eyes. *Caffeine, take me. I'm ready.* "This is exactly what I needed this morning."

"I'm glad." He holds out two still-warm croissants. "Mom made an early breakfast for everyone before they headed out, so I figured you might want one."

I sample a bite. "Oh my God." My eyes close, savoring the explosion of flavor and texture. My tastebuds are in heaven. "How did you know I love croissants? They're, like, the *perfect* lazy-morning breakfast." The rest of what he said finally hits. "Wait, what do you mean, everyone's gone? They've all gone home?"

"Nah. Matthew and Kwan took the boys skiing, Mark and Rebecca went to her parents' house for a late Christmas, and Jo and Andre are in Park City getting in some after-Christmas shopping for their new place."

"Wow. Quiet, huh?" I bite into the croissant, and a moan of satisfaction escapes my lips. The noise I make is frankly obscene, and Luke's mouth quirks into a smile.

"I take it that's good."

"So good," I mumble past my full mouth. "Better than sex."

The second I say it, I know I've gone too far. Better than *sex*? What the hell was I even thinking, bringing up sex? That's Horny Aspen talking again, and she should *not* be allowed access to my mouth. I need to chain her back in the dungeon of inappropriate thoughts.

"Huh," Luke says, drawing the word out. His gaze is on my mouth, and I wipe my lips of crumbs. "I guess you can't have had the best experiences, then."

I take another gulp of coffee in the hopes that it will magically stop my lady parts from buzzing in futile anticipation. "My experiences have been *fine,* thank you."

"Oh? Then that's the world's best croissant?"

Goddammit. How am I supposed to keep my distance when he says things like that and looks good enough to consume? In some ways, it's like our interactions haven't changed, and I've just got a different filter overlooking them. In other ways, I'm certain he's grown more confident. More suggestive. I'm not just imagining that part—he really is more flirtatious now. I wonder, if this version of Luke had been more apparent in the office, would I have noticed him sooner?

Given this is all based on a charade, I shouldn't be enjoying it this much. If he gave me any indication he'd be up for it, I would climb that man like a fireman's pole.

Mind out of the gutter.

He blinks a few times. "There's nothing big planned for today, if you just want to hang out. We could go into town or chill here and watch a movie. Whatever you want."

I have the perfect idea for how to send Horny Aspen to jail. "I have an idea," I say, grinning at him. "How about we start some of the research for the Chinese expansion?"

He flops back on the bed with a groan that makes me laugh. "Work at Christmas? That's your idea of fun?"

"Pretty please?" I lean over him, one hand on the other side of his chest. His face is just below mine now. I could kiss him.

I *want* to kiss him.

Horny jail, horny jail.

His eyes are every shade of brown and green, like sunlight through a forest. I could look at them all day.

"Fine," he says. "But I want it on record that I only agreed under duress."

"On pain of death," I agree, leaning back before I can do something I regret. "I'll get my laptop."

***

We spend most of the day working beside each other on the bed. Luke puts *The Office* on in the background, and we make inside jokes about PAYDAY and Kai as we go. Charlie was right—I can totally see the comparison between Luke and Jim personality-wise. They're both protective, with dry wit and wry smiles, and are adorable, good guys. Like a warm hug after a long day. Though physically, Luke is built more like a Jack Ryan version of John Krasinski than the Jim Halpert edition. He's the best of both characters. More importantly, Luke is real, not playing a role. I feel lucky to know him.

Hunched over a laptop is not how I'd envisaged spending the day after Christmas, but it was my idea, and hanging out with Luke makes it fun. He brings me snacks and coffee and does that thing with his lip when he works. I noticed it at the office, but now it has me transfixed. He sucks his lower lip into his mouth when he concentrates, his teeth *just* visible as he bites down. Then, so slowly it feels like it's on purpose, he releases his lip through his teeth. It flushes red, and I have to keep myself from staring at it.

He has lush lips. How have I never noticed until now?

Amazingly, though we're sitting shoulder-to-shoulder against a mountain of pillows, papers and computers scattered in front of us, we get a lot done, and by the time dinner comes around, I feel like we deserve a break.

I stretch. "That was productive."

"That's what I love to be." He grimaces. "Productive."

I pinch his thigh, and he swats at me. I dig a finger into his side, and he launches himself at me, tickling me ruthlessly. Unable to help myself, I giggle-scream and fight back, pinning him to the bed. Since coming here, so many physical boundaries have been broken. That mythical line that our kiss swept away is in tatters, its ribboning length snapped in places. I don't know what's real and what's not.

He looks up at me, eyelids hooded and lips slightly parted. I'm almost certain he let me win. His shirt is wrapped in my fists, which are braced against his chest, and he reaches up to brush hair back off my forehead. I haven't styled it today, and it's all over the place.

At the touch of his fingers, so light I could almost have imagined it, Horny Aspen claws her way to the surface again. The air between us goes tight. Most of the day, I've been distracted by boring privacy rules and mountains of small print, but when he looks at me like that, Horny Aspen is more than willing to take the front seat in my brain.

I don't know what this man has done to me. One minute, he's a coworker I never daydreamed about, and the next, I'm forgetting where I'm supposed to be looking. Probably not at his mouth.

He's biting his bottom lip again, though. This is practically a fire hazard. And an invitation.

How has he been single the entire time I've known him? Surely, girls have been crawling across broken glass to get caught in his adoring gaze, to laugh at his intelligent jokes, to worship his smile and fabulous health insurance. His love of Warhammer and D&D is a small price to pay for access to kisses like his.

Although, personally, I kind of like all the unique, conflicting aspects that make Luke who he is.

His smile widens, lip pulling free of his teeth, and my brain stutters to a standstill. There is no safe place to look.

"Hey, Aspen?" he says softly.

My stomach clenches almost painful anticipation at what comment will follow after he says my name so tenderly. "Yeah?"

"I'm glad you're here." Another smile spreads across his face.

The butterflies in my stomach flutter in sheer delight. "I'm glad you invited me." My fingers loosen in his T-shirt, and he catches my waist, the tip of one finger grazing my bare skin. I'm on fire.

As I lower my head toward his waiting lips, a sharp rap on our front door startles me. It opens a few inches, and Granny Mae's walking stick pokes through.

"Everybody decent in there?"

I whimper and slide off of Luke as he laughs. We need to start locking our door. My libido can't handle one more interruption from the Simmons clan.

Granny's eyes are narrowed and on us as she tells us everyone's waiting for us at the main house. Dinner's ready.

"We'll be right there," Luke says, and she's gone as fast as she arrived.

Well, that's probably a good thing. Too much tension is bad for a person. Or so I'm told. Right now, I don't think I'd believe it—the only thing I'm hungry for probably can't be found in his mom's kitchen.

At least, not until he follows me in.

"You head on up to the house," he says, looking at the devastation we've left across the bed. "I'll be right behind you."

"Sure you don't want me to help?" The prospect of being alone with his parents, who think I'm the answer to their son's eternally broken heart, isn't appealing. But he just waves me out, so after putting on my coat, I trudge across the yard and up the steps, letting myself through the front door.

"Hello?" I call.

"In here," Granny calls from the kitchen. When I enter, there's a pot bubbling on the stove, but she's the only one in sight. She holds out a leg.

"Help me get these off, will you? I don't have the strength anymore."

I kneel and take a firm grip on one of her worn cowboy boots, then give it a tug. It shifts, and she nods approvingly.

"That's right. Keep going."

"Where's Ruth?"

"She just headed to the bathroom. And Peter is off doing God knows what." She chuckles. "Good to have a day of rest in between the fun."

Granny doesn't look like she's resting, though. I'm not even sure if she knows what rest is, never mind if she's capable of it.

"Those are pretty earrings," she tells me when I've pulled her second boot off.

"Luke gave them to me. They came with the cutest little . . ." I break off, kind of reluctant to share all my bad vibes from that night with a relative stranger.

"He cares about you a lot," Granny Mae says, looking at me intently. I nod, unable to say anything.

It's not that I don't believe it. Hell, I *know* he cares about me. Cares *for* me. We're friends, and again with the line-blurring. It's just . . . He doesn't care for me in the way everyone here thinks he does.

Ruth bustles back in and stops when she sees me. Her smile is warm, and the comparison to my mom, the way she wouldn't ever just welcome someone new into her life like this, makes my throat close.

I haven't heard from her today.

I suddenly, fiercely, wish that *these* women were my family. Not that Mom wouldn't be too, but just that I'd have someone like them to talk to. Talking to Mom about feelings is a dangerous route to take. She drinks to numb her feelings. She's with a man who hits her, for God's sake. And I know she loves me, but it's always been this custody battle between us. Who gets the love or attention? Who doesn't for now because it's inconvenient?

I came along just as she was on the cusp of her big break in music. And my dad, whom I'm pretty sure she adored like no one else in the entire world, left when I was eight. Just dropped out of my life. You don't get to choose your family, and it just so happened that mine didn't have the capacity to give a shit about me most of the time.

"Aspen." Ruth stands in front of me and takes both my hands, her hazel eyes warm and concerned. Luke has her eyes, I notice.

The whole thing is a lot. I've had such a good day just working with Luke. Just *being* near Luke. But he's part of a family I will never have access to, and as soon as I leave here, my broken, messed-up life is going to drain my energy all over again, like a hole in my heart. My chest clenches in preparation.

"What's wrong, honey?" Ruth asks.

Granny Mae takes my arm and sits me down. "There. Now you don't have to think about standing. I know it takes effort sometimes."

Her gruff kindness pushes me over the edge, and I have to rub the back of my hand over my eyes.

"It's nothing. I'm being ridiculous."

"Sadness isn't ridiculous, honey," Ruth says. "You can talk to us."

"It's just . . ." *I want a hug.* "Things aren't so great with my mom right now. She's in a bad relationship—a bad place mentally. And I know that she's going to want me to go over there and play at being a happy family because it makes her feel better, but I don't know if I can. Not while . . ." Not while Tim's there, leering at me because he thinks he can get away with it.

Because Mom has *taught* him that he can get away with it.

Ruth hands me a tissue, and I dab at the corners of my eyes. "You know, honey, we've got two chances in life at having a family: the one you're born into, and the one you get to create as an adult with the people you love. You get to choose."

"You know, Ruth's right," Granny says. "I'm older than dirt. Been living and loving since before your parents were born. Mind if I give you a bit of advice?"

I blow my nose and take a deep breath to stave off more tears. "Sure."

"People are like different parts of a tree. You got some who are briefly in your life, like leaves. They come out in the spring, vibrant and beautiful, but they're only there for a season. There's no counting on them, no depending on them for long-term needs. They give what they can, and as soon as the weather turns or winds blow, they leave."

I can think of so many people in my life like that. There for a season, gone for the next. Scattered like tombstones in the graveyard of my life.

Most of my school friends and exes were like that, actually. We worked right until we tried to fit the jagged edges of our lives together and realized we didn't fit.

"Other people are branches in our lives," Granny says, and although there's other sounds in the kitchen, like the bubbling pot and the quiet way Ruth is setting out the dishes, I'm hooked on her every word. "They are stronger than leaves and offer more support, but you have to be careful with them. It's possible that a storm or two in your life might break them. You can't usually put all your weight on them, or they'll snap."

Mom is a branch person, I realize immediately. She's never been stable enough to be there for me when it comes to weightier issues. And now, there's so much heavy baggage, it weighs on us, threatening to break the branch of our relationship.

Granny looks at me solemnly. "And some people are the deep roots that anchor you in life. If you find a root person, you've got something special. But they can be hard to find because, like the roots of a tree, they're not easily seen. You have to dig deep to discover them. And when you do, their job is to keep you grounded, nourished, and connected. They're vital to you living a strong and healthy life."

Ruth grabs my hand, holding it tightly between hers. "It's okay if your parents are leaves or branches. They don't have to be roots. You will survive. Other roots will come along, intertwine with yours, and strengthen you. The key is to figure out your root people. Focus on nurturing those relationships so it doesn't hurt so bad when the leaves or branches fall away."

Tears well in my eyes. Some people will fall away, and even the thought of it hurts. But my root people? My first thought is Luke, but that's ridiculous, right? I don't know him well enough for him to be my *root person*. I can't put that much stock into our relationship, can I? I mean, up until this week, he's been just my good friend. Yet, he's also the man who has held me every night since I came here, who offered to fly to New Jersey with me to see my mom, who spent all day working to help me with my project.

My best friends are my root people for sure. Any one of my girls would've done similar things to support me, but we've been besties for a long time. Luke has been my friend for a couple years, but he's only been my *close* friend for a matter of days. And already he's done all of this.

The door opens, and Luke comes in with Peter, their arms over each other's shoulders, laughing at some joke we didn't get to hear. They look so happy together, so invested in each other's lives, and my heart squeezes a little.

Must be nice to have a dad who cares. Who thinks you're *worth* caring for.

I refuse to let my hand travel up to the birthmark on my face. When my dad first left, I tried to figure out what was wrong with me. What wasn't good enough. And the only thing that made sense was that I looked different. That was what all the kids at school picked on me for, at least. For *years*, every time I thought about him, I touched my birthmark and wished I was pretty and normal like all the other girls.

Then, I figured that if he didn't want me, I didn't want him either. And I *did* want me. Embracing all the parts of me, even the ugly ones, was hard, but I've managed it. Mostly.

Luke looks over at me, and his face breaks into a smile that's so real, so genuine, so *honest*, that it pushes my sadness away. I smile back, feeling my eyes crinkle just like his.

Right until his mom clears her throat. "So," she says, "is everything ready for Brittany and the rest of the bridal party's arrival tomorrow?"

Chapter Sixteen

Luke

E verything is ready for the bridal party's arrival tomorrow. That is, everything but me. This will be the first time I've been around Brittany in almost two years. As JoJo's lifelong best friend and now maid of honor, she's an integral part of the wedding, and I just need to brace myself for it the way you brace yourself for nasty-tasting medicine: plug your nose, close your eyes, and get through it.

Mom has been flapping around in a panic for the guests, Granny has been throwing out comments like "hashtag BrittanyGate," and Dad has been calm through it all.

It's not that I haven't seen her in passing since the breakup. We're both over what it was. Both moved on. The only thing that *does* matter is how comfortable Aspen feels being around my ex.

So far, she's been taking it in stride.

But as we wait outside in the icy snow, yesterday's melt having frozen again overnight, I can feel her tension. Inside her parka, she's rigid as iron, and I step closer to her.

"It's no big deal," I murmur into her ear. She's wearing a yellow knit hat with the most outrageous, fluffy pom-pom on top. It's adorable, and the kids love it. I love it.

"You say that, but you guys were on again and off again for *years*."

Not since I met you. I don't say it, though.

Aspen isn't easily scared, but if I go out and tell her how long I've been wanting her for, she might just run. And I need her here for when Brittany arrives. Beside me as my girlfriend. Anchoring me. Aspen by my side will solidify once and for all that I've moved on.

Brittany's ego probably won't like meeting the new woman in my life, but hey, mine didn't like being cheated on. That messed me up for a long time. Maybe I'd have made a move on Aspen sooner if I'd been in a place to actually consider putting my wounded heart on the line again. My hope wilted when I was introduced to Aspen's string of boyfriends, none of which were like me, and any dreams of us getting together happened exclusively in the privacy of my head.

Until now, I guess. Because she's right here, standing close enough that our arms are touching, and I want to keep hold of her, reassure myself she's still here, that I'm not dreaming this whole thing up.

I've never been prone to hallucinations, but Aspen as my girlfriend sure seems like a good place to start.

"Last week, this seemed like a good plan," I tell her, regret bubbling up in my chest. "Now, I'm realizing what an awkward position I've put you in. I'm sorry. I'm an idiot."

"It's going to be okay." Aspen's gaze trying to instill calm in me. In both of us.

She doesn't look like she's feeling okay right now. She looks like she's feeling the cold, all pink nose and flushed cheeks and eyes that look like they're seeing too much. I squeeze her hand, threading my fingers through hers. "Thanks again for doing this," I murmur my gratitude. She doesn't say anything, but her eyes soften, just a little.

A car pulls into the yard—a big blue SUV with snow tires. Brittany throws open the door and tosses her hair to one side as she steps out. She's wearing black leather pants that cling to her legs and a long, red coat that cinches tight around her waist. Her hair is long and bleached and perfectly curled.

She looks just as immaculate as she does in all her pictures.

Once, that would've made my heart pound, especially when she glances over and makes eye contact with me. But times have changed. Now, she's nothing more than a hard lesson learned.

And my sister's best friend. I guess she'll always be that, no matter what happened between us in the past.

"Brittany!" JoJo squeals, running forward. The two women dance on the spot for a second, hands flapping, before embracing. They've done this since they were kids, and I don't think I'll ever understand it.

Once they're done with their greeting ritual, Brittany looks across the rest of us, giving Ruth a hug and Peter a huge smile. She knows Granny doesn't like her—everyone knows that Granny doesn't like her—so after a brief, self-effacing smile in Granny's direction, Brit turns to us.

To me, anyway. It's like she hasn't even registered Aspen's presence.

"Luke," she sings, pulling me into a hug. "It's been way too long."

Not long enough actually. I pat her lightly on the back, not wanting to commit to a full embrace. Especially not when my entire family is watching and Aspen is right there. Brittany means nothing to me, and I want Aspen to see that.

"Oh my God," Brittany says as she pulls back and looks up at me. "You look so good. What have you been doing? Soft boy gone hard. I love it."

"Thanks," I say mildly, then gesture across to Aspen. "Can I introduce you to my girlfriend, Aspen?"

I lean a little on *girlfriend* just to make sure Brittany gets the message. She'd old news. Aspen is my future. Or, at least, what I hope could be my future if things go well.

Aspen clears her throat, and Brittany's eyes flick across and down, taking in Aspen head to toe before settling on her birthmark. Her eyebrow quirks, like she's making a judgment, and irritation burns in my stomach.

Then, she flashes her pageant-worthy smile. "I love your aesthetic, Aspen. Jo didn't tell me Luke had a girlfriend. You guys are so cute together."

"I like to think so," Aspen says. Her arm slides around my back, and she hooks her fingers into my jacket. "It's nice to finally meet you. I've heard so much about you."

"Well, I *am* practically part of the family." Brittany waves a dismissive hand. "But enough about me. We *need* to get together and swap horror stories about our Luke."

Our. The word makes me tense, but Aspen just looks up at me, the softest smile on her lips.

"No horror stories from me. All good things."

I could kiss her. And hey, maybe I can. I lean down, and she meets me clumsily in the middle, her face warm and soft against the biting cold, her lips curving into a smile under mine. I don't kiss her the way I want to—there's no way that would be appropriate for a family gathering—but it feels good just to do this.

When I pull away, Aspen's eyes are warm, and I feel like I just drank a whole bottle of mulled cider—every part of me is tingling and light and heady.

The twins accost Brittany, and Oliver looks up at her. "You're wearing a lot of makeup," he informs her solemnly.

"I am," she says, but I guess she knows him too well to ask if he likes it. Oliver won't hold back with criticism if he's asked for it. He doesn't have a filter.

Aspen slides her cold fingers through mine, and Dad calls everyone up to the house to get warm. Mom peppers Brittany with questions about her newest collaborations and updates since her last visit, and Matthew inquires about her latest celebrity sightings. Jo's happy that her best friend has arrived, but I can't help praying Brittany doesn't take the focus away from my sister's special day.

"I'm collabing with KallMeKris," Brittany says, propping herself against the couch cushions and pulling the throw blanket over herself. It's where she sits every time she visits, and the familiarity of it is unsettling now that everything else has changed. "I can't say too much about it, but I'm flying out to Canada in a few weeks for filming."

"Oh, she's *big*," Matthew says, eyes wide.

"Yeah. I reached out to her first, and she was on board to do something fun. My fans will love seeing me do something different, and it's a chance for me to brush up on some of my comedy skills." She glances at me, and I can't help feeling like this boasting is for my benefit.

"Seeing anyone new?" Matthew asks. "Anyone famous?"

She waves a dismissive hand. "I went out with Zayn Malik a few times, but it was never anything serious. He's cute, don't get me wrong, but I want to focus on myself and my career." She looks again at me, and the implication is obvious.

And me.

Except now, Aspen is here, and whatever plans Brittany had are ruined. A tense silence falls, every breath threatening to shatter it.

"Brunch," Mom says briskly. "Who's hungry?"

Brittany tosses the blanket aside and springs to her feet. "I'll help! I know where everything is."

And just like that, things go back to how they've always been.

***

Aspen

Brittany is flirting with Luke. She pretends like she's not, and I pretend that I don't notice, but she is. And I do.

It wouldn't bother me, except she fits in so easily here. Hurrying around the enormous kitchen. getting dishes and cutlery out, prepping salad, washing the knives and putting them back where they belong. With her here, everything is just the same as it was before—they don't have to ask her to do anything because she just does it. Weaving through them like a thread that makes up the tapestry.

I'm the lone needle in the middle. Touch me, and I'll prick.

Brittany smiles up at Luke. She has this way of looking at him like she's seeing him for the first time, and it's really pissing me off. If this woman wants to fight, she's going the right damn way about it.

"Do you remember when we took your air rifle out and smashed all three plates?" she asks, her tone light and bubbly. She's everything I'm not.

And I shouldn't care. I'm the decoy girlfriend. It's not real.

Although right now, I'm the sulking-at-the-table girlfriend because my fake boyfriend is talking more to his ex than he is to me. He's being polite, almost to a fault.

I fold my arms across my chest.

Luke shoots an apologetic look at his mom. "I remember. You were so mad, Mom."

"It was irresponsible of you," Ruth says, giving him an affectionate glance. "But I can't say your brothers were any different."

"Hey," Matthew says from the other end of the table. He has one of the twins—I may never be able to tell them apart—on his knee and is helping him read a Christmas book. "I can multitask, you know. I heard that."

"Then you'll know it's true," his mom says.

Brittany laughs and leans in like she's imparting some great secret to Luke. He leans down to meet her, and hot anger boils in my stomach. I don't want to watch this.

"Do you still have Wilbur?" she asks with a little giggle. "I miss him! Remember we used to head out to the paddock, and I'd say hi?"

Who the hell is Wilbur?

Granny Mae eases herself down onto the seat beside me. "These old bones never let me rest."

I make a noncommittal noise, still watching Brittany and Luke. I can see them together. They'd make a cute couple, her blonde hair against his brown. She's slightly shorter than me, and it's endearing to see him bend down to meet her.

Or it would be endearing if it didn't make me feel sick.

What is wrong with me?

Rebecca tilts me a sympathetic look, and finally, I realize what's wrong. Luke's family all know about his history with Brittany, and there he is, being all cutesy with her while I watch on the sidelines and look ridiculous. I *feel* ridiculous. I want to set fire to her hair and curl up in a hole where no one can find me.

Granny Mae leans in. "The snake is in the house," she whispers. "What are you gonna do, girl, just let her flirt with your man?"

"He's not—" I start to say, but I catch myself.

Today, he's supposed to be.

"She knows just what strings to pull with him," she says, shaking her head sadly as Brittany laughs. It's an annoying, grating sound that I hate instantly. "I'm so glad he's got you now, darlin'."

I flash my polite, I-don't-agree-with-what-you're-saying smile. She thinks we're all happy and in love.

"He seems happy enough," I mutter. Truth be told, he's not doing anything to encourage her. He went over to dry the dishes, just like he always does, and she slotted in beside him. I get the impression that's a place she's used to being.

"He keeps looking at you." Granny shakes her head again.

Brittany winds her arm through Luke's. "What do you think about my tattoo?" she asks, moving her hair back to reveal the tiniest tattoo behind her ear.

This time, I snort. Call that a tattoo? The one on my back is way more impressive.

"It's great," he says, barely glancing at it.

"You like it? I know you're not into tattoos."

Granny Mae leans in, chair creaking. "Same old Brittany, always trying to be the center of attention."

When I turn to Luke again, his eyes flick off of me like he didn't mean to be caught looking, and that decides it.

Guess I'm damn well interrupting their conversation.

I push my chair back and come up behind Luke, wrapping my arms around his waist.

"Oh, he likes tattoos now," I tell Brittany with a coy smile. The version of Luke she thinks she knows is from years ago. When they first met during their college years. He's grown since then. That's what people do. "He's talked about getting one himself, actually." I look up at him and give him a slow, sultry smile, letting my lids fall over my eyes just a little. "He likes my tattoos."

Luke sucks in a gasp. We've talked about tattoos broadly, and he's seen the visible ones on my wrists and arms, but he doesn't know where my more intimate ones are.

The idea of showing him makes me shiver all over.

Brittany's sharp eyes flick to me. "That's cool. I'd love to see your ink."

"Oh, I couldn't possibly show you some of them." My smile is sweet, but I walk around Luke's back until I'm standing beside her, and I twist, one hand still on Luke, so my back is facing her. "I have a few that are in"—I let my voice drop suggestively—"*discreet places.*" Her gaze drops low on my torso, near my hip.

Damn right, girl. Time to back off.

Luke's hand slides around my side, palm flat against me. His fingers are slightly splayed, his hand spanning my ribs, and his thumb isn't too far from the underside of my breast. For a second, I can't breathe.

"Yeah." Luke's voice is beside my ear. More of a puff of air than anything. "I love your tattoos."

Is it just me, or is his voice a little hoarse? I hope it is, because he can probably feel the way my heart is thrumming in my chest, a baby bird in a cage.

I'm nervous about lying to his family. That's all it is. Not the idea of Luke pulling off my clothes and looking at the map I've drawn across my body. My experiences inked onto my skin, written out for him to read, a history of meaningful moments in my life.

I want to feel his fingers trace them. I want him to tell me how much he likes them. I want—

Nope. These are not innocent, good-girl thoughts to be having. Especially around his mom.

"Brittany?" Ruth calls from the other side of the kitchen. "Can you help me with this?"

I don't even look to see what she's leaving to help Ruth with. I turn back to Luke. His eyes are very dark as he glances down at me. No green, just swollen pupils and a heavy, needy gaze that strips me bare in all the wrong ways.

I want him to see my body, not what lies underneath.

I break away with a breathy laugh and snatch a towel so I can help him dry. All the while, I feel his eyes on me.

Chapter Seventeen

Aspen

After lunch, it's time for the bridal shower. I shimmy into a sheath dress that highlights my curves, apply a little mascara and lipstick, and run some product through my short, pink layers. I rush back to the main house just as the men are wrangling the kids into their car seats for an outing to the ice-skating rink. Luke walks out to the driveway, carrying Millie on his shoulders. He flips her down his body in an aerial somersault and gently places her in her car seat. She's squealing for him to do it again, but he's got her firmly strapped into her seatbelt and promises to do it for the ride home. I just reach the car when he's shut her door, turning toward me and scanning my dressed-up outfit appreciatively. He opens his arms and I snuggle in, greedy for one of his yummy bear hugs.

"Damn, you're beautiful," he murmurs in my hair. "And thanks for playing with the kids earlier. They adore you."

"I adore them. I never get to be around kids. I think I was more entertained than they were."

"This is the longest we'll have been apart all week," Luke says mournfully. "I miss you already."

I laugh at his adorable, absurd remark. Secretly feeling the same way.

"Hurry back. I'm going to miss you too," I admit, giving him a quick peck on the lips. His smile beams back at me, crinkling at his eyes. He kisses me again and then swats me on the butt, threatening to not leave if I don't walk away right now. So I do. A Cheshire smile on my face as I walk into the decorated barn filled with guests.

The heaters are combatting the cold, and delicate flowers adorn the tables' centerpieces. We gather in a circle of chairs, JoJo in front of the wooden arch, which is now covered in florals. She is radiant.

Most of the time, she's eclipsed by Ruth's energy and efficient capability, but today, her joy is giving her a halo all of her own. She's beautiful, though she's not confident about it the way Brittany is.

Brittany's appearance is a commodity to her. *Like and subscribe for more. Buy into whatever she's selling.* Her vibe doesn't fit the Simmons' warm, authentic energy at all. I'm guessing she wasn't always this way. The fame and pressure to keep a following must be intense, and I don't envy her.

The plan is games, then gifts. Brittany is making her presence very felt, laughing and talking more than anyone else. It feels like a pissing contest, and I don't want to play. Not today, when the party is supposed to be about Jo.

I opt to help Ruth with hosting and sort through the presents. There are gifts from friends and family, both here and out of state. I make notes of them so she can easily thank them later.

One is marked from Luke and me. My name is printed beside his in his neat handwriting. It's been a long time since I've seen him write my name out in his own hand, but every line, every curve, every loop is familiar, like he's done it a thousand times before. I smile at the memory of how we met through a mail mix-up, and the witty pen pal he became, exchanging dozens of letters before finally meeting. I've kept them all.

"Why don't you give that one to her first?" Ruth asks, nudging my shoulder with a kind smile. So gentle, so accepting, even when I'm a fraud and don't deserve to be here in this special family moment.

But I don't have a choice. Adrenaline is almost feverish inside me as I carry the gift over. Jo beams up at me, and as she unwraps, I think about Luke. How easy it was for him to wedge me into his family, filling the cracks with our relationship.

Adding my name was a move of quiet assurance. No big deal to him, I guess. Part of the pretense. Natural.

But I feel like this gesture, more than anything else, has blown me wide open.

"Thank you!" Jo squeals, holding up an engraved cocktail shaker and a collection of crystal cocktail glasses. Stuff for setting up a home with.

I've never let myself want that before. Home has never been a restful place; it's never been safe, but with Luke, it's different. He makes me feel safe, gives me a place where I can be myself. And being part of a family like this—it makes the idea of a home feel appealing. They have traditions and come together often, and no, it's not perfect, but all the flaws are spackled over with love.

Maybe, if I wanted, I could have that. I could have *him*.

It's a dangerous, wanting, heady thought.

Luke isn't like any of the other guys I've been with. I've always been drawn to alphas, to the borderline toxic—someone who I think won't break in the storm of my life. Someone who won't fall apart when things inevitably end.

Someone who won't make *me* fall apart when things inevitably end.

But Luke hasn't broken under the weight of my emotional baggage, and he's gotten so much more of it than the other guys I've been with, even in this short time. Maybe he's not dominant in the traditional sense, but he still loves and protects his family in a benevolent alpha way.

I'm getting a glimpse at what being part of his inner family circle means, to what being *protected* looks like.

I want to cling to this feeling and never let go. Maybe he's my "type," and I've been shortchanging myself with assholes because feeling like this, tender and vulnerable and open, is so fucking terrifying.

I hand out the rest of the gifts in a daze, smiling mechanically at JoJo's genuine exclamations of joy, and always moving, keeping my hands busy so they siphon some of the thoughts that are bubbling in my mind. But eventually, it has to end, and during dessert, Brittany finds me.

"You and Luke, huh?" She heaves a sigh and looks at me. Under the cultivated exterior, I see a girl about my age, maybe slightly older. Not some crazy, terrifying Wicked Witch of the West. Perhaps a wounded heart on her own flawed journey to finding love and acceptance. "You guys look good together."

"Thanks." I don't trust her compliment, but I smile anyway. "He's a terrific guy."

"He really is." Brittany's eyes cast downward as her smile falters.

As if on cue, Luke bursts through the barn door and starts with the cleanup, bringing trash bags for all the wrapping paper. Brittany's eyes follow him.

Look what you're missing out on. I have to force myself not to say it.

"I never realized how good I had it when I was with him," she says, quietly enough that only I can hear her. "He's something special, you know?"

"I know." I smile empathetically, glad she realizes what she threw away.

"Treat him right. Don't make the same mistake I did." She nods and glances back at me. Her blue eyes are pale and fierce, and when she sighs again, I feel it like a punch to the gut. "He's the one that got away."

***

As the afternoon fades into long shades of purple and orange sunset, I curl up on the sofa in front of the fire in our cabin, checking through my messages. Luke is at the main house so I have a few minutes to myself. Lina, Annabelle, and Charlie have been blowing up the group chat and demanding answers. I send an emoji in response to their increasingly unhinged questions, and almost immediately, my phone lights up with a call from Lina. I press it to my ear. No way am I video calling her where anyone can hear.

"Aspen!" Lina shrieks. "You have been *radio* silent."

"Nice to hear from you too," I say dryly.

"What's going on? I need all the details. *All* of them," she emphasizes. "Where are you? Can you talk openly?"

"Nope."

"That means you've slept with him, doesn't it? Admit it."

"Lina, leave her alone," Annabelle says, joining the call with the drowsy voice of someone who's just woken from a wine-fueled nap.

"For your information, Lina"—I pause, just for effect—"no. We have not."

She makes a strangled sound of disappointment. "Your vagina probably has cobwebs by now."

"Thanks for that beautiful image," I say.

"You're not asking the real question." Charlie has arrived, apparently. Were they all sitting by their phones, waiting for me to resurface from my fake dating adventure? "What I want to know is what Luke is *like* as a boyfriend."

Oh boy. Where to even start?

"He's . . . Okay, he's amazing," I admit. "Super sweet. Very attentive. As a fake boyfriend, he's far superior to most of my real ones."

"That's *awesome*!" They launch into the word like it's some kind of target and they're the missiles, and I hold my phone away from my ear as they babble all at once. The gist of it is that they want details.

"His family is lovely," I say, firmly staying away from the *Oh, by the way, Luke and I are sharing a bed, and actually, I think I'm crazy attracted to this man, and it turns out there's nothing I want more than to be part of a family like his because they treat me like I belong, and my emotions are all over the place because I don't know if I'm lonely or whether this is something else. But Luke is sexy and sweet and I'm so crazy jealous of his ex, because she knows what he looks like naked, and I can't think straight. Also, I'm terrified of liking someone this much.*

"Don't tell me about his *family*," Lina says. "Tell me about his abs."

"How did you know he has abs?"

"I knew it!" She crows. "And you've seen them! Tell me you've seen them."

"No," I hiss. "I have *not* seen them."

"So, how do you know?"

"We were slow dancing, and—"

"Slow dancing!" Charlie makes a victory whoop. "Alert, alert."

Annabelle sighs. "Can you guys not be sensible for one second? Maybe she doesn't *want* to sleep with him."

Uh-huh. And the moon is made of cheese.

"Wait, really?" Lina sounds genuinely confused. "You mean to tell me you are spending the holiday with that fine hunk of a man who appeared to be very into you at the cantina, and you don't want to make a move?"

"Maybe she's falling for him," Charlie teases. "She *loves* him. She wants to *kiss* him."

I don't know what to say. My silence is an admission, but I can't think of anything to say. And to tell them I don't love him, while true, would just be confirmation that I *like* him.

Holy shit, I'm in too deep.

"Look," I finally say. "We're colleagues. When we get back to work, we're going to go back to being coworkers. I don't want it to be awkward. So what's even the *point* of thinking about stuff like that? It's not going to happen. Even if I wanted to, you guys know I don't have experience being in a real relationship. I wouldn't want to screw it up and lose the friendship I have with him. I'm doing a friend a favor, remember?"

The words sink low in my stomach, pressing me into the sofa. I grab a cushion and hug it. That was the arrangement all along. Reminding my friends helps remind me too.

Besides, with Brittany around, there's no guarantee he won't find his way back to his ex. She's been part of the family for so long, and she obviously regrets breaking up. He might say he doesn't want her now, but I've seen what men do.

Luke isn't like those men.

"So, you're not gonna go for it?" Charlie sounds almost disappointed.

"No! No, I'm not gonna go for it. There's nothing to go *for*. We're just . . . Look, it'll all be over in a few days, okay? I helped him out, he helped me out, and things will go back to the way they were before. Okay?"

"If you say so," Lina says, but her tone sounds unconvinced.

That's fair, I guess. I'm not sure I believe me either.

***

Luke

It's late by the time we get back to the cabin after family dinner. I haven't had much of a chance to get Aspen to myself, but now she looks exhausted, her eyes drooping closed.

"You were incredible today," I say as she slumps onto the bed. "Helping Mom out with everything. I know she appreciated it." *And I do too.* "Sorry about . . ." I wince. "Brittany."

Although, the way Aspen behaved around me, even if she just thought she was protecting me, was hot. For a second there, I forgot how to function.

The tattoo conversation flashes through my mind. I've come around to them recently. I never used to be interested in them, but Aspen's tattoos opened my mind to the idea.

Now, knowing *where* they are, I don't think I'll be able to sleep at all.

She props herself up on her elbows and blinks at me with sleepy eyes. "So. Brittany."

"Do we need to talk about her?" I search her eyes, rooting out what she's really trying to say.

Her brows crease, and I already know I've said the wrong thing. I perch beside her, easing off her shoes and tossing them to the floor.

"Okay," I say, softer now. "We can talk about her if you want."

"She's pretty into you."

"No, she's not." I press my thumbs into the arch of her foot, and she lets out an involuntary moan.

The sound shoots straight down my spine and to my groin, and I have to shift into a more comfortable position. If she notices, she doesn't say anything—she just lies on her back and stares at the ceiling, eyes fluttering closed. I repeat the motion, and another moan slips out.

"Holy shit," she mumbles. "That feels so good."

"What did you want to say about Brittany?" If I can think about all the negatives of my ex, maybe it'll turn me off enough that I don't rip Aspen's clothes off right now. Because damn it, concentrating on what I'm saying is hard enough as it is.

"Oh. You know, she sees you as the one who got away. Told me to hold on tight and not to lose you." Her voice is drowsy, and her eyes are closed now. A good thing, because it means she doesn't see the smile that spreads across my face at the thought of Aspen taking the advice. But her next words wipe it away again.

"Is that what she is for you?"

"Aspen." Cautiously, I slide my fingers up her ankle to her calf and massage there, too. She lets out another little moan of pleasure. "Brittany isn't the one that got away. She never was. She's the one I released."

"Eventually. But for a while, you kept going back to her."

"That's because I was young and stupid and didn't know any better. I thought that's what relationships were—dogged determination and a refusal to see how bad the other person is for you. Everyone has flaws, so I figured it was just my job to make it work. Pick up the pieces, you know?"

She doesn't say she knows, but I keep going, because this is important. If there's even a *chance* of Aspen deciding I'm worth taking a leap for, she has to know I'm not all hung up on another girl.

Especially not Brittany.

That ship sailed long ago. Even if Aspen never spoke to me again, I'd still not be interested in Brittany. Once you cheat, there's no going back.

"She's not the one that got away, truly," I repeat, waiting until Aspen finally tilts up her head to look at me. "If she was the last girl in the world, I'd be a monk."

"Luke." She tosses a pillow at my head. "Don't be ridiculous."

"I'm not. I mean it. I don't ever want to be with her again."

Aspen isn't the kind of girl to pout, but there's definitely a sulky look in her eyes when she says, "She was flirting with you."

And yeah, that just makes me dig my thumbs into her feet more firmly. She's painted her nails pink. I love knowing that about her. A detail no one else would know this time of year.

She did it for her. Pink is her signature color.

I'm not a foot guy, but the sight of her little toes, all pink-tipped and pretty, and the noises she's making as I massage them, sends my mind wandering into dangerous territory. There's a reason they say massages lead to sex. No guy could do something like this to the woman he's attracted to and *not* want more.

But there's only one rule. Only one. No sex. I can do anything but sex. And I'm almost positive that there's no potential there for loopholes.

"Brittany can flirt all she wants," I say, not daring to look Aspen in the face in case she reads more there than just reassurance. "But all that means is she's lonely because she and her boyfriend split. There's a good chance they'll get back together."

"You're really good with your hands, you know that?" Aspen grins. "Yeah?"

"Yeah." She shuffles farther up the bed, holding a pillow to her chest. She's not a short woman, but sitting there with her arms wrapped around that pillow, tired after a long day, she looks tiny.

"Mom was a massage therapist," I say. "Rebecca says that's one of the main reasons she married Mark."

I could be wrong, but I think I see a flicker of interest in her eyes. "She taught him too, huh?"

"She taught all us boys. Kwan hasn't talked about it, but I'm sure he's happy."

Her eyes drift closed again. "What about Brittany?" she asks, and although she's not looking at me, she seems tuned in, like she's listening to my breath and monitoring the movement of my hands.

"Well, that was probably the reason Brittany stuck around for so long," I say. "I was super nerdy back then. Same as now, except I've filled out a little since going to the gym with Kai."

"Don't talk to me like you weren't attractive back then." She yawns. *Back then?*

"Let's just say the best wines mature in their later years."

Her laugh is more of a snort, and she lets out another brief, delicate sound that heats my skin and warms my blood. I want to know all the noises she makes—whether she'd sound like this if I had my hands in other places. Her body is a map of unexplored lines, of hills and valleys and curves I don't know yet.

I inhale, forcing my hands to stay where they are.

"I understand," she says sleepily, "why Rebecca likes it."

"Yeah?"

Her smile is a ghost on her face. "Yeah." Like a cat, she stretches and settles back down. Her breathing softens. "You know," she mumbles past lips that barely move, "we should probably talk about when we get back into the office."

I tense without meaning to. That's a conversation we need to have—and sooner rather than later. No one knows about my plan to relocate. I didn't want the fuss that usually surrounds a goodbye, and it didn't make sense to draw it out.

But Aspen needs to know. If we're even going to have a *chance* of making this work, I need to tell her. And soon.

With the way her breathing has evened out, though, she's about asleep. Probably not the perfect time to reveal I'm going to be moving out of state.

Tomorrow. I'll sit her down and tell her tomorrow.

Chapter Eighteen

Luke

The next morning is a circus. Pure chaos. Mom and Rebecca are making everyone breakfast, while Dad has taken over playing with the kids to give Matthew and Kwan a break. They're sharing a peaceful coffee at the table with Jo. Andre isn't up yet.

Brittany, unfortunately, is.

Mark and Granny are absent, probably doing chores on the ranch, and I can't help feeling like their absence is entirely deliberate. Mark loves his family, but he prefers the quiet most of the time. And Granny had to share a bunkhouse with Brittany and the other bridesmaids last night.

I can't imagine either of them enjoyed that one.

"Lukey," Brittany calls as we walk in. She's "playing" with Millie, which involves sitting beside Millie while on her phone. "Hey."

"Lukey?" Aspen mutters. "More like pukey."

"Good morning, sleepyheads." Rebecca ushers us over to the table, where she's placed plates of steaming pancakes for us. "What are you two up to today?"

Waking up beside one another has become habit now. She gravitates toward my warmth, and there's nothing I want more, asleep or awake, than to be holding her. I already know that when we head back home, I'm going to miss this. Miss her.

Time's running out. I need to talk to her about my move to San Jose. If things are moving in the direction I think they are, she needs to know before it looks like this is something I've deliberately kept from her.

Mom chimes in before we can even respond. "We are thinking of having a board game marathon. We could start with Pictionary and maybe some Catan later. I'll make some caramel popcorn. Are you guys in?" The earnestness of the invitation doesn't outweigh my desire to decline.

I glance at Aspen, gauging her reaction. Her expression is as grim as mine, confirming that neither of us wants to spend the day cooped inside, and with Brittany.

"Are those snowmobiles?" Aspen asks in a bright tone, with what appears to be an impromptu idea. "Behind the shed."

It would be a shame to throw away this opportunity to escape.

"Want to go snowmobiling?" I ask. "I know the perfect place."

***

We pack warm. I collect everything I think we'll need, and she teases me about it. *Once a Boy Scout, always a Boy Scout.* I pretend to be annoyed, huffing a sigh and rolling my eyes, but I can't stop my smile.

Now, her arms are wrapped firmly around my waist as we skim across the snow. I show her the paddocks, tell her a bit about my family history and the ranch over the scream of the engine. Wilbur is our prize bull. He's sired hundreds of offspring in his lifetime, but now, he's living out his final days in peace.

Aspen absorbs all of it.

I climb the mountain, engine straining as we weave through the trees, and when we finally reach the top, she hops off the snowmobile and stares down into the canyon below. Our breaths spiral in the crisp air, and the sky is a perfect cerulean blue, marshmallow clouds hovering below the mountain peaks. We're enveloped by mountains—the Wasatch Range on one side and the Oquirrh Mountains across the valley. Sometimes, I forget how fortunate I am to live in such a beautiful place. The air is crisp in our lungs, and Aspen's eyes are wide as she takes in our picturesque surroundings.

Never mind the view. I could watch this expression on her face forever.

"Luke." She spins and looks up into my face. "This is incredible."

"Yeah. It's one of my favorite places. Like you can hold the world in your hands." I cup my palms to show her, and she nods.

On top of the world. I didn't understand that saying until I came up here. The world as I know it is so small compared to Mother Nature's creations. It gives perspective, I guess.

I've wanted to bring Aspen here since I've known her. Something about her made me think she'd love it here, and I've wanted to see the expression on her face as she sees this view for the first time. The dawning wonder written across it, the way her eyes widen and reflect the glimmer of the snow. The way her mouth curves into a slow smile as she absorbs the beauty around us. Her reaction didn't disappoint.

Almost automatically, like she doesn't notice she's doing it, she leans against me, back to my chest, and I wrap my arms around her, resting my chin on top of her head.

I need to tell her about my job opportunity in California. Then, I need to find a way to tell her that I've been in love with her for two years and that I desperately want to make this work. This charade isn't enough for me. This week has shown me what it could be like. Seeing

Aspen interacting with my family, waking up with her in my arms every morning, acting like a couple, has made it clearer than ever that I want to take a shot at really dating her.

"Thank you for bringing me here," she murmurs, her voice almost lost in the stiff breeze and rustling trees.

"It's my pleasure." *Here goes.* "Aspen, there's something I need to tell you—"

"Hey, look over there," she interrupts, pointing to the left, and my eyes follow her finger. "Are those going to be a problem?"

Gray storm clouds are rolling in from the north, heavy and thick.

Damn it.

The weather said there was a chance of a snowstorm this afternoon, but I figured we'd be back by then. But by the speed these clouds are moving, drawing across the sky like blinds, it's going to hit a lot earlier than that.

"We should probably get going. The weather here can turn on a dime."

She gives the clouds a long look and sighs. "Can we come back again?"

"Of course. Anytime." *Come back, keep coming back, never stop coming back.*

We climb on the snowmobile, and I guide us back down the mountain, not taking the scenic route this time. Aspen buries her face in my shoulder blades, and her arms are bands of steel around my waist.

The wind picks up, cold and biting, flicking shards of ice and snow at us as we follow the path through the trees. My fingers are numb even through my gloves, and I squint through my visor. I increase our speed. The frozen air burns my lungs, and I grip the handlebars even more firmly. Adrenaline pounds through me, and Aspen's arms tighten around my waist as we turn a corner.

Crack.

Impact shudders through us. The engine whines; the snowmobile tips sharply on its side, hurling us through the air. I try to gauge impact, and in the few seconds I have, I take hold of Aspen's arm, holding her tight against my body as we topple sideways into the snow.

Chapter Nineteen

Aspen

My body aches. Snow burns my face below my goggles with cold, though the majority of me is lying on something soft. Luke.

I scramble back, patting him down. If I landed on him, he's probably got a broken bone somewhere. Maybe several. The snowmobile is on its side, engine still running, and its throaty hum is all I can hear aside from the crackling by my ears as snow tumbles out of my hair.

"Luke!" I brush my gloved hands across his face helplessly as he sits up, wincing. I'm right; he is hurt. My mind spirals immediately. He's probably got three broken limbs, and I'll have to make a handmade stretcher and pull him all the way back to the house.

"Aspen, it's fine. I'm fine." He rolls his shoulders to illustrate and only winces a little. It's enough to stave off my overly dramatic imagination. "We hit something."

"What do you think it was?" My eyes are fixed on Luke's micro-movements in case he's downplaying his injuries to keep me calm. That would be such a Luke move.

"I dunno." With clumsy, labored effort, he manages to get to his feet and examines the snowmobile. It's a red monster, with great snow treads and handlebars that look like they belong to a motorcycle. I'm not sure how old it is, but it's seen its fair share of bumps and scrapes by now.

One of the treads looks. . . bent.

Luke sucks in a breath as he assesses the damage. The wind has really picked up now, sending tiny bits of ice stabbing at my exposed skin. I tug my scarf up tighter around my chin.

"I think we hit a fallen log," he says, nodding back to where something dark juts from the ground. The snow was scraped off by the impact. "Pulled the tread right off."

"Can you fix it?"

He gives me a grim look. "No."

I fumble for my phone. According to my GPS and tenuous signal, we're still eight miles from the house. I'm no Boy Scout, but that doesn't feel like an easy hike to make. I'm wearing boots and wrapped up warm, sure, but that's a long way, and now snow is spiraling from the darkening sky.

Thirty minutes ago, it was *sunny*. Typical Utah weather.

Luke's mouth sets in a hard line as he looks back up the way we came. "I think there's an old pioneer cabin back there. Are you okay to walk?"

"I'm fine. I landed on *you*, remember?" Another gust of cold wind shudders its way down my scarf and up my cuffs, and I shiver, wrapping my arms around myself. The sky has darkened. The temperature has dropped *dramatically*. Another reason why trying to trek home would be impossible.

He gingerly reaches for me, tucking my hand through his arm. The bag he brought is already over his shoulder.

"I'm fine," he says in answer to my unasked question. "Come on. When the storm really sets in, we won't be able to see a thing."

He doesn't let go of me the entire trudge uphill. We follow the snowmobile's tracks, peering through the ever-thickening snow until he spots what he was looking for: a dilapidated cabin, tucked between the trees. There's a cell tower positioned on the ridge above us, and by some miracle, Luke's phone has a signal. He talks to his dad, explaining the situation and the early onset of the storm, while I examine our surroundings. We really are in the middle of nowhere. The shack—let's call it what it is—is set on a flat-ish piece of land and is made, predictably, of wood. The building leans a little to the left, and the roof sags. Some planks are missing from the front steps, and a window pane is cracked. It's probably well over one hundred years old. Maybe closer to a hundred and fifty. It looks its age.

Can cockroaches survive in the cold? Probably. I think I read somewhere they'd survive a nuclear blast.

I shiver again, and Luke mistakes it for the cold.

"It'll be warmer inside," he says, climbing the rickety steps and examining the front door. The whole thing looks one stiff breeze away from falling over, but one side is already coated in the snow that's now falling sideways, and it's still standing.

Maybe inside wouldn't be so bad.

He jiggles the handle, and to my surprise, the door just opens. Inside, there's nothing but dust and dim light. He ushers me inside first, then closes the door behind him.

There are windows, more or less, but they're so ingrained with grime, barely any of the gray light filters through. The other set—the side facing the wind—is thick with snow and only lets in a vague glow.

Luke is pulling more gadgets out of his pack, settling on a silver foil rectangle that is the size of a pack of playing cards. He unfolds it several times until it turns into a small, tarp-like sheet.

"Wrap this emergency blanket around you. It'll help you retain your body heat." *Bear Grylls, eat your heart out.* "I'll find some kindling."

"Are you *insane*? This entire place is made of wood." And it looks like it's on its last legs.

He kicks something in the corner that clangs. It's a metal drum, rusted and in about as good condition as the rest of this place. But Luke is pleased, dragging it to where there's a small hole in the roof. In a few swift motions, he snaps a chair that's seen better days. Then, and I kid you not, he brings *flint and steel* out of his bag and sets a tidy fire going. As cool as you please.

This is Luke in peak Boy Scout mode, and I have to admit, I'm impressed as hell. And a little turned on.

Out of the driving wind and snow, I'm already feeling warmer. The fire sends dancing light across the wooden walls, and although this place rattles with every gust, it's survived this long. I imagine it's seen worse storms than this one.

Of course, the light also illuminates the dried-up carcass in the corner. A rat, probably. I don't let myself give it more than a passing glance. There are also a few cans, wrapped in worn labels and coated in rust, that I wouldn't touch if you paid me. Clearly, no one has been here in a while, but I suspect hunters have made use of this place over the years.

We both crouch by the fire, knees brushing.

"My dad should be here in about an hour with a trailer for the snowmobile," Luke says.

"Is he angry?"

"That I hit a fallen log? Nah." He shrugs, and his shoulder knocks against mine. "These things happen. He knows I didn't do it because I was being careless or stupid. We'll get it fixed on up."

"Your parents are pretty understanding, huh?" I shuffle even closer. "Must be nice."

He wraps his arm around me under the makeshift blanket, and I shuck off my gloves, sending my cold fingers questing under his jacket and sweater to his T-shirt. Warmth. He shudders, and I snicker. His breath comes faster as I press my knuckles to his side.

Every time I touch him, I'm astonished by the muscles going on under his clothes. If I had definition like this, I'd flaunt it to the world. And this is *definitely* worth flaunting.

"So." I blow out a breath and watch it dance around me. The storm notches up a gear. "Is this a first for you, or are you used to sheltering from a storm with girls you're pretending to date?"

"This is a first."

"What part?"

"All of it."

I bite my lip to hide my grin. No way I want Luke knowing how much I *like* the idea of being his first. The first for this, anyway. I know Brittany has been a big part of his life, and he's admitted to dating other people as well, but no one else has done this precise thing with him. Like exploring uncharted territory. When he adds it to his map of memories, it'll be under my name.

"Are you hungry?" he asks. "I brought granola bars."

I laugh, the sound clashing against the howl of the storm. "Of course you did."

"I didn't want you to get hungry."

"You're a really good guy, you know that?"

He shifts even closer to me, and I take the opportunity to burrow deeper under his jacket. Our legs are in the dirt, but it's this or a table so rickety I'm pretty sure it's held together with cobwebs and prayers.

"Do you like really good guys?" he asks, his voice so low, it's a murmur. The wind drowns it, takes the words and smashes them against the walls, but I can still hear them. They rumble through me.

I never thought I did like good guys. They were never my style. I thought they'd be dull, and it'd require more vulnerability than I thought I was capable of.

It's just . . . being with Luke has taught me how incredible it can be as well.

"I think so," I whisper back. I say the words against the skin of his neck—that tiny fraction of space visible between the collar of his jacket and the low sweep of his hat. I don't know when we became this close, but I don't want to move. "I'm beginning to understand the appeal of them. You've done more nice things for me while we're not dating than anyone who's *actually* dated me."

His laugh is a whisper of air. "Maybe you've just been dating assholes."

"Maybe I have."

He doesn't say anything more, but I feel his arm around me tense and tighten. His other hand is on my leg, and his fingers flex. Just once.

The silence begs for my honesty. The shack shudders around us, but the only thing I notice is the thud of his pulse under my nose. Fast and strong.

"My dad left when I was little," I say. People know this about me, of course. They ask and I tell them the truth, but this is maybe the first time I've said it unprompted. "He and my mom had been fighting for a bit before then, but they'd always make up. Until one day, they didn't. He just walked out. Didn't even say goodbye." The hurt of it still stings after all this time. Luke curls me into him even more, and I shuffle forward until I'm on his lap, legs curled around his hips, our bodies pressed close together. I don't want him to see my face, so I rest my cheek on his shoulder.

"I'm sorry." I feel the vibration of his voice more than hear it. "That must have been hard."

"It makes me scared, sometimes, to think about forever. Forever doesn't exist for me. I don't have happily married parents or siblings. Or permanence of any kind. Dating assholes means I'm less likely to get hurt." And, if I'm honest, their flaws mean I'm less self-conscious about mine. Who cares about an absent father and a disfiguring birthmark when the guys you're dating have the emotional depth of a puddle and are just interested in casual sex?

Luke eases me back so he can look me in the face and waits for me to make eye contact. When I do, he says, "It doesn't have to be like that, Aspen."

I shake my head, my mom's mantra automatically coming to my lips. "All men leave eventually."

"That's not true," he says, fiercer than I've ever heard him. "Look at my parents. My dad freaking adores my mom. Kwan is devoted to Matthew, even though I think he's crazy for it. Mark would die for Rebecca." His gaze searches mine like he's trying to tell me something. "And I'm not a quitter, either. When I'm interested in someone, I'm all in."

The thought makes my chest ache, like my heart is swelling and there's not enough room for it beside the doubt and the fear, so I focus on the color of his eyes. The firelight brings out the gold, burnishing it until it gleams.

I can't address what he just said, the things it feels like he's promising me, so I just whisper, "You have beautiful eyes." My fingers flatten against his cheek, and he blinks in surprise. His mouth softens into a smile that I come to match, and I grow bolder, tracing his bone structure. High cheekbones, strong jaw, deliriously long eyelashes. He's a work of art, a masterpiece of a man, and I'm in awe.

His eyes are dark now. The green is gone, the gold banished to the outer ring.

I am lost in them.

"Aspen," he murmurs. His lips move underneath my hands, and I feel the way he swallows. This close, I can feel almost everything. "If you were mine, I would never let you go."

Chapter Twenty

Aspen

*I*f you were mine, I would never let you go.

The words reverberate around my chest as I look up at Luke. Because if he was mine, I would feel the same way.

He could be mine, I think. At least now. I know enough about men to know when a man wants me, and my attraction isn't one-sided right now.

I press my cold nose against his neck, and he sucks in a breath. My fingers and toes tingle with heat. It prickles all over me, burning at every spot his body is touching mine. His hands are both resting on my hips, holding me in place.

And I don't care that we're in one of the most dilapidated buildings I've ever set foot in. Or that we're in the middle of a snowstorm. Or even that there's a dead rat in the corner. I want to kiss him. All those things that have been bubbling inside me for days are overflowing, and I can't remember how I'm ever supposed to stop myself.

If you were mine, I would never let you go.

I never set out wanting to be his, or to ever be anyone's. Now, I'm greedy, the hand under his sweater grasping his soft T-shirt, and I don't want what we are feeling right now to end.

When I look back up at him, he's staring at me as though he can sense my every thought and is patiently waiting for me to respond to his declaration.

If you were mine, I would never let you go.

We're feeling the same things, wanting the same things.

His eyes are almost black. The wind howls.

I lean in and kiss him.

At least, I think I'm the one to do it. Our mouths collide with just enough force for it to be awkward and urgent. Our lips are messy, our teeth clack as we find our rhythm together. This is different from the other kisses we've shared—those perfectly poised things in front of his family. This time, it's raw, heated. One of my hands is in his hair, tossing his hat aside so I can thread my fingers through his soft curls. I run my fingernails along his scalp and feel his soft moan into my mouth. His breaths are whispers, and I swallow them, deepening our kiss. If I ever worried about him kissing me back, I do not have to worry.

I *really* do not have to worry.

He kisses me like a starving man faced with a banquet. His lips are hungry, needy, moving against mine with almost frightening intensity. It's clear that he wants this—maybe has always wanted this.

I slide my fingers up inside his T-shirt. His skin is soft; the muscles underneath hard. His fingers flex on my thighs, and I beg him, silently, with my mouth, to move them higher. Touch me, touch me, *touch me*.

There's roaring everywhere, all around, and it has nothing to do with the storm.

He breaks away for breath and kisses my neck. His stubble is the perfect length to cause goose bumps everywhere it touches. Sloppy, open-mouthed kisses, with just a hint of teeth, that cast shivers all over me. I shimmy closer and stop when I feel the impressive bulge that's conveniently making contact between my legs. Even through his thermals, and thick snow pants, I can feel it.

I roll my hips, pressing myself against him. He finds the underside of my sweater, pushing it up past my thermals, fingers dipping underneath. His other hand is spanning my thigh, tracing my fleece lined leggings. I can feel every flex of his fingers, every hesitation, every rasp of his calluses through the thin material. The friction is delicious on my skin.

I'm incoherent with want for this tech-nerdy, wood-chopping, flannel-wearing, undercover lumberjack. Who'd have thought.

I want our clothes off. Now.

"Hey." He catches my wrist with one hand. The other is still on my hip over way too many layers. "Stop. Think about this for a second."

"I am thinking." Horny Aspen is, anyway. And right now, I think Horny Aspen is the only Aspen that exists in my body. "Don't try to tell me you don't want this."

"You know I do."

"Then kiss me." I reach up and plant a kiss in the crook of his neck. He shudders, and the fingers around my wrist tighten. "If you want to, then what's stopping you?" When he doesn't say anything, I trail kisses across the line of his jaw to his ear. "I want you, Luke," I breathe against the shell of his ear.

"The rule—" Luke's swallow is audible.

"I've changed my mind. There are no rules." Seriously, what do I have to do to convince this man to sleep with me? "Sex is on the table. Maybe even on *that* table." I gesture toward the piece of furniture in question, and he shakes his head.

"It would collapse at the first thrust. The last thing I want is to risk injuring you."

"Against the wall, then?"

"Aspen." He huffs a laugh against my hair. "I really don't think this is the best place."

"Why? The fire is warm enough that I could stand to shed a few pieces of clothing. We don't have to get fully naked." I'm practically begging now.

"Aspen," he says, more firmly this time. "Stop looking at me like that."

I take his bottom lip between my teeth and bite. Not hard enough to draw blood, but hard enough to elicit a shocked gasp from him. "You know you want to."

"That's not the problem; trust me."

"Then what *is* the problem?" I look up at him, tracing his familiar features with my eyes. How could I have sat opposite him for two years and not noticed the smile lines in his cheeks, or the way his brown eyelashes tangle, or the sinful gleam in his eyes? He's perfectly gilded by the licking flames and so unrelentingly handsome. "Are you worried about it being just once? Because let me tell you, I am *more* than up for continuing this back at our cabin. Several times, even." With my most sultry smile, I trail a fingernail down his neck, tracing his collarbones, and he shivers. "Maybe even when we get back home. We can have a torrid office affair." That doesn't sound so bad. Actually, sneaking around like that sounds *hot*. "We could have hot sex in storage closets and my car during lunch hours."

He licks his lips. His pupils dilate even more. He likes that idea, I can tell. But he still doesn't bite. "What about your habit of only dating assholes?"

"Well, this doesn't have to be dating. It can just be sex." Even as I say it, I'm not sure that's true. Sex with Luke might just kill me, especially if he keeps looking at me like that. I dig at his loosened scarf, throwing it aside so I can further explore the soft skin at the base of his neck. His pulse thuds unevenly there, pale skin throbbing in the dim light. "Or maybe you'll convince me to try out something more long-term—like a real girlfriend."

His groan sets fire to my libido. "We need to talk about this. There are some things I need to tell you—"

"Stop overanalyzing. We can talk later. *After*." I finally find the zipper for his coat and pull it open, shoving it back. His gray sweater is sculpted to his body. Those shoulders. I think I'm salivating.

"I've been thinking about this moment for way too long to waste it here," he says, his voice low and grating. "I want to have you on a bed."

That sounds hot. But a bed is a very long way from here, and I want him *now*.

"What about right here in your lap then?"

"*Aspen*." The pleading in Luke's voice is wavering.

"So that's a yes?" I attempt to assume the sale.

He kisses me again, his lips urgent, opening my mouth so his tongue can curl against mine. Teasing, teasing, always teasing. I'm alive with want, heat pooling between my legs. It's never been like this with anyone before, like fireworks. My body belongs to him; he can have me, do whatever he wants with me.

I rub against him, in case that helps change his mind, and he groans into my mouth. "Fuck, Aspen."

I don't think I've ever heard him swear before, and it's so sexy I almost lose my mind.

"Take me." I'm babbling, placing one of his hands on my breast. Too many clothes. We're wearing too many. Shit. *Shit*. "Luke, please. I'm all revved up and nowhere to go."

"Don't quote Meatloaf at me," he says with a shaky laugh. "We can't. There's a dead rat in the corner, for heaven's sake."

"Just close your eyes," I plead as I dry hump him in his lap.

"I don't want to have to get a tetanus shot after I make love to you for the first time." His voice is strained. He's been craving this as badly as I have. Maybe more. I'm sure of it.

That's what Luke is for me now: a craving. I'm an addict, shameless and needy.

A thought bursts through my horny haze, and I break away to look at him. "You said you've been thinking about this moment for a long time. You said *making love*."

His eyes are hooded. There's no green there now, just dark, naked lust that takes a second to clear. His thumbs swipe up my ribs, dangerously close to the underside of my breast. My nipples have pinched, hard and aching.

"Yeah," he says distractedly.

"How long?"

"Long enough."

I huff, frustrated. That's not an answer. "Luke. Tell me."

He sighs, but at least he doesn't move me away. His thumb is still moving, drawing restless circles across my ribcage, under my sweater. I can tell he wants to be against bare skin. "You remember how we first met?"

"When you sent that family Christmas card to the wrong address? I remember."

"And after becoming pen pals for a bit, we met up in that Starbucks?"

"Yes," I say impatiently. Of course I remember. "What's your point?"

"I wanted to date you then, when I first got you the interview with Kai. But you'd just started dating someone else, and then we became colleagues, and the timing never worked out."

I lean back so I can see his face. "Seriously?"

"Don't tell me you had no idea."

"I had an inkling you might've liked me at one point, but you never did anything about it, and I just assumed I read the signals wrong." That, and I wasn't interested in a work romance with a guy who is so obviously sweet and good and wholesome. That sounded too much like the start of something serious.

Now, if he's confessing what he's confessing, it still does, but I'm in a different place. I *like* Luke. A lot.

"Two years?" I ask, trying not to sound too incredulous. "And you never said anything?"

"I never thought I stood a chance before." His fingers creep lower under my shirt to the bare skin along my waistband, and I shiver from want. Smoke from the fire dances round the room, swirled by the wind, before finding its way to the hole in the roof. "But there's something else I need you to know before this goes any further."

I freeze. "What?"

"I'm transferring to San Jose in January to oversee the expansion there," he says in a rush. "It's the kind of opportunity I've been working toward my whole career, and I'm the only one Kai trusts to lead it. Plus, we'll be working in Go, which no one else on the team is familiar with, and he's trusted me with a sense of his vision."

I let out a long, slow breath, trying to feel my way through my disappointment. Luke is moving to California to work on Kai's big, new project. I knew Kai was expanding and setting up a new office in San Jose. Everyone in the office knew about it. A few other people said they were transferring, although as I understand it, there will be a few new hires as well.

It's a big deal. He's right that this is the opportunity of a lifetime. A chance for him to do the things he's been working toward all his career.

In *California*.

"Aspen," Luke says gently, his hand finding my face and cupping it, "I know this is a big shock. I just needed to tell you before things went too far."

"Before we had sex," I say numbly.

"I don't want either of us to get hurt, so maybe it's better if we stop here before we take this to the next level. Your friendship is too important to me to throw it away on something fleeting." That thumb rubs across my birthmark and the uneven skin there, and I still, half wanting to pull away, half wanting to lean into the touch. "The thing is, I don't want casual sex. If I'm going to be with you, I want the whole thing. A real relationship."

I push back from his hand so I can think. "First, you tell me you've been pining after me for two years; then, you tell me we need to stop? You're giving me whiplash, Luke."

"I can't face another breakup, Aspen," Luke says, and I immediately think back to Brittany. She has a lot to answer for. "If we have sex, and I find out how good we can be together, and you decide you don't want anything more, that would wreck me. If this isn't going to work long-term, then I don't know if I even want to start. I'm not that strong, Aspen."

"So, you're chickening out? You're scared."

He raises an eyebrow. "And so are you."

"Excuse me? I'm the one who's been trying to have sex with you."

"Sure, but if you weren't scared of something real, you'd have offered me more than a quick fuck against the wall and an office fling." He runs a hand through his hair. "Are you willing to try a relationship?

Because I can't be casual with you. I want everything—the good, the bad, the ugly." He doesn't say he wants forever, but I hear it anyway. My stomach ties itself in knots.

What he's asking for is too much. I don't have forever to give—nothing lasts forever, even if I wanted to make this moment stretch the rest of my life.

"You're leaving," I say, knowing I should pull back even further, extract myself from his lap, but I'm unable to. "I want to tell you I'll be anything you want, but long distance is a lot to ask. It's really hard. Especially at the beginning."

"I know." He gives me a sad smile. "The timing sucks. Let's take a step back, then. You don't have to make a decision right now. Just know that if you want to give it a real go, if you want something with me, I'm all in."

My mind is reeling. My body is still aching for him, but over the howl of the wind, I hear an engine. And so does Luke, by the resignation clamping the corners of his expression.

"That'll be my dad," he says, gently lifting me from his lap to standing. "We should go."

No. Stay here with me. Don't let reality in.

He stands up and crosses to the door, letting reality in with a burst of cold air that puts out the fire. I trace the pattern of the smoke with my distracted gaze, trying to figure out what I want.

How much I want it.

If I want it enough to be with Luke despite my fears and flawed motherly advice. A real relationship. Long distance. With a good guy.

A chance at happiness or heartbreak. The possibility of either—or both—is as shockingly cold as snow sluicing down the back of my neck, and the ride home is in silence.

***

We arrive back to find Andre's family has arrived and dinner is on the table. The groom's parents are nice, in a quiet way. I think they're overwhelmed by the sheer *volume* of Luke's family. There are so many of us and so few of them. Honestly, I'm not paying much attention—I'm replaying our conversation from the shack, dissecting each secret and desire we revealed.

Occasionally during the meal, our thighs nudge or our hands brush, and I'm filled with electricity and anticipation. It's buzzing through me, stronger than any alcohol.

All I can think about is his hands on me. His mouth on me. The wet heat of his tongue and the sharp nip of his teeth. A loop of sensations playing over and over in my mind.

I shiver just thinking about it.

"Oh, you must be chilled to the bone," Ruth says sympathetically. I look up to see all eyes on me.

Oh no. Not good.

"I'm fine," I start, but she's already smiling kindly at me, an idea on her lips.

"I know just the thing: a soak in the hot tub."

"You never offer a hot-tub party when I visit," Matthew says indignantly.

"I'd love to go for a soak," JoJo puts in, and that's more or less the end of it. Matthew and Kwan are obviously keen, and thirty seconds later, a full adult hot-tub session has been planned. Which is . . . typical. Just typical. The Simmons family has a knack for innocently intervening where Luke and I are concerned.

Luke sends me a long-suffering look, and I glory a little in the knowledge that he's going to find this just as hard as I am. Less clothes and more skin contact is the exact opposite direction we need to be going in if we are trying to cool off our attraction.

"We don't have to go," Luke says as soon as we're back in the cabin. "If you think it's too much after . . ."

I rifle through my bag for my bikini. This isn't about us. It's Jo's wedding, and we can't be the ones to disrupt that, even if things have gotten complicated.

"They expect us to be there," I say. "We can't back out now."

"We can *always* back out."

"I came here so I could act as your girlfriend and protect you from blind dates and exes. What girlfriend is going to turn down a hot tub?" I gesture wildly because if I was a *real* girlfriend, a hot tub is the last thing I'd turn down. "This is JoJo's wedding weekend. It's a family thing, so we should be there."

Luke gives me a long look, and I know he's thinking about the shack and all the things we shouldn't be thinking about. Especially if this isn't going to happen. If *we're* not going to happen.

"Okay," he says. "If you're sure."

"We can act normal, right?"

"Right."

Wrong. There's no more acting normal. I know what it's like to kiss Luke until I'm feverish with it. I know what it's like to have his hands on me. To feel his arousal against my most intimate parts.

Albeit covered in clothes.

Now, we'll be wearing far fewer layers. But we'll be with his family. And there's no way either of us is going to get carried away.

His gaze heats as he looks at me, and the only thing I'm sure about is the fact that I'm not sure about anything at all.

Chapter Twenty-One

Luke

This was a mistake.

For multiple reasons. I should have manufactured an excuse for why we couldn't attend. Insisted that Aspen and I were way too tired for a stint in the hot tub with my family. Set the cabin on fire, perhaps.

But I didn't, and now we're here, Aspen nearly naked except for a strip of bikini that leaves almost nothing to the imagination. The only thing grounding me is the cold night air against my wet skin. Aspen's tattoos are now on display for my feasting eyes.

There's an anime-looking character on her back, an Aspen tree on her shoulder, and lines of Sanskrit on her ribcage, just below her breast. And something small and delicate on her hip bone that I'd like to investigate later. I'm curious to know the stories behind each marking, to have a deeper understanding of her past and how she became who she is.

"Scoot over," Mark says as he lowers himself into the water. Aspen scoots closer, her leg brushing mine. Brittany, in a bikini that seems designed to push her boobs up to her eyeballs, squeezes in too, and Aspen wiggles onto my lap to create more room.

Matthew launches into an open admiration of Brittany's latest posts and TikTok videos, and Dad starts a quiet conversation with Kwan. Granny, Mom, and Rebecca stayed inside to watch the kids and host Andre's family. Aspen, by degrees, relaxes against me, molding our upper bodies to each other. The water bubbles around our chests, and I adjust, sinking lower in my seat so she'll be more comfortable. Her hand reaches down, brushing my thigh in gratitude.

I don't know why either of us thought it would be a good idea to torture ourselves like this.

No, I knew from the start this would be a bad idea.

JoJo and Brittany's conversation drifts to the wedding, while Andre asks Matthew and me some inane questions about our jobs.

Aspen sinks further against my chest, her head resting against my cheek, my arms cradling her to me. I do my best to focus on the conversation, but I can't stop thinking about the way she kissed me in the shack.

Before, I could kid myself that she was just pretending. But now, I know better. She wants me almost as much as I want her—she was prepared for me to have her then and there, almost at the point of ripping my clothes off, and even though it's not the same as knowing she wants a relationship, it's something.

More than before.

Absently, I toy with her newly discovered belly-button piercing, caressing the small jewel at the end of it. Her breath catches, and my hands still. She runs her nails lightly up and down my thighs, encouraging me to start up again, so I do, exploring the soft shape of her bare stomach. As Matthew talks and I add the occasional comment, I lazily trace the outline of her upper thighs with my other hand.

My finger brushes the edge of her bikini line, and she shudders, pushing back into me until there's no hiding how much I'm enjoying this.

How turned on I am.

She freezes, just for a second, and I think I've gone too far. No, I *know* I've gone too far—I'm the one who told her to stop in the shack. These boundaries are mine, and right now, I'm crashing through them.

The feel of her skin against mine is addictive. The soft way she catches her breath, the way she wiggles against me, like she's trying to provoke a reaction.

Neither of us is paying attention to the conversation, especially now that Kwan's joined in and directed it away from us. My every nerve is focused on the places our bodies are connected. Her back arches, and I think she's going to pull away but realize she's opening her legs a little wider, granting more access to her body. Aspen turns her head slightly so that her nose rubs along the line of my jaw, encouraging me to continue touching her.

How far can we push this? My family is right there.

JoJo throws a comment to Aspen, who gives a languid response, and the heat between us cranks up a notch as I slide my fingers under the waist of her bikini. We definitely shouldn't be pushing it this far.

I shouldn't be pushing it this far.

She grinds against me again, and my fingers tighten convulsively around her waist, digging in just enough to anchor us in this moment.

The water bubbles around us, warm and soft, gratefully concealing everything we're dangerously doing.

If she doesn't want to be all in with me, doesn't want this to continue after the wedding, it's going to crush me. I'm playing with fire, but even that thought isn't enough to convince me to stop. Nothing can make me give up on what this could be. That's clear now. I said something about waiting, but there's nothing in me that wants to delay even a second longer.

My fingers dip down a little further, into forbidden territory, and she bites back a gasp as I encounter her slickness.

My mind goes blank. There's a roaring in the back of my head, a primal need that transcends all the millennia of advancement and sophistication.

She's wet *for me*. She wants me. I knew that logically already, but there's a difference between knowing something and having the evidence irrefutably placed before you.

I want her. Need her. Now. Despite what I said earlier.

She leans her head back so her lips are by my ear. "How soon until we can leave?"

My blood is racing. No amount of calming thoughts are going to help when she's right here, pressed up against me like this.

"Soon," I murmur back. "Now, even."

"I'm kind of tired," Aspen says as soon as there's a lull in the conversation. "I think I'm going to head to bed."

Matthew pouts. "Already?"

"Yeah. It's been a long day, what with the snowmobile accident and everything."

"Oh, I forgot about that," JoJo says with a guilty look. "Yeah, you guys get some rest. We'll see you tomorrow."

I remove my hands from Aspen, so we're back to being PG. Mostly. "See you tomorrow, Jo." With Aspen in front of me, shielding my crotch just in case anyone is looking, we clamber out of the hot tub and wrap towels around ourselves as we head back to the cabin and into uncharted territory.

***

Aspen

We're barely back through the door before we're in each other's arms again. I don't know what prompted him to change his mind, but I'm not about to argue. Not when his fingers are running through my hair and his mouth is on mine.

Frantic. Needy.

Standing on the bearskin rug in front of the fireplace warms our damp skin. His wet hair is slicked back, allowing me to take in his whole face. The firelight dances across his beautiful features. I take a moment to trace them lightly before my impatient lips crash into his again.

We're both on the verge of combusting. I could lose myself in him. The scent of him, the feel of him, the way he says my name, raspy and gruff, lingering on the *s* like he wants to keep it on his lips longer. He kisses me like he's known there was no other conceivable outcome than us being together.

"Aspen," he says again, cupping my face in his hands. I can't bear how tenderly he holds me, like I'm precious, something he treasures. My heart is ripping open, every guard and barrier I've put up coming apart, and Luke is the only thing holding me together. "I've lived my life being cautious, and I can't do that anymore. Will you risk going beyond our friendship tonight?"

"I can't promise tomorrow," I tell him, though inside, I'm screaming yes.

"Can you promise me tonight?" His fingers are warm against my cheeks, and there's no escaping this.

"I want you. I care about you." So much more than I ever would have imagined. "Can you be with me tonight and not worry about what comes next?"

For a second, I think I've pushed it too far. His eyebrows meet in the middle as he searches my face. But then, he nods.

"Yes. No regrets."

I could never regret this. But I don't have time to express that because he's kissing me again, and everything I haven't said percolates under my skin. A little collection of secrets I've gathered over the course of being here with him like this. The way he smiles, slow and sure like sunlight breaking out from behind a cloud. The delightful skim of his fingertips across my skin. The way I love how he touches me. I'm giving parts of myself away, and he doesn't know how many. Not yet.

Maybe I'll tell him.

But that's tomorrow's problem. Now, we only have tonight.

His hands are everywhere. Exploring my curves, every inch of skin the bikini has left bare, murmuring compliments, how I'm beautiful and perfect and tempting. How he's losing his mind over me.

Meanwhile, I'm melting into a puddle of want, aching so badly I don't know how he can't hear it with every pounding thump of my heart.

"Not here," he says eventually, reaching down to kiss me. "I don't want our first time to be on the floor."

I grin up at him. "But there aren't even any rats here."

"Call me old-fashioned, but I want you in my bed, Aspen."

What girl could say no to that?

I let him lead me across to the bed and lay me down, yanking off his swim shorts as he goes. I eye the rigid length of him for the first time.

So that's *what's been pressed up against me all those times. Impressive. Stunning.*

I'm ogling him, and I can't even bring myself to feel bad. Nothing about this situation feels bad. Who would've thought I'd ever be in this kind of situation—and want it this ferociously.

Want *him* this ferociously.

With two strategic pulls of string, I'm out of my bikini, and he exhales shakily as he looks down at the whole of me, naked and bare in front of him. If there was ever a time to be self-conscious, this would be it. But the admiration in his eyes buoys my confidence. I'm sprawled out on the bed in front of him, and he's devouring me with his mouth. His lips are everywhere, tasting every inch of my skin, a ravenous exploration of my body.

I'm basking in the heat and light of his roaming hands. I feel adored and cherished as he climbs on the bed, hovering over me. His erection twitches, and I can't help my smirk as I look up at him.

"Is this where you want me?" I ask.

"Right there. Don't move."

"Not even to do this?" I spread my legs, and his throat bobs as he looks at me. I know I'm wet. I've been wet since he first started touching me—never mind how innocently—in the hot tub. I must be glistening with it now. He takes his time tasting and testing what makes me gasp in pleasure. He's hijacked all of my senses. I close my eyes and surrender.

Minutes later, his gaze rises from between my legs and fastens on my breasts. Then, finally, to my enamored expression. His eyes are hooded.

"Keep looking at me like that, and this won't last as long as I want it to," he tells me shakily.

"Get up here and kiss me, and you won't see how I'm looking at you at all." I reach down and take his hand, tugging until his body presses me against the sheets. Delicious weight. Sinking under it, the weight of him and wanting him and the fact that this is finally going to happen, I wrap my arms around him and hold him closer.

After tonight, everything will be different.

I don't care.

We're skin to skin. The feeling of us pressed together is exquisite, firing all my nerves, tickling all my senses until I'm in overdrive.

When we kiss, our mouths are frantic, like he's just as overwhelmed as I am. It's urgent and bright. I think he wants to go slow, but our hands are all over each other. Breaking the kiss, he leans down, and his teeth scrape against my nipple. I arch against him, spreading my legs further and wiggling until his fingers find me and he can finally finish what he started.

"Aspen." His voice is half-laugh, half-disbelief. "Damn, you're so wet."

I mean to reply, but he strokes me again, pressing one finger inside, and all I manage is a whimper. He laughs and does it again, and I hold on tight, nails digging into the skin of his bicep. It's a pleasure to be touched this way. The other guys I've been with viewed foreplay as a means to an end, the end being getting inside me, but Luke takes his time, like every moment here is a privilege.

As he works me, I reach down to touch him, exploring his length with my fingers. The tighter I'm wound, the more fervent my hands, until his breath is as fractured as mine. Eventually, when I'm at the point of snapping entirely, he reaches down to still me.

"Not yet," he says, harsh against my cheek. "Do you know how long I've wanted this?" He punctuates his words with a soft bite of my nipple that has my orgasm beckoning closer. I shake my head, even though I do know. He told me. Since that first meeting. "It's been months. Years. I've dreamed about doing this to you."

My eyes roll back in my head, and I squeeze them closed. One of his fingers swirls lazily around me, holding me right on the edge.

"Luke." I'm scrabbling for his arm, trying to force his hand exactly where I need it. He seems to know and is avoiding the spot. "Luke, *please*."

"Tell me exactly what you want, sweetheart."

Sweetheart is enough. I never thought I was the kind of girl to love endearments, but hearing him say it in that rasping voice of his sends me spiraling over the edge. I'm falling so violently, I lose touch with reality. All that exists in my world is sensation—and Luke. Even in this place of pleasure, he's here with me. My body is out of control, but he holds me through it, through every wave and convulsion, the hazel warmth in his eyes grounding me to this moment. To him and what we've shared.

When I come back to myself, it might be minutes, hours, days later. I reach up to touch his face. Strange how tenderness feels natural here in this bed with him.

"Luke," I say. My voice doesn't sound like my own. "Let's do that again."

Chapter Twenty-Two

Aspen

Luke's mouth works it's way up my torso, pausing on my breasts, then kissing me on the mouth, a hard and fast peck, before rolling off me. I'm about to complain when I see him reach into the nightstand where I'd shoved the lingerie and condoms. I send my friends a silent thank-you. Maybe I won't murder them after all.

"Good thing we have these," he says, letting me take the little packet and roll it on. "I didn't come prepared. I didn't think—"

"Me neither." I grin and lie back, letting him cover me with his body again.

His erection teases my entrance, and I'm almost certain I've died and gone to heaven.

"Is this all right?" he asks, the concentration on his face making him look a little strained.

"It's better than all right," I tell him. "It's amazing. Don't you dare stop."

He laughs a little then, focused and lovely, and firelight gilds his body as he presses, testing the water. At the feel of him slipping inside with a sudden rush, my eyes roll back in my head. Okay, yes, this is good. He's giving me space and time to adjust to the feel of him inside me, then providing just enough friction with his languid strokes to have me quivering around him. The feel of him inside me eclipses everything that's come before.

I thread my fingers through his hair and softly nibble on his chin, my lips tingling with the feel of his scruff against me.

This is a good look on him. Naked, above me, with a few days' stubble scratchy on his jawline. He groans shakily and drops a tender kiss on my forehead without breaking his stride.

We're fused together, body and soul, and I might explode from the sheer energy running through me right now.

Sex with a new partner doesn't usually feel this good or this connected. So intimate, like the space between our bodies is just filled with everything unsaid. Everything we don't have to say.

There are so many thoughts I want to share, but I feel the words settle on my skin, like sweat. Like assurances, sweet and lovely. Like the knowledge that this isn't going to be a one-time thing. I already knew he couldn't do that, and neither can I.

Having him here, now, confirms I'm going to want this more than once.

This moment is transforming us. We will never be the same after this.

The thought is terrifying, but he holds me hostage with his eyes, not letting me run away from my feelings. Instead, our gazes lock, reflecting the pleasure we're feeling, making it brighter, more consuming.

Luke has taken down almost every piece of my protective walls, and he doesn't even know it. He searches my micro-expressions for confirmation that I am getting maximum pleasure from his talented efforts.

"Look at me sweetheart," he says when I try to glance away. "I want to see you."

You do, I want to say. *You see all of me.*

"Damn, Luke, this is amazing." I babble, because it is, it really is. I feel another orgasm building. "Holy shit you're going to make me come again."

Despite the concentration on his face, he grins. "Isn't that what fake boyfriends do?"

I raise my eyebrows and give a pointed glance at what he's doing to me. "Does this feel fake to you?" I tease.

The way he looks down at me, all heat and vulnerability, tells me his answer before he gives it. "No," he says. He slides against my body with his, my sensitive nipples brushing against the smattering of hair on his chest, and the friction is everything. "This is so much better. Being with you is everything I hoped it would be and more."

In a show of tenderness that melts every last part of me, he brushes his knuckles across my cheek before grabbing my ass and angling me into a deeper position, picking up his pace. His cheeks are flushed and his eyes are bright, and aside from the pleasure on his face, there's something else there, too. Happiness. He's genuinely *happy*.

Why that's enough to send me over the edge, I don't know, but it is.

I shake, losing control of my limbs again as I break around him. Softer this time, in rhythm with those smooth, rolling thrusts that have been pushing every pleasure button inside me.

He follows me soon after, and we cling to each other. It feels as though this unified pleasure should mean something bigger, but I'm beyond thinking right now, only feeling.

Meaning, the future, feelings—it all goes into tomorrow's box.

No regrets. That's the only thing I can be certain of as he collapses to my side and I cuddle under the welcoming shelter of his arm. Tonight, tomorrow, forever, there will be no regret.

***

Morning finds me wrapped in Luke's arms. The dawn light is gray, dipping under the blinds and painting the floor with the absence of color. I'm pressed against Luke's bare chest, body tucked against the cradle of his arm, his hand cupping my ass and my ear above his slow-beating heart.

I feel soft and warm and relaxed.

Sex has never felt that connected and meaningful before. It's as though he reached inside me and flipped a switch, and I don't know how to switch it back off. I don't know how to go back to viewing him as my platonic workmate. A colleague. A friend.

We're more than that now. I still don't know where this is going, but it feels like it might have a direction. A destination. Luke wants it to, at least, even if he accepted just this one night.

When I return from using the restroom, I snuggle back into my favorite spot beside him. He stirs under me, arm tightening around me, and I press my face into his collarbone, inhaling so deeply it's almost a snort. I love that we're wrapped around each other like this. I never want to let go.

"Good morning, Gorgeous," he murmurs.

I smile into his skin. "Good morning."

Technically, it's tomorrow, but given we're still in bed, I don't think we need to worry about that right now. All those decisions and realities can wait a little longer. I'm not done exploring the treasure trove that is Luke.

"How do you feel?" he asks, fingers gently tracing the skin on my shoulder.

I'm scared to use too big a word to describe how I'm feeling right now, so I settle for, "So good. Last night was . . . It was incredible."

I feel rather than see his smile. "It was," he agrees.

"I didn't know sex could feel like that."

"Like what?"

Putting this into words feels like too much, but I can't hold them back in this quiet, hushed air of the morning after, where we haven't stepped out of our bubble into reality. "Like I felt it here, too." I touch my chest and his gaze follows the movement, eyes softening. His fingers skate across my skin again in gentle, reassuring gestures that soothe me.

"That's how it was for me too." He shifts, reminding me that even though his voice is soft, other parts of him aren't.

Answering warmth blooms inside me, and I smile to myself before kissing his neck, his shoulder, down his chest. I kiss along his torso, paying special attention to every dip and curve of his body. So many muscles. Biceps and pectorals and abdominal muscles. I kiss them all. Down toward the hollow above his hip bone and the hair dusting the triangle that points toward his groin.

His hand finds my hair and rakes across the longer sections, running them through his fingers. "What are you doing?" His voice is raspy. But his taut arousal proves that no matter how sleepy he is, he's very ready for what I have planned.

"You spoiled me yesterday." I lick around his navel, loving the way his stomach muscles tense. "Now, it's my turn."

"Oh." He half sits up. "*Oh.*"

Yesterday, he made me fall apart first. I want to do the same to him. I want to make him incoherent, and then, when he thinks he can't take anymore, I want to show him all the things we haven't done yet.

He might be skilled with his hands, but I know what I'm doing with my mouth.

"Don't move," I tell him, dancing lower until I'm trailing the tip of my tongue along that line of hair. "I'm busy."

"Right. Yeah." His eyes are dark, and he's watching me greedily. I can imagine that he's committing this to memory, engraving it in stone so he doesn't forget. Almost the way I am, pressing this memory between the pages of my mind so I don't lose the color.

I curl my hand around his hard length, and he catches his breath, sitting up so we're almost nose to nose.

His face fills my vision.

"Hi." My voice is breathless.

"Hi," he echoes, a smile crinkling the corners of his eyes.

"You should lie back down. I'm just getting started." Also, I probably have morning breath and don't want to inflict it on him.

He takes my chin in his hands. "One thing first." Gently, so gently I almost don't feel it, he kisses my birthmark, then my forehead, then my lips. I'm caught by his eyes, deep and dark and ringed by such gorgeous lashes, I'm in awe.

"Good morning," he murmurs. He kisses me again, stealing my breath and all thoughts I had about seducing him. Luke has a way of kissing me that just dives straight to my core. It's immediate, liquid want from the moment his hands cup my face and his tongue darts across my lower lip.

I kiss him until the gray dawn light is tinged with gold and colors are reappearing in our bedroom. When I break away, my plans for this morning have become more than just wanting to make him feel good with my mouth.

Yesterday's sex has heightened everything. I want to burrow under his skin and never surface, to swim in his veins and pummel his heart the way he did with mine.

"Let's wake up like this every morning," I say.

His smile is dazed and beautiful. "Deal."

"Now, lie down. I told you; I'm not done." I push his shoulders, and he lies back. I position myself between his legs and look up at him past his arousal. At my perusal, it twitches, and I test my tongue against the very tip. He groans. I like that. I do it again, then take him in. As far as I can. His hips jerk, and his fists tighten in the sheets.

Why have we not been doing this right from the start? I never want to stop.

I withdraw and look at him. His hair is mussed across his face. His eyes have entire worlds in them, and his mouth is parted. His breath is short and fast.

"Damn, Aspen."

"I love it when you say my name." I never meant to say it, meant to keep that piece of me tucked away, but he has it now. His smile does something to my heart.

"Aspen."

I shudder against him and close my eyes. Having him in my mouth like this is one of the most intimate things I think we could ever do. I control his pleasure, and I do so with abandon. His hand finds my hair, but he lets me take the lead. Lets me lick and suck and tease until I can feel the tension coiling in him. He tells me to go slow, to give him time so he doesn't finish this too early, but I can also sense the impatience in him. His body is crying out for more—*yes, yes, yes*—even as he's telling me that I'm too wonderful, that he wants me too much, that he's been dreaming of this for such a long time and he doesn't want to finish anytime soon.

I look up and hold his gaze as I flick my tongue over him. He shudders, and his eyes roll back in his head.

"Careful." His voice is a rasp.

"I want to devour you, Luke Simmons."

He stares at the ceiling like he's praying to God for mercy. "Dear Lord, you have no idea what you do to me."

I smile wickedly down at him wrapped in my hand. "I think I have some idea. And you love it."

A strange look comes across his face that I can't read. After a moment, he nods. "Yeah. I do."

I crawl up his body, wrap him in the condom he's pulled off the nightstand, and sling my leg over him, pressing him into the bed. I'm slick and ready, and I don't need any further preparation as I slide down onto him. His eyes flutter closed, and he says something like, "God, *yeah*."

God, yeah. That's accurate.

"I have an idea," I say as I press down until he's fully inside me. My hands are braced against his chest, and I'm looking at him, raw and vulnerable and breathtaking. "Let's never leave this bed. Not for the rest of the vacation." *Or the rest of my life.*

"I think I want you in more places than just the bed," he says, reaching up and taking my nipple into his mouth. I arch into him, my mind providing me a thousand images of what that would look like. On the sofa. On the rug before the fire, the heat scorching our bare skin as we fuck like animals.

Against the wall. In the shower, all hot and wet and soapy. There are so many options, and my imagination is not skimping on *any* of the details.

I grind against him as his thumb finds my clit and rubs. My thighs clench. My hips jerk forward, pressing into his touch.

"Are you trying to kill me with pleasure?" I accuse him. "Death by sensory overload—is that possible?"

"No dying allowed on my watch. Not until you're old and gray and we've done this a thousand times." His other hand palms my breast, and I move faster on him, hitting that precious place inside me. The noises I'm making are melodic and obscene. "You are so damn incredible, Luke."

We're hovering on the precipice of something more, something so large and terrifying, I can't articulate it. All I can do is lose myself in the darkness of his eyes and the way his mouth curves into a slow smile meant just for me.

"And you're beautiful," he tells me. "So damn beautiful. Inside and out."

Inside, I am mush. He has illuminated and seen all the worst parts of me. I'm utterly bare to him.

"I need you." Another confession I don't intend to make, but I mean it. He's broken through all my walls, and now, there is nothing between us but electrically charged air.

"Aspen," he says, hands on my hips now, not urging me faster but anchoring me, assuring me of how much he loves this. "Is this good?"

"It's sublime." I'm incoherent, babbling adjectives, grasping for ways to accurately describe the emotions coursing through me. Every word feels too weak, too diluted. "I never want to stop. Please don't stop."

He makes a low noise in the back of his throat, a groan, maybe, a sound of desperation, and closes his eyes. "Sorry, babe, but I'm close."

"That's okay. So am I." I grasp the headboard and roll my hips fervently. Our mutual gasps of pleasure are in unison this time. It's only our second time together, and already, it's mind-blowing. I can't imagine what sex by the end of the week will feel like.

There, I've done it. I've thought about tomorrow, and it's just more of this.

We are drawing out every moment, not wanting the connection to end. Luke smiles up at me, and that's enough to tip me over the edge.

I clench around him hard, locking eyes with him as his hands guide my hips to keep taking pleasure from him. This isn't the soft, rolling sensation of yesterday; this is a wild, unrestrained feeling, a swell of sensation so great it crashes over me and tumbles me headlong through the waves. I can't breathe; I don't know which way is up. I've lost control of all my limbs, my breathing, every blissful thought, and it's only Luke that's keeping me grounded. Luke, who's holding on just as tightly, murmuring sounds of encouragement and appreciation, and whose rigid posture and focused expression display his determination to hold back his release until I've had mine.

Luke sucks my nipple and I'm so incredibly sensitive it's almost too much, and by the way his breath rushes out of him, it's overwhelming for him, too. His hands squeeze my breasts, my ass, anything he can get his hands on. His eyes are unfocused, the leash of control in the dust behind us.

"I can't last much longer," he warns me.

"Then don't." I grind into him, watching as his eyes roll back in his head and his breathing fractures. "You've given it so good, now it's your turn to take."

His groan echoes through my bones, and I link our hands together, pinning them on either side of his head as I ride him headlong into his release. I feel the way his body shudders, the way he tenses, the low sound of pleasure he makes at the back of his throat. He's beautiful like this, and I hold him through it until he goes limp underneath me, covered in a sheen of sweat and an aura of satisfaction. I feel irrevocably changed.

We're breathing hard in sync as we try to find our equilibrium again, and I randomly remember the mug I got him last Christmas for Secret Santa. The Excel spreadsheet one he drinks out of every single day, even though he blushed so hard when he unwrapped it that I was worried for his wholesome heart. I can't stop the laugh that bubbles up and out of me at the memory.

Luke rolls to one side, his arms still around me. I guess he wants to stay in this afterglow as much as I do.

"What?" he asks, giving me a wry look. "Giggling after sex is not exactly encouraging to my ego."

"No, no." Laughter is escaping me in breathy gasps. I can't control it—my ribcage is spasming. Easier to laugh about this, about how all my preconceptions about Luke were so wrong, than to think about what this means. "I was just thinking . . . the mug I got you . . . Freak in the Sheets."

He toys idly with my hair. "What about it?"

"I was so *right*."

His laugh is sudden, barking out of him explosively, and all I can think is that I want to never stop hearing it. His face is lit up with amusement and pride.

"Well, you weren't so bad yourself," he teases.

"Not so bad? I've seen fried chicken get better reviews." I playfully slap his bicep.

He finds the spot between my ribs, the one he coasted over before, and tickles me until I can't breathe. Then, before I have a chance to recover, he kisses me deeply, and just like that, I'm mesmerized by his touch. It's an excellent distraction technique.

"I don't believe in leaving reviews without sampling more of the menu," he says, biting my earlobe, a movement so erotic, I am instantly imagining what round two before breakfast would look like. "How about we give it another go?"

I'm all ready to start anew and explore a multitude of pleasure paths with him when his phone rings. We stare at each other with identical expressions of frustration.

"It's JoJo," I say, sitting up and pulling the blanket to my chest. "Take it."

Luke sighs and grabs the phone. "What's up?" he says, managing not to sound curt, even though everything about his body language speaks of extreme irritation. Then, his expression clears, and his eyebrows shoot up. "You did *what?*"

Chapter Twenty-Three

Aspen

I t's a beauty emergency. After getting drunk in the hot tub last night, JoJo and Brittany convinced each other that bangs for the bride would be a good idea. To no one's surprise, they woke up today and realized it was *not* a good idea. Jo is having a breakdown, not wanting to go through with the wedding, Brittany is running around worrying about how to fix it, and one look at the situation tells me there's only one thing to do.

I call Annabelle.

Annabelle, accompanied by her "assistants" Charlie and Lina, who I just *know* are desperate for an update on the Luke situation, arrive in less than two hours. Ruth and Peter are sweet, offering them beds in the bunkhouse with Granny Mae, Brittany, and the other two bridesmaids. While Annabelle gets to work on JoJo's hair (which really does look terrible), Lina and Brittany head into town for last-minute preparations for the bachelorette party. Granny Mae shows Charlie and me the equestrian stables on the other side of the ranch, seeing as Charlie is horse-girl extraordinaire, and I don't have anything better to do.

"You mean there's another barn and full equine facility just over this hill?" Charlie asks, voice full of enthusiasm. I trail behind, listening to a voicemail my mom left yesterday. She was pulling out of her driveway, sounding tipsy, and hit her mailbox, the voicemail cutting off.

This morning, sober and repentant, she messaged me to let me know what had happened and that she's fine. But that doesn't change the fact that she was drinking and driving.

This has been going on long enough. *This time*, she's fine. But what about next time? What about the time after that? I've been making excuses for her for too long, and this has to stop.

She needs an intervention.

And I have to be the one to provide it. Tim won't—if anything, he encourages the drinking, because she's easier to control when she's drunk and her defenses are down. There's no one else in her life that would care enough to help me arrange it.

It's frustrating that this is happening now of all times, when things are going . . . Well, I don't know how to define it, but they sure are going.

While I'm here, I need to focus on the now. Her bad decisions aren't my problem to solve today. And when I leave here, I'll let myself think about Mom and what needs to be done. One major emotional hurdle at a time.

For now, that's Luke. And the mind-blowing sex.

The *sex*. That word seems inadequate—I feel like there needs to be a bigger word to encompass everything that happened between us. I feel different, like that was my first time, not just with Luke, but ever.

He kissed me goodbye earlier with a promise that we'd speak later. I already know it's going to be about the future, whatever that entails. Before we left the cabin this morning, he suggested I could move out to San Jose as well, to join the team Kai is setting up there. Kai would probably be on board if I wanted to.

And for a second, I was tempted. Really tempted. But the reason I moved to Salt Lake City was to put down roots near my best friends, the only family I can rely on. I've made a life here. And I promised myself long ago that I would never uproot my life and career for a guy, especially not this early in a relationship. We're not even *officially* together. Not in real life. It's too soon to make that sort of commitment.

Credit to him, he just kissed me and said he understood. Just like I understand that this move is the best thing for him and his career. That just doesn't solve the problem of *us*. If we fit into the lives that we already have.

If we want it to.

The scariest thing is that I think maybe I do.

I follow Charlie and Granny Mae into the equestrian barn. Horses snicker, and the air is warm with the scent of horses and hay. There's a wheelbarrow full of evidence that someone was mucking the stalls recently. It's a full-time job, looking after horses. I wonder how long Granny Mae can continue doing it.

Charlie is having the time of her life, peppering Granny with questions about the horses, how many riding instructors she employs, what training philosophies she uses, and a dozen other questions that mean nothing to me. We spend some time in the barn before heading out to the snowy paddocks, Granny still explaining horse-related things.

My mind circles back to how messy this could get if things go wrong. I've never really had my heart broken before, but if we got together, there's a chance that could happen. There's a strong chance I would break his.

So many things could shatter. Am I willing to take the risk?

Charlie grabs my hand as we walk back to the main house, Granny Mae striding ahead like age is just an outdated concept she has decided to ignore.

"You need to tell us *everything*," Charlie hisses. "And if you dare claim that you and Luke are fully platonic, I'm going to bury you where you stand."

"Like you'd be able to dig a hole. Ground's way too frozen."

"I am *very* persistent."

I believe it. *Persistent* is Charlie's middle name.

"Later, okay?" I say. "Might as well tell you all at the same time."

"That means there's something to tell!" she crows.

Despite all my best efforts, a grin tugs at my lips. "Shut up."

"You caught feelings for him. I knew it!"

I nudge her hard enough that she almost falls into the snowbank on her other side. Granny Mae's stride hasn't faltered, so hopefully she hasn't heard. My friends are as subtle as a brick to the face.

"Hush," I say, pinching her arm for good measure. "You can't *say* things like that."

"Fine. But you better not keep us waiting long."

***

As it happens, my chance comes at the beginning of the bachelorette party. Luke and I have barely had a chance to do anything except exchange a quick kiss between the day's chaotic busyness, and Annabelle is losing herself in congratulations about JoJo's hair. Before, her uneven bangs looked like a child had gotten hold of craft scissors and attacked her hair. While wearing a blindfold. Now, though, her sleek bangs are lightly curled, shorter in the middle and longer at the sides. They look elegant, which is an achievement in itself. The rest of her hair falls in soft waves around her face, and her stress lines have faded into a smile. Annabelle also did her makeup for the party, and now JoJo looks every bit a bride, just without the dress. She's beautiful, and I can tell she *feels* beautiful, too.

The bachelorette party is held in the bunkhouse for the sake of Rebecca's comfort, and Granny Mae, who is tossing back flavored martinis like a pro. The men are headed into town for a casual bachelor party at their favorite sports bar.

"You did a fabulous job," Lina tells Annabelle as we all sit together on one of the bunkbeds. I'm pleasantly tipsy. JoJo and Brittany and the pair of bridesmaids are laughing together in the opposite corner. Lina really hit it off with Brittany earlier. And I'm forced to admit that even though I want to maul her every time she looks at Luke, maybe she isn't so bad in her own way. She's just not so good at love.

Which I guess I can't be mad at, seeing as it's the reason I'm here.

Annabelle preens, touching her tightly coiled curls with a smug smile. "I know. I'm a genius."

Charlie brings us all back new drinks, and as Brittany dances to Taylor Swift on the other side of the large room, I fill them in on my newest mom predicament. The initial worry faded when she messaged to say she was fine, but the anger has remained, banked because of today, but still hot. Slowly burning me up from the inside out.

"She needs an intervention," I finish. "And that's going to be my job, and I'm really dreading doing it."

Annabelle takes my hand and squeezes. "I'm sorry, honey. That sounds so frustrating."

"I just don't know how to approach it. Or if she'll even listen. It feels futile."

"All you can do is your best," Lina says, serious for once as she looks at me with those dark, liquid eyes. "You're a good daughter. At the end of the day, she has to *want* to change. All you can do is encourage her to take those steps."

"We're with you every step of the way," Annabelle says.

Charlie takes my other hand. "But you can't let this ruin what's going on with Luke, okay? Your mom doesn't deserve to take up all this headspace when you've got so much else going on."

"So much else?" Lina looks between Charlie and me. "What do you mean, so much else? Have there been *developments*?"

Charlie's right. I just need to compartmentalize.

"Yes," I allow. "But not all good."

"What?" Lina folds her arms and narrows her eyes at me. "But you're glowing."

"That's probably the sex," I say.

"I knew it!" Charlie fist-pumps the air. "I knew you guys slept together. Annabelle, didn't I say I knew?"

"You did, but you think everyone is sleeping together."

"No, just with Lina."

Lina sticks her tongue out at Charlie and turns back to me. "I need to know everything. Was it good? Was *he* good? He looks like he'd be good in bed."

"Very attentive," Charlie agrees. "And there's obviously something between you. There was right from the start."

I scoff. "No, there wasn't."

"Yes, there was. I saw it. I knew."

"Yeah," Lina agrees, letting her head fall on Annabelle's shoulder. "The way he looked at you. That man was very interested. Couldn't you tell?"

Annabelle taps my hand impatiently, almost spilling my drink. "Tell us about the sex."

I'm blushing, which doesn't usually happen. We've talked about sex before, all of us. We've all had our escapades, and we've all over-shared them. But this is different. And I don't know how to talk about all the other stuff. Feelings aren't exactly my strong point.

"Oh my God," Lina breathes. "You're falling for him, aren't you?"

I look at Charlie helplessly, and she gives us all a firm nod. "Well, we all knew it was inevitable. If you don't mind me saying, girl, your taste in men sucked. This is a good thing."

"I haven't told you the bad stuff yet."

"So?" Lina prompts. "What's the bad stuff?"

"He's moving to San Jose." I pinch my nose. "I don't know if I can handle the long distance. The sex was incredible, but it was more than sex. It was bigger than just a physical connection."

Annabelle leans toward me, making sure I'm listening before she speaks. "I've wanted you to experience that kind of connection for so long. Something real and meaningful. I'm so glad you finally got to, and with a good guy like Luke. I'm happy for you." She squeezes my hand.

"Still, maybe this was meant to be a way for us to have a really great goodbye instead of a really great beginning." My wavering voice gives away my emotions.

"You slept with the poor guy, and now you're going to throw him to the curb like yesterday's newspaper?" Charlie demands. "Do you not know how into you he is?"

"Yes," I whine, "but the long distance. I don't think I'm cut out for it."

"Everything is worth trying at least once," Lina says.

"You need to fight for what you want," Charlie says. "Come on, Aspen. Remember when your old boss was sexist, and you quit on the spot and found yourself a new job in a new city?"

"That company folded two months after I moved here," I remind her.

"My point is you can be brave."

"You've always let guys go before things can get real," Annabelle says. "Now, this stuff with Luke got real before you ever knew it would, and now you're afraid. But this is a chance to step out of your comfort zone and get what you truly want: to be loved."

I want Luke, but I don't want to break my heart over him.

I never, ever want to become like my mom.

"Are you going to stick to your same unhealthy patterns, even with Luke?" Annabelle asks gently. "Are you really going to let him go?"

"What if it doesn't work out?"

"But what if it does?" Lina says. "You're obviously crazy about him, or you wouldn't be scared, and you wouldn't be conflicted."

"Do you love him?" Charlie asks.

"Unfair question. Next."

"That's a yes," Charlie says to Annabelle in a stage whisper. Then, to me, she asks, "And is this thing with Luke worth fighting for?"

"Obviously, it is," Lina interjects before I can deflect. "Look at her trying to find ways to deny it."

"Hey," I say half-heartedly.

"Courage is doing something even when you can't control the outcome," says Annabelle, the mother hen. "And for what it's worth, I think he might be the one for you."

For the first time in a very long time, the idea of someone being "the one" doesn't fill me with a sense of panic. Yes, the idea of him leaving is scary. Everyone leaves me. But the idea of him being right for me? That slots into my mind like it was always designed to be there.

No one can ever promise forever, but maybe, just maybe, I can figure out a way of giving him tomorrow.

Chapter Twenty-Four

Luke

Mark leans over the pool table, face tight with concentration. Matthew elbows me playfully.

"So," he says as Mark hits a red straight into the pocket. Andre boos. "Tell me how things are going with you-know-who."

I groan and take a swig of beer. "You can say her name, you know."

"But this is more fun." He's had more drinks than the rest of us, and his face is flushed. He even tried out a tequila shot for the first time in about ten years. Just as gross as they used to be, apparently.

Me, my two brothers, and my two brothers-in-law are the only participants in our cozy bachelor party, and it's nice for the five of us to have some brother-bonding time. Kwan and Andre come from very different upbringings than my brothers and I, but thankfully, we've really hit it off. Right now, Andre and Mark are vying for the prize of first place and best pool player. Loser has to buy drinks for the rest of the evening.

To be honest, I want to talk about Aspen, but I don't know how to without revealing that it never started out real.

"You look happy," Matthew prods.

"I am."

"But?"

I stare into the bottom of my beer, where the dregs hug the curved corners of the glass. "I told you guys about this new opportunity Kai gave me, right? The one that involves moving to California?"

"No." Matthew's voice is a dramatic, hushed whisper. The music changes, dropping into some classic Bon Jovi. "Bad Medicine." It'll be apt if I don't get my act together. "Please tell me she knows."

"Of course she knows. And that's the problem." I groan. "No, that's not the problem. The fact that she knows isn't the problem. The fact that I'm going isn't even the problem. I *want* to go. This is the kind of thing I've been working toward."

"But?" Mark prompts, looking up at me, focused on something other than the pool table for the first time this evening.

"But she's not sure if she wants to continue the relationship long-distance." It's the closest to the truth I can get without revealing everything. "But I like her, guys."

"Let's be honest here," Matthew says. "You *love* her. You want her to have your babies so there's an army of them wandering around. Just like Mark. Right, Mark?"

Mark grunts, still looking at me. "Do you love her?"

I loved her before, but I'd convinced myself I could walk away. Now, I've gone and done the one thing I said I would never do—made myself vulnerable to a woman again—and I'm in deeper than I've ever been before.

There's a good chance Aspen's going to rip my heart to shreds. She has a Pentagon-level defense system around her heart to protect herself. Even from me, I think, despite my Herculean efforts over the past few days.

But I had to try. I couldn't help it; I had to know what it would be like to be with her, even if the consequences are a broken heart.

Which they very well may be.

"Yeah," I say in answer to Mark's question. They're all looking at me with varying degrees of drunken sympathy. "I love her."

"So, make it work, dumbass," Matthew says. "Does she know you love her?"

"Yes. Maybe. Probably."

Mark points the cue at me. "Have you told her?"

"Women like to hear it," Andre offers. "At least in my experience."

If I tell Aspen I love her, she might run away from that alone. I've never met a woman so afraid of commitment before.

Trust me to fall for the only woman I know who doesn't want a shot at a relationship.

"Talk to her," Mark says, bending over the pool table to take another shot. "Communication, man."

Andre nods seriously, then gestures to the bartender for another round. I guess we'll need it. "What's the worst that can happen?"

Matthew rolls his eyes. "Idiot," he says, clapping Andre on the shoulder.

"The worst that can happen is we break up in time for me to move to San Jose," I say, not really sure how Andre's missed that one. "If we don't figure this out before I leave in a little over a week, that's it. I don't think we'll get another chance. I won't be around to help her change her mind."

"She likes you," Mark says.

"Right." Andre holds up his beer. "So, what do we do when girls like us?"

"Speak for yourself," Matthew mutters, and I laugh. He's a good-looking guy, and he's had his fair share of women being interested before he came out. By now, he's an expert in letting them down gently.

Something I've never mastered.

Then again, I've never been outgoing enough for numerous women to really be interested. And it's only been the past couple years that I've come into my own, mentally and physically.

I down the other half of my beer. "We don't have to talk about my problems," I say. "This is meant to be a fun evening."

Andre slings an arm around my shoulders, then reaches up to sling his other arm around Matthew. He grins at me, the expression slightly sloppy from the several beers and two shots he's already consumed this evening. "We're family, right? This is what family does."

Mark abandons the pool table and finds us a corner booth. He and Matthew bring the drinks over, and we all pile in. They look at me expectantly.

"I like Aspen," Matthew slurs. He's definitely the most wasted of us all. I'll remind him of this when my head isn't spinning so much. "You better not mess this up."

"Apart from reminding her how great we are together, there's not much else I can do, is there?" I say. "It's her choice whether she wants to be with me. The ball's in her court." I lean down until my head is resting against the table and whatever someone else spilled here earlier in the night. All I can smell is beer. There's some country music going, and I can hear the unmistakable sound of someone dancing on a table, everyone cheering them on.

"I'm doomed," I mumble.

Matthew pats me on the back kindly. "We already knew that."

"I didn't tell Jo I was moving overseas for ages," Andre says. "Partly because I'm a moron with the empathy of a baboon, as she told me, but also because I was scared she wouldn't want to handle the long distance." He slices his hand across his neck.

"Bet she took that well," Mark muttered.

"Lost it at me," Andre says cheerfully. "But once she knew the situation, instead of cooling things off like I'd feared, she did the opposite. She told me that if I was serious about making this work, I needed to marry her, and fast. So, you never know. It might go better than you think."

Aspen and JoJo are such radically different people, I can't even imagine how differently that same conversation would go.

Aspen has been surrounded by people who leave her. An absent dad, an unreliable mom, and a string of exes who clearly weren't interested in sticking around. The last thing she wants right now is marriage. From what she's said, she's only just figuring that this thing between us could be real and good if she allowed herself to have it.

She just has to get over the fact that it's going to be long-distance for a bit.

"Talk to her," Mark says again. "Tell her how you feel."

"No promises." I toss the remainder of my drink back. "But I'll try."

Chapter Twenty-Five

Aspen

I t's well past midnight when I open the door to our cabin and sneak inside. Everything is dark, blanketed in the stillness that only comes just before dawn. Luke's heavy breathing fills the silence.

The bachelorette party finished over two hours ago, and I tucked up beside Charlie in one of the bunkhouse beds. As I lay drifting in and out of restless sleep, my head spinning, I became aware of two things.

One: if I don't have much time left here, I need to make the most of it. With Luke.

Two: I should take medicine and hydrate ASAP before I wake up with a hangover.

Hence, me sneaking into the cabin at four in the morning, my hands clumsy with the leftover burn of alcohol in my system. I stumble across the floor to the bathroom, where I clink the glass against the faucet as I pour myself a drink, then spill droplets messily down my chin by gulping it down too fast.

It wasn't until talking with the girls that I truly appreciated how much I like Luke. Like, really like him—in a sneaking way that came up behind me. I didn't know how invested I'd gotten until I was already in too deep.

And when I was sleeping beside Charlie, I realized how much I missed sleeping next to Luke. Waking up beside him.

Being with him.

Long distance is terrifying, and I'll admit that the idea of being with someone who I *know* is leaving is debilitatingly scary.

But it's Luke. If anyone will stick around for the long haul, it's him. He makes me feel safe and like maybe we have a chance.

Maybe I can be loved. Maybe I'm *worthy* of being loved. By him and his family.

Maybe we should give this thing a try.

I put the glass down and walk unsteadily back to the bed. The sheets are smooth and cool against my skin as I slide under them. Luke's lying on his back, but when I cuddle up to him, his body burning even through his T-shirt and boxers, he shifts.

"Aspen?" His voice is soft in the darkness, all husky and sleepy goodness.

"Hey." I wiggle even closer, if possible. He's so warm. I slide my arm over his stomach, and he wraps an arm over my shoulder, planting a kiss on the top of my head. His breath smells like beer, just like mine probably smells of margaritas. The thought makes me giggle, and I lean up to kiss his scruffy chin.

"What are you doing here?" he whispers. "I thought you were spending the night with the ladies?"

"I missed you."

There's a beat before he rolls onto his side and gathers me into his arms, burying his face into the crook of my neck and breathing me in. He's just as much of an addict as I am, it seems.

"I missed you too," he says, the words almost a groan. "So much."

When we kiss, it starts familiar and comfortable but quickly spirals to sensual and ravenous. Insatiable. I'm drowning in his magnetic energy. His hands skate languidly down my arm and over my hip to my thigh. I'm buzzing with drunken delight at rediscovering his body, and he buries his face into my cleavage.

"I dream about you every time we're apart," he murmurs.

"Were you dreaming about me now?"

His eyes are dark. There is no oxygen left in my body.

"Always, Aspen. Always."

I catch his face in my hands, my lips yearning for his. There are so many words bubbling up inside me, words like *stay* and *love me* and *be here*, but I don't dare so much as whisper them. Instead, I tell him with my fingers, butterfly light as they skate across his jaw and down his chest, all the way down until they wrap around his hard length. I tell him with my lips as I kiss his neck and mouth words against it.

Never stop wanting me, I beg him silently. *Let's make this work. I love what we have.*

He returns the favor, pulling me up and over him so my legs straddle his hips. I stretch over to the nightstand drawer, grabbing a condom and rolling it on in one swift movement.

Luke undresses me first with his eyes, then with his hands. There's no corner of me left untouched. Luke has all of me cradled between his fingers, and I wonder if he knows that he has me captured. His hands knead my breasts as I sink down onto him. Full to brimming. I look down at him, and he's watching me with an expression in his eyes that makes my chest fold in on itself. I whisper his name under my breath as I undulate my hips. One of his hands comes up to grip my hip, gently following my lead, his fingers pressing in with urgency.

I want both his hands on me.

I reach for his hand as he sits up, steadying me with an arm around the small of my back. We're chest to chest now, and I can't do much more but continue to press into him, keeping my abbreviated rhythm. Even so, the pleasure is blinding.

"Aspen." He gives me little biting kisses along my neck. Never quite enough. They're addictive in the best kind of way. "I'm so glad you're here with me. You're incredible."

"I like that you're sentimental when you're drunk." I bite his shoulder.

"I like that you find your way back to my bed when *you're* drunk."

"Me too." I moan before capturing his earlobe between my teeth and nibbling.

Our skin is slick with sweat. I wrap my arms around his neck and look into his eyes as he guides me up and down, finding the perfect spot inside me and hitting it again and again.

My heart is too big for my body. Too big for either of us. If it wasn't for his hands on me, I would float away.

My orgasm sneaks up on me. One moment, I'm marveling at the crinkles at the edge of his eyes, the ones that deepen when he smiles, the way he looks sexy even cloaked in night and sweat, and the next, I'm swept away by a rush of pleasure so intense, I see stars. Luke groans as I clench around him, and I feel his arms' firm resolve as he holds himself together and cradles me.

"Hold me forever," I hear myself say as the aftershocks fade. He rolls me over so he's on top, balanced on his elbows. I think his eyes are glassy with tears, but he kisses me before I have a chance to properly see.

He pushes into me with more certainty than before, and the world is spinning. The only thing that makes sense is Luke. Here now. With me.

Luke Simmons.

"God, I love you, Aspen," he says against my mouth as his rhythm fractures.

When he falls, we fall together.

Chapter Twenty-Six

Aspen

I *love you.*

The moment I wake, that's the first thing I remember. Luke is still sound asleep, passed out from a combination of alcohol and exhaustion, and I slide out of bed as easily as I slid into bed only a few hours before.

I haven't slept much, but I'm so wired, I have to force myself to put on boots and a coat before heading outside into the bitter air to clear my head. Even with the snowfall over the past couple of days, the path to the barn is cleared. There's a bite to the crisp air that sneaks down my collar.

I love you.

I probably shouldn't be freaking out over this. It's all happening so fast, and I knew he cared about me—love isn't a step too far from that. I've never been in love before. Is that what I'm feeling too?

I've always thought love was an illusion. It's like a mirage, something you think you can see until you get close enough that reality shatters your perception. And you realize that whatever it was, it was never love.

My breath billows around me as I take a long, deep breath. My head and my heart are on opposing sides, trying to puzzle out the truth.

Luke said it like he meant it. Like he put his entire soul into those three little words.

So many things this week have been new revelations. The sex is spectacular, but more than that, he's caring and thoughtful and makes me feel safe. No one else has made me feel like that. Maybe that's what love is. This feeling of belonging. Of being cherished, being someone's priority.

"Aspen?" JoJo comes out of the main house wrapped in a faux-fur coat. "Are you okay? You look cold."

"What are you doing up? We went to bed so late."

"Nerves, I guess." She looks across to the barn, which is draped in icicles. "I know I need to sleep more so I don't have huge bags under my eyes, but I'm just so wired, you know?"

I know. I really, really know.

I put my arm around her. Already, she feels like a younger sister. A beautiful person in every way, but with that vein of insecurity running through her that makes me want to protect her. I understand why Luke is so close to his family—with a family like this, who wouldn't be?

"Everything good with you and Luke?" she asks as I lead her toward the bunkhouse. Andre shouldn't see her this morning, on their wedding day. "I mean, you guys didn't fight, did you?"

"No. I'm just . . ." I look at her. "How did you feel when Andre said he was being deployed overseas?"

"Oh." Her eyes crinkle with understanding as she looks at me. "Luke's job."

"I mean, it's a big deal, right? Andre leaving."

"I guess so. But I trust him. I just wish I could go with him, you know?" She sighs and looks at me. "How have you and Luke decided to handle it? Are you going to transfer too?"

I want to make things work, but I can't commit to moving across state lines with him. Everything is too new. We need time.

"We're just trying to figure out if we can make it work long-distance, you know?" I say, aiming for breezy and missing. "It's too early to make those sorts of decisions yet."

"Well, I think you'd make a great sister-in-law," she says, looping her arm through mine as we head back inside the bunkhouse.

I love you.

For the first time, it doesn't feel like a complete impossibility.

***

I'm the most feminine I've ever felt in my life.

We're all getting ready in the bunkhouse, with Annabelle and Lina doing everyone's makeup. They're not going to stay for the wedding, though they were invited, but they're helping out anyway before they leave. As they lean over the gorgeous bride, spraying her face with a makeup setter and cooing over her, I stare at my reflection.

They styled the longer hair on the top of my head in soft, beachy waves, and Annabelle brought her professional makeup kit and used a magic, cinema-grade foundation to cover my birthmark. I guess having a friend who previously worked on movie sets as a makeup artist has its perks. That, added to the cerulean-blue wrap dress I brought that matches my eyes, makes me look especially pretty.

I am beautiful, and I really feel like it today.

Around me, Ruth is blinking rapidly, trying not to smudge her mascara. JoJo is her only daughter, and it's clear just how proud she is. It's heartwarming to see: a mother who doesn't have favorites but celebrates each kid for their special place in her heart.

The sense of love surrounds me. Ruth strokes my cheek and tells me I'm beautiful in the same way she says it to JoJo. Brittany focuses on applying her own makeup and beckons me over for a selfie.

"Luke has good taste," she says as she looks at our smiling faces, satisfied. I don't quite know what's going on, but this feels like an olive branch. Maybe she's finally letting go of any aspirations of reconciling with Luke, accepting that he's mine.

We've only been apart for a few hours, but already I miss him, which is ridiculous. And being here, with his family, preparing for a *wedding*, is making a lump swell in my throat. Everyone is treating me like I'm one of them without even questioning it. Because of Luke, I'm a part of their family.

I want to be. So much it hurts. I ache with this need to be accepted by these wonderful people, to share my life with them. My home life was never like this, and my heart breaks as I realize what I lost out on. This is *real*. And if I play my cards right, I can have a part in it.

This could be mine. Luke might've fallen first, but I want to let him know I've caught up.

The second I have a spare moment, I pull on my coat and run out to find Luke, my heels unsteady on the frozen ground. The snow is holding off, and faint sunshine bathes the world in pale, glittering light. Luke is already waiting outside the barn, greeting friends and family members with a smile and directions to their seats.

I stop walking. His groomsman suit is light gray, a white rose tucked into his pocket. Annabelle cut and styled his hair, too, so it's no longer slightly too long. The product she combed through his hair has lifted it off his face and given him a more distinguished look. I'm going to miss running my fingers through it, but holy mother of God, he looks fantastic. His stance is casual, confident in a suit that fits him so perfectly, it must have been tailored to his exact size. When he smiles, his entire face glows.

More than anything, I want to run up to him, throw my arms around his neck, and confess all the riotous feelings demanding a prison break from my heart. I can't keep hovering in limbo—let's make this real. I want *him*. I want this future: the family and the barn wedding with a handful of people I know and love, who will watch me pledge my life to the man I adore.

Tears, hot and sudden, fill my eyes the exact second Luke looks at me. His smile widens, and I hurry to his side, praying I don't turn my ankle in these ridiculous shoes. He can't lose that smile because of my clumsiness.

"Excuse me," Luke says to Andre's parents. Then, in full sight of everyone, he pulls me in for a kiss. I wrap my arms around his neck and kiss him back enthusiastically.

"I'm sorry I left this morning before you woke up," I say before he has a chance to say anything. "I ran into Jo, and she was nervous and needed to be with us girls."

His expression clears as he looks down at me. "I was going to make you a coffee, but Mom told me I wasn't allowed to go in and see you."

"Of course you weren't. Groomsmen and bridesmaids don't mix." It's honestly amazing that JoJo has known me for a handful of days, and already, I'm an honorary member of her bridal party. "Though you're adorable."

I love you. The words pop into my head and onto the tip of my tongue, but I force them back. I don't think now is the time to test them out and see if they ring true.

"Thanks for spending your holiday here with my family. With me. My days are always better when you're in them," he says, swiping his thumb over my birthmark. I realize he's never seen me without it. His gaze searches mine, and he bends to kiss the skin, which no amount of foundation can smooth. "You didn't need to cover this up," he murmurs, and my heart breaks wide open at this tender admonition. "You're beautiful to me either way."

"We need to talk," I blurt out. "About us. To figure stuff out." I link my fingers through his so he knows I mean it in a good way. "What this could look like."

The smile that breaks across his face is the most beautiful thing I've ever seen. "You've decided what you want?"

"I have."

"Okay, then, Aspen." He says my name like it's something special, and I know I will treasure the sound for the rest of my life. "It'll have to be after the wedding."

"That's okay. I know this isn't the perfect moment to talk, but—"

His lips press against my earlobe, and he bites down gently. Goosebumps erupt on my neck and arms. "I can't wait to get you alone again."

"Luke!" I swat at his arm and laugh despite myself. The sky is a perfect blue, the wedding is here, and I'm finally about to get my happy ever after with a man I never thought I would ever love. "I mean so we can *talk*."

"I know what you mean," he murmurs, lips against my neck. And even though it's only been hours since the last time we were intimate, my body is warm and wired already, and I'm half tempted to look around for a quiet space. Five, ten minutes. We could work with that.

The talking can come after. It's just details, anyway. The yes has already been decided.

"Excuse me," a tremulous voice interrupts. Luke gives me an apologetic squeeze before releasing me, turning to who I can only assume is a distant relative wanting to greet him. I walk down the aisle, wondering what it might be like if I was to one day wear a white dress and do this. After watching Mom go through so many boyfriends and failed relationships, I told myself marriage was off the table.

But maybe, if the table looked like this, I could do it.

I don't let myself imagine Luke standing next to the pastor in the groom's spot and instead find my allocated seat, one row back from where the bridesmaids are going to sit. I've been placed with his family. Luke is going to sit beside me when his usher duties are over. We're probably going to hold hands the entire ceremony. Like a real couple. I smile to myself in anticipation.

There's a rustle, and Granny Mae sits beside me. "How's it going, sugar?" she asks me. "You look like a woman that's just had an epiphany."

"I've not been to many weddings," I admit. "This is maybe the first in several years."

"Well, they've done it right, in my opinion. The people Jo cares about are here, she's standing before God, marrying the man she loves." Granny gives a firm nod, and it feels like a stamp of approval. "Held at her parents' farm. And you mark my words, she'll be happy with him."

"You think?"

"Every successful partnership comes from two puzzle pieces that are a true match," Granny says, turning and looking at me. It's the same look Luke has inherited, although I'm a little nervous of what Granny Mae will find when she peers directly into my soul. "JoJo is clever, she's eager, and she's kind, but she's flighty. She can be a worrier. Andre steadies her."

I remember what Granny said about trees. "He's her root person."

"Exactly. But while Jo might look like a branch from the outside, she's fiercely loyal to the people she loves. If you're ever in trouble, all you need to do is call on her, and she'll come running."

"You must be very proud of her," I say softly.

"That I am. It's the role of a grandmother, I think, to be proud of my grandchildren, and to steer them right if they ever go wrong."

I've never had a grandma before. This is another missing piece I never knew I craved.

Luke slides into the seat on my other side and takes my hand, threading our fingers together. I press my palm against his.

I love you.

I don't think I can ever not think it when I look at him now. I'm just not sure if that's his voice in my head or mine.

Andre takes his place in front of the wooden arch, and after a few minutes, music starts playing. Turns out, Andre's siblings are musical prodigies, so one is on the cello and one is on the violin as Jo walks down the aisle. She's beautiful. Ruth lets out an audible sob, and my own eyes fill.

Andre looks about ready to faint. He's smiling so wide that my cheeks ache in sympathy, and when he takes JoJo's hand, he mouths *I love you* to her.

Luke hands me a tissue, and I dab at my eyes. I never thought of myself as an emotional person, but tears keep leaking as the happy couple signs the register to the sound of Matthew crooning a country ballad, and at the end, when JoJo and Andre kiss, I cheer and whoop along with everyone else.

Luke keeps hold of my hand the entire time.

After the ceremony, we head inside for a big dinner while some of the men get the barn ready for the reception. The food is catered from a local farm-to-table restaurant, and it's perfect. I chat with Ruth and Rebecca, whose ankles have swollen something terrible, and get to know Matthew's husband a little better. Kwan's got a wicked sense of humor, and he's a calming presence to be around. A counter to Matthew's more chaotic energy.

I begin to understand what Granny was talking about. These people are two halves. Rebecca and Mark balance each other out—she's bright and chatty, while he's quiet and kind. Ruth is sweet and talkative and a bit of a busybody (out of love, of course), and Peter has the gentle energy of a rambling stream. He'll get there when he gets there, and nobody's about to rush him, not even his wife.

I wonder what Granny's husband used to be like. Maybe he was an effusive sweetheart with a red face from too much wine and a loud laugh that brings joy to everyone who hears it.

I eat and speculate, Luke by my side, and all too soon, it's back to the barn. The chairs have all been moved aside, and the floor is cleared for dancing. The bride and groom wrap their arms around each other and sway to Restless Road's "Growing Old With You". The love in their eyes turns me into a puddle on the floor.

That. I want that. I never thought I did, but being here has shown me that I really, really do. I just want to be adored by someone who thinks I am the most important thing in their life.

It's possible. These people have proven it's possible.

"Wanna dance?" Luke asks, extending his hand toward mine.

I take it, and our dance is an imitation of when we did this the first time—except then, this was still new and unfamiliar. Now, I know Luke. All his mountains and valleys. All the internal trails that lead to hidden places within his soul. All the quiet strength that he keeps tucked away, and the abundance of skills I never knew lurked under the surface.

I love you.

The words are so close to bursting out from me, so I kiss him instead. And I think he must understand what I mean, because when we break away, he says, "Let's leave early."

"You don't think Jo will mind?"

"After the speeches, she wouldn't notice if we both turned into pumpkins," he says with a wry smile. "And I want to talk to you, Aspen. About us."

"I know. Me too." A rush of nervousness has my throat closing, but the soft movement of his thumb across my shoulder blades reassures me. He presses his cheek against mine, and I close my eyes, letting myself experience this moment as it is. Just this. Just us.

"I want to stay like this forever," I breathe, so quietly I don't think he hears it. I'm not even sure I want him to.

But then, his hands tighten around me, and I feel his cheek rise as he smiles against my hair. "I'm hoping that can be arranged."

My own smile hurts my cheeks. JoJo and Andre have the award for happiest couple here, but I like to think Luke and I come in a close second.

Chapter Twenty-Seven

Aspen

"Attention, everyone," Peter says the second the music ends. Luke raises his head, and I nestle into the welcoming curve of his body as we both turn to where Peter is standing at the back of the barn.

"Speech!" someone calls, and everyone laughs. There's an air of relaxed happiness that makes me lean my head against Luke's neck. His hand settles on my waist. We're totally entwined.

"It's time for the speeches," Peter says, holding out his hand. "Starting with me, to get it out of the way." Another ripple of laughter. I think the champagne I've had has gone straight to my head. I'm swimming, and Luke is my anchor. "This has been the most incredible day for everyone here. I'm blessed to see my favorite daughter get married, surrounded by so many of our family members."

"Hey," Matthew calls with false indignation. With a wave of fondness, I grin across at him, and he winks back.

"We're also so incredibly grateful that so many of you live close by and could attend and that we could have the wedding before Andre's deployment and Luke's job transfer to California. I know today will stay in my memory as one of the happiest moments of my life."

My phone vibrates inside my purse, and I peek at it discreetly. *Cliffside Hospital* flashes on the screen. It has a Jersey area code.

Mom.

Peter is still talking, but all the joy of the moment has been washed away. There's a pounding in my ears.

I need to take this.

"I'm sorry," I mutter to Luke, gesturing to my phone and to the door. He nods as I slip away and out into the fresh, sharp air. Fear pounds over me, black and all-encompassing. I'm lost under it.

"Is this Aspen Shaw?" a calm voice asks when I answer.

"Yes," I say, fighting to keep myself steady. Restrained. "Who is this? What's this about?"

"This is Cliffside Hospital in Hackensack, Jersey," she says. "Your name is listed as Tina Shaw's next of kin, and we're calling to inform you that she was admitted for lacerations and a severed tendon this morning. She's scheduled for surgery later this afternoon."

Lacerations. A severed *tendon*. I grip the phone to my ear. "What? *Lacerations?*"

"That's right, ma'am. I understand she's had an accident, and her hand went through a pane of glass. The surgery is minor." The woman has a nice voice, professional but kind. She probably makes these kinds of calls a lot. "But she will be under general anesthetic, so there is a risk."

"Right, okay." My voice doesn't sound like my own. "And that's happening today?"

"Yes, ma'am. She's scheduled for surgery in a few hours."

I need to get to Jersey.

"Okay," I say. "Thank you for letting me know. Can you call me again to let me know how the surgery goes?"

"Of course," she says sympathetically. "Is there anything else you need?"

"No. I'll—" I don't know what I'll do. It's JoJo's wedding. "Thank you."

"You're welcome. We'll let you know the outcome of the surgery and her projected release date as soon as possible so arrangements can be made to pick her up."

"Thank you. I'll check back in later today," I say numbly, and the line goes dead.

Mom is in the hospital. While I've been here trying to figure out whether I can navigate the most important romantic relationship of my life, my mom has been putting herself in goddamn danger, once again taking up extra bandwidth in my life with messes I'm left to clean up.

Guilt is hot and vicious in my chest as I turn and stare, unseeing, at the barn. I've let myself get caught up in what could be, and I've forgotten what is.

My mom is what is. A hot mess.

I need to find a flight, get out there as soon as possible.

But Luke . . .

Torn, I hesitate for another moment before heading back inside to find him. The speech is over, thankfully, and guests are milling about as old country classics spill through the speakers.

Ever since I first saw Luke's Christmas family photo two years ago, all in their ugly sweaters and big grins, I've had this longing in my stomach to meet them. Now that I have, it's only highlighted the difference between them and me. Luke's parents and mine.

That difference is stark. Gaping.

I need to find Luke. The refuge in my storm.

Lost, dazed, with a pressure in my chest I don't know how to handle, I spin on the spot, searching for him. Finally, I catch sight of him by the buffet table, two glasses of punch in his hands. Waiting for me. I stride towards him.

Brittany sidles up beside Luke before I reach him, a smile on her pretty face, blonde hair perfectly curled to her shoulders, in a bridesmaid dress that hugs her curves to perfection. I look good today, but Brittany—she looks fantastic.

No birthmark on her cheek. No large tattoos, pink hair, alternative fashion sense. Just seductive beauty that she knows all too well how to use.

"Alone?" she asks Luke, flirty and sweet. When she holds out a hand for the punch, he passes one to her.

"Aspen will be back soon," he says. "She just headed outside to take a call."

Their backs are to me, unaware that I'm behind them. Brittany nods and takes a sip of the punch. This is my moment to interrupt them, but I'm rooted to the floor, and the next second, she's speaking again. "You know, this is the first time we've seen each other since . . ."

"Since the final breakup," he finishes gently. "I know."

"I wanted to apologize for the way I behaved and treated you back then. I've been in therapy, and that's something they recommended. To take ownership of my actions. I was a bitch to you, and I don't blame you for ending things. I know I put you through hell, and I'm sorry."

"You did put me through hell," he says, still calm, watching her with that Luke way of his. "But I appreciate the apology."

Tell her to go away. This thing with my mom is burning me up inside, and I know he doesn't know, but seeing him talking to Brittany is becoming too much to handle.

"Part of my therapy is also learning to speak my truth," Brittany says, and every instinct in me is screaming that I should *stop her*, but I can't seem to formulate the words in time. "When Jo got engaged, a part of me hoped that we could reunite at the wedding."

"Brit," Luke says, voice weary, but she holds up her hand, cutting him off.

"I've missed you," she insists stubbornly. "You're the best guy I've ever dated, and I wish I could go back in time and change things, but I can't. When I got here and saw you had a girlfriend, I told myself I wouldn't meddle in your love life. Not if you're happy. But Jo told me that you're moving to San Jose and Aspen isn't going with you. Your relationship isn't at that level yet, which is why I'm willing to risk saying this." She takes a deep breath. Luke steps backward slightly, and although he doesn't say anything, he doesn't walk away either. I guess he's in shock. I'm in shock too. I thought Brittany had given him up. I thought she had accepted he was mine.

"Aspen is great," she says quickly. "And you guys seem happy together, you do. But if it's too new and not committed enough to take the next step, then please keep your options open. If things don't work out between you two, you and I could start over. We have history, and a solid foundation we could build on again. My job is flexible. I could move to San Jose in a heartbeat. I want one last chance to make things right."

Brittany puts a hand on his arm, and that's it, the end of what I can bear.

Today has been too much. I've got whiplash from this morning, all the thoughts and feelings I had about Luke then, to the wedding and the all-encompassing joy of this family, to the shock and worry about my mom's injury, and now this underhanded move of Brittany's.

All my fears and insecurities are triggered. And maybe I'm overre-acting, but I don't care. I need space so I don't explode from the sheer breadth and depth of my tumultuous feelings, and I leave the barn to walk back to the cabin.

Luke can't know I overheard him. That I *eavesdropped*. It would imply . . . what? That I don't trust him?

It's not *him* I don't trust; it's Brittany. She clearly wants him back, and she's prepared to do anything she can to get him, including going behind my back to steal him from me.

Not that he's even necessarily mine. We never did have that conver-sation. And if it's a competition between Brittany and me, is there a small chance she'd win him back? Yes, she cheated, but she *has* been in therapy. Maybe she's really grown and changed since then. My mom has taken back men who've treated her worse. And Brittany has so much history with him—way more than I do. She's not a commit-ment-phobe. They're not even together, and she's prepared to move to San Jose, for God's sake.

Men always leave; that's been my life experience. I was just be-ginning to hope this time would be different. That Luke would be different.

I do love him. The revelation is bittersweet.

A bitter laugh escapes my lips as I burst into the cabin. I love him, have maybe been unconsciously in love with him for a while now but tricked myself into thinking he was just a friend. And just when I'm figuring this out, the universe throws Brittany into the mix, campaigning to get him back before I can declare my feelings.

But seriously, fuck Brittany. That is some underhand action, and if Luke does end up getting back with her, she better not break his heart again.

Okay. Compartmentalize. There's only so much I can focus on at a time, and right now, Luke can't be part of that. Being distracted by Luke has been what's kept me from giving my mom the attention she needs if we're going to solve her drinking problem.

So, first things first: a flight back home. I grab my phone and sit on the end of the bed, squinting through the stubborn tears that insist on falling as I search for flights to New Jersey. The first available one is tomorrow morning, and I book it, knowing Luke or Peter or *someone* will drive me back down to Salt Lake. It's just that kind of family.

Next: packing. I throw clothes into the bag haphazardly, leaving the condoms but taking the lingerie. I'm wearing some of it now; I put it on this morning, intending to surprise Luke after our little talk.

So much for that.

Chapter Twenty-Eight

Aspen

I'm about packed when there's a knock on the door. I open it to find Granny standing on the steps.

Obviously, it wouldn't have been Luke. He'd have just come in.

"Couldn't help but notice you're crying," she says, not unkindly. I scrub at my face and sniff. "What's the matter?"

Oh, you know, just my life falling apart.

"I need to visit my mom," I say, looking around the room at my mess of belongings. I forgot to pack the bikini, so I stuff it in the bag. "She's in the hospital. It's a long story."

Her face softens. "I'm sorry to hear that, honey. Do you want me to find Luke?"

"No!" I must say it too fast, because she stiffens, confused. "I mean—no. It's fine. I'll talk to him later."

"He'll want to know about this."

If he's not flirting with Brittany.

I chide myself for the stray thought. He wouldn't do that. I know him too well to think he'd essentially cheat on me, especially when he knew we were going to talk about *us*.

"It's fine," I say, a little too bitterly. My emotions are all over the place; I can't keep them in. "Brittany's making a pass at him. Thought I'd leave them to it."

Granny's eyes flash, and for a second, I think she's going to storm back into the barn and challenge Brittany to a duel, but her features settle back into calm. "Well, I can't speak for Brittany or her actions, but you know Luke. He would never betray your relationship."

"We're not actually together," I blurt. I'm too emotionally over-whelmed to stop myself. My insecurities bubbling to the surface and betraying me. "Luke and me. We were never a couple. We just pre-tended to date so everyone would stop trying to set him up on blind dates or worry about him and Brittany getting back together."

"Is that right?" Granny tilts her head, her lips disappearing as she holds back saying anything more.

"Yes. So, he's not my man, and I don't have any right to get in the way of him and Brittany if that's what he decides."

"And you think that's what he wants?" Granny folds her arms as she looks at me. "Did he say that?"

Now doesn't seem the right time to admit that I didn't stick around to hear what he said. I just wanted to escape the situation.

The coward's way out.

So, fine, I'm a coward. But my mom is in the hospital about to get surgery, so I think it's understandable. I'm not my best self right now.

"That boy isn't interested in anyone else," Granny says. "You might think your relationship is fake, but the way he looks at you isn't. And the sex didn't sound fake either."

I blush so hard you could fry an egg on my face. "You . . . heard that?"

"I'm old, not decrepit," she says tartly. "And I have ears."

"I'm so sorry."

"You don't need to apologize to me for living your life to the fullest." She looks at me critically, and I collapse on the couch, wrapping a throw blanket around myself like it'll keep me together. "Is this because he's moving to San Jose?"

"Long-distance is a hard way to start a relationship—" I start pathetically, but Granny takes hold of a fire poker and jabs the fireplace's embers viciously, the sparks stopping me mid-sentence. I'm not even sure where I was going with that.

"Let me tell you something, Aspen. Luke is my grandson, and I've watched him grow up. All the awkward years, all the years he thought he was in love with that girl, Brittany." She says Brittany's name like it's a disease. "And he's never been like this with anyone before."

I sink deeper into the couch, wrapping my arms around myself. My cheeks are wet. I think I've been crying all this time and didn't even realize. These past few days, Luke has been the one anchoring me, and now, without him, I feel untethered. Drifting.

"Do you love him?" Granny asks, the words dropping like hot coals in my lap. I want to scream and run away.

But this is my truth.

"Yes," I whisper. The words settle in my chest like they've lived there this whole time.

"I thought so. There hasn't been anything fake about the way you two interact with each other."

"It's been just over a week. How can I *trust* what I feel? How do I even know this is real?"

The way my chest aches tells me this is real. It's just . . . new and scary.

"I could point out all the signs until I'm blue in the face, but I can't convince you," Granny says. "Only you can do that."

I shake my head because this entire conversation feels ridiculous. Overblown. "It happened so fast."

"And? It's been longer than that for Luke. You know it, and I know it. Your friendship laid a better foundation than most marriages I know. You're not just friends; you're coworkers. You've spent more waking hours with that man than any other person in your life, and you're telling me you don't believe in your feelings because you've only just realized them over the past week?" She snorts derisively. "One of the bravest things in life is to risk it all to be with someone you love."

"But that's just it!" I drag a hand through my hair in frustration. "Risking it all. I can't risk it all. Breaking my heart over him—that's not something I'm willing to do." Even though it feels like my heart is already cracking wide open.

That's not just Luke's doing. Not just the fact that he's moving. It's my own vulnerability that's suffocating me here, and the fact that Brittany has wormed her way between us in my head. My insecurities are saying all the things that Luke never has.

For five years, he kept choosing her.

Even if he doesn't choose her again, what's to say he'll permanently choose me?

Everyone leaves. He's going to *San Jose*. He's going to put those roots down in California while I stay here in Utah, and I don't know how to handle that right now. Everything is confused in my head.

Mom in the hospital, not handling life. My fledgling relationship with Luke in a fragile place.

"You're a root person, Aspen," Granny says. "But root people become so because they have true grit. They stick around when things get tough."

The fight goes out of me. All the anger—at Luke for making me fall for him, at Brittany for trying to steal him, at myself for getting into this predicament—fades away, and my shoulders slump.

"I don't know how to do a serious relationship." The words burn on their way out. "No one has ever shown me."

"Let Luke show you."

"And if it doesn't work?" Impatiently, I brush away the tears that won't stop flowing. "I won't come back from that, Granny Mae. I just won't. I've depended on and lost too many significant people in my life to just . . ." God, this is hard. "I'm better off alone, I think. Maybe that's the lesson I've learned from life."

Knees cracking, Granny crouches in front of me and takes my hand, clasping it between both of hers. "Do you know the tree you're named after is the most resilient and interconnected phenomena in the world?"

I sniff. "My parents didn't name me after the tree. They named me after the city in Colorado where I was conceived."

"Happy accident, then." Her smile creases the skin around her eyes, deep like cracked leather. The marks of her life are scattered across her face, and I wonder, briefly, what I'll look like when I'm old. "The longest-living single organism in the world is an aspen grove. The largest one actually exists just a few hours south of here, called the Pando. It's almost ten thousand years old."

"I didn't know that," I mumble, my head spinning from the abrupt turn we've just taken. What does a tree have to do with anything?

"It's reached that age because it's a survivor. Despite all the adversity it endures, an aspen with deep roots can survive just about anything. It's the last thing to burn down in a wildfire; the first to sprout from the ashes. And it's common to find groves of them in the paths of avalanches, because even though their trunks get knocked down by the force of the snow, their root systems remain and rebuild." She squeezes my hand. "Do you know why?"

I shake my head.

"Because they're interconnected. The Pando has a root system that spreads out over one hundred acres. They're not just trees—they're one organism, one living community. The trees can communicate, and if one is sick or thirsty, the others can pass long nutrients and water through their root system to aid them. They survive because they're not alone. They have each other."

"I—"

"You have your own aspen grove around you," Granny says, her gruff voice gentler now. "Look at your friends that came running when you called. Look at all of us here. The Simmons clan has embraced you with open arms. Look at Luke. What you two have built over the past years. These are your roots. You're not designed to be alone, sweetheart. You're built to thrive. You're a Pando."

For once, I'm speechless. My heart hasn't stopped hurting, but it's been given an infusion of love and light. Granny's wisdom makes me feel seen. She's pressed on my biggest insecurities, and like a splinter, she's taken hold of the end and pulled them loose. An exposed wound, hollow and raw, left in its place.

The door bursts open and Luke blows in, along with a flurry of fresh snow.

"Aspen," he says, sounding both concerned and exasperated. The exasperation melts when he sees my face. "Sweetheart, where were you? What happened?"

Granny climbs to her feet. "Have a good talk," she advises us both, to Luke's bewilderment, and leaves the room, shutting the door behind her.

"My mom's in the hospital," I say, avoiding his gaze. "I found a plane that leaves tomorrow and got a ticket."

"Your mom? What happened?" Luke crosses the room swiftly and sits down beside me, gathering my hands in his.

"I don't know, but I can only assume she was drunk and something . . . I don't know." I suck in a breath and exhale it slowly.

He wraps me in his arms.. "I'll come with you."

"No." I don't mean the word to come out as harshly as it does. "I think I need to do this alone." I break our embrace and lean back, needing some distance for this conversation.

His hands reaches up to tuck a rebellious strand of my flattened curls behind my ear. "Are you sure?" he asks tenderly. "I can be there for you. Support you."

Part of me wants that, but if he comes with me, that adds a bunch of complications I don't think I'm ready to face. So, I go for the easy, cheap way out. "I heard Brittany talking to you."

Luke leans back, his eyes assessing me for clues as to where this conversation is headed. Finally, one eyebrow raises. "You did, did you?"

"Before we figure anything with *us* out, you need to work out your feelings for your ex. Stay here. Work out what you want and explore who would be the easiest person to have in your life."

"Work out what I want?" he repeats, shaking his head. His nostrils flare, and it occurs to me that I've never seen him angry before. "How the hell do you think I don't already know what I want?"

"Brit—"

"Did you even hear what I said to Brittany?" he interrupts, standing. "Or did you just listen to part of the conversation and storm off to sulk?"

I'm not sulking. I'm hurting. There's a difference, I'm sure of it, even if I can't think of it right now.

"I told her that we're done," he says. "That I'm committed to you. That I'm *in love* with you. So, you don't get to stand there and decide what's best for me and what I need to do when I've already done it. I've already made the decision. It's you I want. Even though I'm totally pissed at you right now." His lips pin together, and real hurt flashes across his face. "Is this you looking for a way to sabotage us?"

"No," I snap, jumping to my feet.

"You sure? Because it sure feels like it. Damn, Aspen. What we have is fantastic. And I mean it when I say I'm in love with you. I'm so fucking in love with you that it's going to gut me if you walk away now."

He's right—this isn't about Brittany.

The problem, laid bare between us in the wake of our anger and his confession—and mine, though I still haven't dared say it to him—is that I don't know if I'm enough.

I don't know *how* to be in love. How to be loved. How to stick around when things get tough. And Luke deserves better than that.

"I need to stage an intervention with my mom," I say, my voice small, my gaze lowered to the floor. It's an avoidance if ever there was one, but what do you say when someone tells you they're in love with you and it's just too much for you to handle? "I don't know how long it's going to take. I'll have to request personal time off from Kai. But it might interfere with your move, and I just can't—" My voice chokes on the word. "I don't have the emotional bandwidth to think about us and my mom right now, Luke. I'm sorry."

His eyes are raw and empty, and I catch my breath at their haunted beauty. He's hurting, and that alone is almost too much to handle.

I'm my mother's daughter. All I know is to run when things get bumpy.

But that's something I'm now realizing I need to work on. I don't want to be that girl anymore.

Look where it's gotten Mom.

When he stands and wraps his arms around me, I don't resist. I hold tight to him, breathing in that fresh-cut pine scent, and I think about how much I'm going to miss him.

"We'll talk about us when I'm back," I say into his shoulder. "Even if you're gone by then. I'm not saying this is the end, I just need a break."

"I don't ever want it to be the end, Aspen. We can make it work."

"I'm not running from you," I whisper, feeling tears start again. "I promise I'll give it some thought. It's just been a lot, in such a short time. I need to process all of this."

His fingers dig into my waist. "Come back to me, and let's sort it out together. That's all I ask."

I have no words left. They've all been corroded by grief and loss and this awful, awful feeling of goodbye. So, instead, I stretch up. Brush my nose against his, feel the soft exhale against my cheek as he closes his eyes. One hand slides to my shoulder, the other slides around the back of my head, cupping me. But still he doesn't move. Doesn't pull me in.

I'm the one to close the distance. There's a low groan deep in his chest, then he's holding me close, kissing me. We're both open wounds, and this salve soothes our torn flesh. His touch feels so terrifyingly good that the moment he pulls back, the second this is over, I know I'm going to crumble.

I don't let myself think of *after*.

His hands are urgent, pulling me closer, and I deepen the kiss, pulling him into me, blurring our lines so we're one and the same. Both aching, both desperate, both scared. The only thing I want is to melt into him, to unspool time so it pools around our feet and winds around us and never lets go.

The selfish part of me wants to. Selfish Aspen, like Horny Aspen, wants Luke the way she has never wanted anything in her entire life. She craves the ease of his love for her. She needs the balance he brings to her life. Selfish Aspen wants to forget about her mom, who has upheaved her life once again, and pull Luke to the bed so he can make her forget.

Luke is the one to pull away first. His eyes are wide, but they haven't lost the heartbreak. I think he sees it in my eyes too, because he touches my face, sighing, trying to collect himself.

It's a losing battle. A lost battle.

"I'll miss you and your amazing hugs." I squeeze his middle one last time.

"They'll be waiting for you." It's as close to *I love you* as we're going to get. By the sad smile on his face, he knows it.

I nod, swallow, and step away. He drops his hands, and I sling the strap of my bag over my shoulder. Everything about the world feels lighter, more unstable. I've left something behind me, here in this room. A lot of things. I don't know if I can ever get them back.

Chapter Twenty-Nine

Luke

A spen left for home before the wedding reception was over. She ordered an Uber instead of waiting until morning to hitch a ride with Dad and the newlyweds. She thought a clean break was better, and although I didn't like the abrupt turn of events, I'm grateful to have avoided sleeping in the same bed without being able to snuggle her.

Now, there's not much I can do except hope she gets her shit sorted out and comes back before I leave.

Either way, it's out of my hands.

Which, unfortunately, doesn't stop this from feeling shitty. Life can be like a tsunami. One moment, you're riding the waves; the next, you're sucked out to sea and spat out on a deadly shoreline.

All the wedding guests have left. The day passes in a blur of cleaning up the reception aftermath and putting the barn back together. The fog in my head is half hangover, half heartbreak. Cleaning requires no brainpower, just muscle, so my mind keeps drifting back to worrying that Aspen is across the country dealing with some heavy family stuff, alone and unsupported.

I yearn to know her family the way she knows mine. To meet her mom and learn their family dynamic. It would unlock so many answers about Aspen. But she isn't ready for that, and I hate feeling helpless. When I made the decision to move, it was so I would have control over my own choices. So I would get over her and reclaim my heart.

Instead, I took a risk and gave her everything, hoping the gamble would pay off in the end. I'm getting a master class in patience.

After dinner, Mom and Rebecca colluded together to put on a cheesy Christmas movie, knowing the kids would be entertained for at least an hour and give them some peace and quiet. Rebecca, I'm pretty sure, just wanted an excuse to rest without having to go to bed already.

Bright images flash across the darkened room. Rebecca is already dozing off, her head resting on Mark's chest. Millie is asleep on my lap.

Granny hands me a whiskey and I toss it back, the fire burning away some of the numbness. Millie stirs but doesn't wake up.

"She told me everything," Granny whispers, leaning in. "That you pretended to be a couple to keep your mom's shenanigans at bay."

Shock jolts through me, but I manage to mask it with a raised eyebrow. "And?"

"And how long have you loved her, Luke?"

At this point, I shouldn't be surprised that she can see straight through me so effortlessly. If she had a superpower, this would be it.

"Long enough. Almost as long as I've known her, despite her never feeling the same way about me."

"She loves you too."

"You think?"

"It's why she's so scared. Look at this through her perspective. She told me no one in her life has taught her how to stick around when the going gets tough. And now that she cares for you, you're leaving too. It's triggering her deepest wound."

Shit. I wince in sympathy, bowing my head against Millie's hair, which smells of shampoo and hay. "We're going to talk when she gets back."

"Show her you understand her fears. Make sure she knows you're going to be there for her emotionally, if not always physically."

"I know." I toss the rest of the drink back. "I'm done playing it safe now anyway. I'm all in at this point."

"Good." She nods, satisfied. "It's about damn time you step up and give love a chance again after that girl broke your heart."

No need to ask who "that girl" is.

"Thanks, Granny," I say dryly. "An inspiring pep talk, as always."

"And don't you forget it." She prods me in the arm. "I've got more of that whiskey in the bunkhouse if you want a nightcap. For old times' sake."

Anything is better than moping, and it feels like returning to the way things used to be. A breath of familiar fresh air. "Sure," I say, putting a sleeping Millie back on her dad's lap. "Let's go get shit-faced. For old times' sake."

***

Aspen

I get to Jersey after Mom's discharged. The hospital rings me to let me know that she's recovering fine and has been sent home, so home is where I go once I'm off the plane.

She lives in an aging suburb, in a small apartment that she moved into after I left home. Once the Uber drops me off, I stand for a moment and stare up at the blank windows. It's late—my flight landed as the evening sun set—and the world feels oddly hushed.

I have a key, so I let myself in and climb the stairs to her floor. Number four. I rap on the door, knuckles aching. Being here feels like my nerves are stretched too tight, ready to snap any second. I know what I need to say to her, I know what she needs to do, but that doesn't mean it'll be easy.

It especially doesn't mean she's going to want to listen.

I knock again and finally hear footsteps. If Tim answers the door, I'm bolting. If he's the one she called after he's helped get her deeper into this pit, then I can't help her anymore. Not while he's in her life.

Love shouldn't feel like this, like my chest is constantly collapsing, a black hole where my heart should be. I've seen Luke's family. It *can* be easy. Or at least easier.

All I've ever wanted is to get to a place with Mom where it can be like that.

But first, she needs rehab. Professional help. I can't be the one to help her truly recover.

The door swings open, and it's not Tim. It's not Mom. A face I haven't seen in over twenty years stares at me, lined and graying and haggard, but still so familiar that I know I would recognize it anywhere.

My dad stands in the doorway, dressed in a white tee and plaid pajama pants. He's standing in my mom's apartment. My *dad* is standing in my mom's apartment, and she's nowhere to be seen.

We stare at each other a beat too long, my shock mirrored on his face.

"Aspen," he says.

I barge inside. "Where is she?"

"Keep your voice down." Dad closes the door behind me. He doesn't lock it, like he can sense I desperately need to know there's an escape route handy. I'm suffocating; I can't breathe. "She's sleeping."

"Why are you here?" I cross my arms and plant my feet.

He holds up both his hands. "I think you and I need to talk, honey."

"Don't *honey* me." My heart is pounding too fast, and I point my finger at him. "Why are you here? Did she *call* you?"

His gaze is steady as it holds mine. "It wouldn't be the first time. Come into the kitchen and we can talk."

I don't want to talk to him, but I can't leave Mom alone here with him. This isn't how I pictured my visit starting. Now that he's here, everything I'd planned to say feels wrong. But I have to do something, to step up and make sure she's okay. I'm so confused and surprised that I don't know how to proceed.

I point at the tiny kitchen table. "You have five minutes to explain before I walk back out of that door."

"Okay," he says, remarkably calm considering I'm angry enough that I want to throw something. Before, if you'd asked me to draw his face, I wouldn't have been able to recall what he looked like beyond the most banal of details. Blonde hair, thin nose, square jaw. But now, I can see the way time has cut into his face, carving an older man from the one I recognize. He's well into his late fifties now, and he looks it. Deep lines gouge his forehead and mouth. Hair puffs from the neck of his T-shirt. I always remembered him being a big man, but he looks small and fragile now. One strong word from me, and he'll blow away.

As soon as we're in the kitchen, I slam the door and yank out a chair. It's a long-as-hell day, and I'm too tired to keep standing for this.

"You said Mom called you," I say bluntly. "Why? She never forgave you for walking out."

"Not for a long time, she didn't," he says gently. "But there are a lot of things you don't know."

I fold my arms. "So, get talking. Why, after all these years, are you here now?" The low self-esteem I carried for years creeps back into a knot in my stomach. The insecurities are faded now, like old wallpaper, but sometimes I can still feel the pattern they left on my soul. The sense of not being worthy.

He looks at me seriously. "I think I'm here for the same reason as you, Aspen. So let's lay down our weapons, okay? I know you're mad at me, and I get that. You have every right to be, but I came here because your mom needs help."

"Not from you."

A sad smile flickers across his face. "I understand why you'd think that, but I think she does. In fact, I think I might be the only person who cares about her that can help. She needs to know that it's possible to come out on the other side of addiction. I've been there in a way you haven't, and I never want you to be, not ever. I know you want to help, but you don't understand what it's like. You haven't been where she's at."

"I don't want anyone I don't trust around her right now."

He looks at me again, for a long, long time, before sighing.

"Let me make you a coffee," he says, standing up. "And we can keep talking."

"I still don't think you should be here," I blurt out from behind him. "You left us once. Now, you're going to what, mess with Mom's head and make her trust you so you can make promises and then let her down again? I'm not going to allow that."

"You sound just like your mother, you know that?" He finishes preparing my coffee and hands it to me, the frothed milk in what I think is meant to be an artful swirl. He grimaces. "I never did get the hang of that."

"Don't talk to me like we're friends."

"Right." He sits back down and waits for me to speak.

I take a sip to avoid looking at him. Mom's place is a mess. There are bottles everywhere, and she's taken up smoking again, if the thick odor in the air is anything to go by.

I don't know how to do this. Be here, with Dad, like this, like nothing happened.

"Tell me something," I say, and I can't help the way my voice breaks. "Was I not good enough for you?"

Something shatters across his expression. "Aspen, no—"

"I know I don't look like normal girls." I touch my fingers against my birthmark. The skin is slightly rougher than on my other cheek, reminding me it's there even when I can't see it. "Did you look at me and think that I wasn't what you signed up for?"

"No, honey. It was never about the way you looked. God, no." He looks so appalled, I'm almost tempted to believe him. "You were beautiful. *Are* beautiful. The reason I left had *nothing* to do with you and everything to do with me." His throat works as he shakes his head, and his fingers tremble. "I never wanted you to feel like that, Aspen. I'm sorry—so sorry. If I could go back and make it right, I would. I would sacrifice everything I have if I could take away your pain."

I take a scalding sip of coffee so I don't have to look at him. I wish he could have taken away all those years of self-doubt as well, the times when I looked in the mirror and despised what I saw. All my life, I've had to fight against the tiny voice that told me I wasn't enough—pretty enough, clever enough, *normal* enough—for my dad to stay.

"I left because I was an addict and out of control. I needed help. I couldn't stand the shame of putting you in danger," he says, the pain in his eyes matching his confession. "Did you know, once you tripped over a broken beer bottle I had dropped and left on the floor, totally spaced out of my mind? You cut your foot wide open."

He was like Mom is all I can think.

"I couldn't see straight to drive you to the ER." He shakes his head, regret shadowing his face. "Our neighbor had to drive us both there. You needed stitches. There was going to be an investigation into my suitability as a father after that, and I knew I needed to leave for you to be safe. I didn't want you taken away or put into the child protective services system."

Now that he's said this, the faintest image comes back to me. Pain, my foot wrapped in a T-shirt, too much blood. The faint sting of antiseptic. Questions posed gently but hammering into my skull. "I didn't remember."

"I never wanted you to remember. That's too much of a burden for a child to bear."

"I'm not a child any longer."

"I know," he says softly. "That's why I reached back out to your mom a few years ago when I was sober long enough to not be a liability in her life. She refused to give me your contact details, but she's kept me updated on the basics of your life. We've stayed in touch. I'm sorry for walking out all those years ago."

"Sorry isn't going to cut it." My lip trembles slightly.

"I know. It'll take time to make it up to you. But I want to, Aspen. That's why I'm here—because your mom needs me, and because I want to make up for all the shitty things I did to both of you."

Luke's family has taught me life doesn't have to be all weeds and no roses. But you have to tend the flowers so they don't wilt and die. I saw that every day. Mark massaging Rebecca's swollen feet, Ruth making meals for everyone, Granny offering advice like a peddler with jewels in a box.

Love takes work.

My love for my dad never died, even when I hated him. It's a thorny, half-dead shrub in stony ground, but it's survived the years of neglect. I'm just not sure it will ever be enough for me to forgive him. There's so much pain there. A lifetime of hurt and anger and hatred that I can't just brush aside.

"Why did Mom call you?" I ask. "I don't mean why are you guys talking again, but what are you here to do?"

"The same thing as you, I imagine." His smile doesn't reach his eyes. "To make sure she gets the help she needs. I've been there before, sweetheart, and I had to drag myself out of the dark hole by myself. It wasn't easy, and I relapsed. A few times. It would have been easier if someone who understood that level of hell was there to help me." He steadily holds my gaze. "I want to help her make it to the other side."

A crossroads lies before. Whether to let my dad help.

Whether to send him away and tackle this by myself.

I'm so *tired* of being strong all on my own.

"Okay," I say. "How are we going to do this?"

Chapter Thirty

Luke

The office feels wrong without Aspen here. It's my second day back, and although I have a bunch of things to wrap up before my last day at the end of the week, I can't seem to concentrate. Usually, she's sitting across the aisle from me, reading me ridiculous and dubiously sourced facts from online articles and generally trying to distract me. Now, her chair is empty.

I should get used to this. When I'm in California, the desk will always be empty.

But somehow, it feels worse like this.

Kai strolls through the office, and I half-heartedly pretend to do some work. I'm not going to hit my deadlines before I leave. By then, it'll be someone else's problem.

He perches on the edge of my desk. "You look like shit."

"Thanks."

"I thought you and Aspen were—" He makes a crude motion with his fingers. "You know. Didn't you guys hook up?"

"I didn't take her to my sister's wedding so we could hook up."

"So that's a no?"

I sigh. Luckily for me, half the office is working remotely today, so there's no one close enough to hear our conversation. "We did sleep together, yes. But I'm moving to San Jose, in case you've forgotten."

"She can transfer," he says with a wave of his hand. "I'm the CEO. I can make it happen."

"She doesn't want to."

"Oh."

"Yeah." *Oh* is kind of an understatement. "It's fine. She's just with her mom right now, so we haven't had a chance to work out what comes next. If *anything* comes next, or if an amazing holiday vacation is all we get."

He rubs the side of his nose. "Yeah, she called me to ask for time off. Sounded pretty upset."

"She is."

"Have you tried, I dunno, talking to her?"

I roll my eyes. "Amazingly enough, that did occur to me. I offered to go with her to help out, but she didn't want me to, and so here I am."

"Not working," he says, looking at my screen.

"Pretending to work," I agree.

"She'll come around," he says with confidence I don't feel. "Maybe she just needed a bit of time. And look, worst case scenario, you can just fly back home for visits."

"Yeah, I know. It'll work out how it's supposed to, I guess. At least, that was my family's feeble advice."

He claps me on the shoulder. "You're a solid guy. She knows that."

The issue is that solid guys aren't exactly her dating MO. And the *real* issue is that her experience with men hasn't exactly been stellar. She's too used to giving up instead of working on making a relationship work.

Sure, I know I'm different, but she has to really trust in us for this to be successful.

A text buzzes in from her. *Thinking of you*, it reads. Maybe there's some hope for us after all.

I type a reply. *Thinking of you too. xo*

***

Aspen

It's weird, having a truce with my father after I vowed as a kid to never forgive him. Dad and I spend hours researching potential rehabilitation treatment centers in the area, and in that time, we gradually answer questions about each other's lives.

Things have changed in the twenty years he's been gone. He's got a steady job now, with savings, and both of us pledge money toward helping Mom get clean. It's not cheap to fix your life, but between us, we just about have enough to cover the expenses.

But there is one thing I'm sure about. For this to work, Mom has to be prepared to help herself. If she isn't, I'm mentally done. I don't have the emotional energy to give to someone who isn't ready to receive it.

Luke helped teach me that.

By the time Mom shuffles out of her bedroom, Dad and I have cleaned the place, and I'm dead on my feet. She blinks at the two of us standing together.

"Aspen," she croaks. "You came."

"You were in the hospital, Mom. Of course I came."

"I'll leave you two to chat," Dad says, more diplomatically than I could have imagined. When he leaves the apartment, silence fills the space between Mom and me.

I should have prepared a speech. Because now that it's just us, I'm *tired*. Tired of being the one who has to pick up the pieces again and again. Tired of being the parent because she's so caught up on mourning the dream career that never panned out.

"This has to stop," I say in a low voice.

"It was just an accident—"

"Were you drinking?" I demand. "Or high?" She flinches, but I keep going. This needs to be said, like forcing someone to vomit when they've ingested poison. "You cut yourself so badly, you needed minor surgery. The day before that, you drove into your mailbox. You were drinking and driving, Mom." I start to pace, unable to stand still. "You think that's okay? Normal behavior? *Acceptable* behavior?"

"I don't know why you're talking to me like that," she mutters, grabbing a blanket and wrapping it around herself as she lowers herself onto the couch. "I'm your mother."

"Then fucking act like it. Don't call me up asking for bail money or to come to pick you up from the hospital because you hurt yourself. Let me visit you on birthdays and Christmases without me having to worry if your scumbag boyfriend of the month is going to sexually assault me. Or whether he's going to hurt you."

"Aspen, I—"

"I'm tired," I say, voice cracking. "I don't want things to be difficult between us. I don't want to dread when you call because I think you might ask for money. I just spent Christmas with the loveliest family I've ever known. They're not perfect—I'm not saying they're even close to that—but they love each other, and they provide a safe space for everyone to be themselves. And I need that. I didn't know how much I needed that until I saw someone else have it."

Mom's eyes are wet, and I see the hurt in them. "I don't make you feel safe?"

"Not when you're drinking, Mom. Not when you allow men to hurt you." I don't know what I'm intending to do until I'm bending down, kneeling in front of her, pleading for her to hear me. "I love you. I love you so much, and that's why I'm here. That's why I'm doing this. Because this *has* to stop."

"It's not so bad," she says weakly, but even I can tell she doesn't believe it. The evidence has gotten away from her now. The proof is in the bandage on her arm, the mailbox out front.

"Let's stop lying to ourselves, okay?" I whisper. "Please?"

She starts to cry, great racking sobs that jolt through her body like she's holding a live wire. For a second, I freeze. Luke's family are into hugs, but that's never been how it is between Mom and me. But she needs it, so I hold her. It's unfamiliar at first, but grows comfortable. Nice even. I stroke her thin, straggling hair and tell her that it's going to be okay. We're going to get through this together.

She's sober now, I know. And maybe talking to her when she's sober like this is how I'm going to get through to her.

"Dad and I are trying to work together to get you help," I tell her. " I don't know why the hell you called him, and I don't know why you've been talking to him for years without telling me, but he's here now."

"I want him here," Mom says.

I want to argue against that, but I can't. "Okay. Then I guess I'll get over it. But I don't understand what's going on between you two. And don't ask me to forgive him, Mom. I don't think I can do that. At least, not now."

"I know, baby." This time, it's her turn to stroke my hair. I lean into her fleeting, motherly affection. "I know."

We stay like that for a long time. And when Dad comes back with ingredients for a late dinner and an email response from one of the rehab centers, I think that maybe, just maybe, things might turn out okay.

***

It takes another couple of days before we find a place close by that can take her, and then it's packing and sorting and getting ready to drop her off. The residential treatment facility is nice, and the staff there are both friendly and efficient.

"I know it's going to be difficult," I say as we sit in the waiting room. The wall sports several brightly colored paintings, and the chairs are harder than they look like they should be. Someone has spread outdated magazines on the table. The lemony smell of cleaning spray hangs in the air.

Mom is pale. This is the first time in her rock-star career that she's really had to come to terms with the fact that she has a problem—one she can't fix by moving again, or swapping bands, or hooking up with a tour manager.

I curl my hands in my pockets as I watch the nurses. There's a handsome one with kind eyes that reminds me a bit of Luke, and my stomach clenches with homesickness for him.

We've texted over these past few days. I've tried to make sure the lines of communication stay open.

Rebecca had her baby the day after I left. Momma and baby girl, Sadie, are doing fine.

I miss the Simmons clan more than I could've imagined. I especially miss Luke. Sometimes, when I lie awake at night, I almost kid myself into thinking he's lying there beside me.

That's what I want, I've decided. Even if it's only sometimes. Weekends and vacations and time we've stolen away. If that's all of him I can have for now, I'll take it. If he still wants to be with me, I will move heaven and earth to make it happen.

All I need to do is get back to him so I can tell him.

My flight is booked for this afternoon, and I should get to Luke by early evening. Today's his last day at work, and I'm so sad I missed it. We've arranged to meet in the cantina, where Kai is hosting a farewell party. It's our team's unofficial hang out spot and the perfect place for his send-off. It'll also be our first time back there since we hatched the fake-girlfriend charade.

Only, this time, I'll be asking to be his real girlfriend.

My dad offered to drive me to the airport, but I decided to get an Uber. We're still in our fledgling truce, but every conversation has been about Mom. I'm not ready for anything more just yet. Maybe in time I'll share my few good memories and influences I inherited from him. My eclectic taste in music, my love of manga, my aversion to eating anything slathered in BBQ sauce or peppermint flavoring. Secrets to share another day. Baby steps.

While we wait for my ride, Dad tests the waters, almost as if he can sense my ruminations.

"I've been waiting a long time to give you something. Now seems like the right moment. Would that be okay?" His eyes find mine, probing for my reaction.

"Sure," I hesitantly respond, hoping this new truce doesn't blow up in my face.

He pulls out his phone and hands it to me. There's an email account there, filled with unopened emails. Almost one hundred of them in total, all from him, from what I can see.

"When I left, I opened this account for you," he says. "Aspenshaw94. On your birthday, Christmas, whenever I missed you, I'd write you letters. Like a journal of sorts. Then, I'd send you an email, a place to hold my thoughts and memories until you'd be ready to hear them. Some even include photos." His face twists with genuine hurt that makes my chest ache in sympathy. My throat is thick; tears sting my eyes. "I missed all the best bits of you growing up and becoming your own person. And I'm so sorry, Aspen. You deserved better."

"Yeah," I say, scrolling through the subject lines before handing the phone back. "I did. I do."

"I'm going to text you the account details. It's yours to read through whenever you want. I know it's not a replacement for fatherhood, but I hope it can be the beginning of a new start for us."

He wants my forgiveness. He wants to be involved in my life again. I don't think I would've even considered it before, but the Simmons family has shown me that family can be a good thing. I'm willing to start with this baby step.

He texts me the information when I leave, and while I'm waiting for my flight to come in, I scroll back to the beginning of the emails.

He didn't lie. He really did set it up a long time ago—almost twenty years.

Hey baby, the first email reads. *It's your birthday today and I can't see you to say happy birthday and give you all the kisses in the world. I miss you so much. Happy birthday, kiddo.*

The next one is from a year later.

Ten today! I can't believe my beautiful baby girl is so old. Double digits! I bet you've done so much growing up since I've been gone. I think about you every day.

On and on it goes. Birthdays, Christmases. Over the past ten years, he's attached pictures, too. Blurry ones of himself. Things he thinks I would like, though he has no idea.

Here's a pretty picture of a tree, he's written in a random email that doesn't correspond to a significant time or date in my life. *Look at the colors. It's beautiful, just like you.*

The leaves are a deep, burgundy red. A little like my birthmark, I suppose, although mine tends toward pink, and these colors are more on the orange spectrum.

Then again, if he hadn't seen me in years, how well could he remember the color of my birthmark? My memories of him had faded, although that was because I'd forced them out. Bleached them with sunlight like an ancient photograph until all that remained was faint lines.

The one that really makes me cry is one sent five years ago.

This is it, baby. I've been sober three months and going strong. I know this is the one that will stick. Thinking about my beautiful daughter has helped me get through this. I love you so much. I'll do it for you. Maybe when I'm further along in my sobriety we can talk.

It's too much to think we can ever go back to being father and daughter in the traditional sense. But the knowledge that he didn't abandon me, that he's been thinking about me all these years, heals some part of my heart. Maybe I do have a chance at a family after all.

I am a Pando, and these are my roots.

I pull out my phone and text Luke. *I'm on my way*, I write. *Wait for me.*

Chapter Thirty-One

Luke

The cantina is crammed, full of hot bodies, loud conversations, and flowing alcohol. Drinks are on Kai tonight, and most people have taken advantage of it. Normally, I might have too, but I don't want to be buzzed when Aspen gets here and we *finally* have a chance to pick up where we left off.

"You're moping," Kai says, swinging a chair round and perching on it backwards, his hands braced against the back.

"No, I'm not." I take a sip of my beer. "See? I'm drinking."

He narrows his eyes. "Slowly."

The wait might actually kill me. If it doesn't, Kai's pestering will.

Amy takes to the stage, doing her best Taylor Swift routine, although her eyes are glazed and her movements are a little too loose.

Beer and margaritas are flowing. Someone has ordered a tequila sunrise. This is a celebration.

I'm getting the promotion I always wanted. My career is successful.

And no matter what Aspen chooses, I'm going to celebrate it.

I drain my glass and hand it to Kai. "Wanna get me another?"

"That's the spirit," he says with a grin, sliding off his chair. I'm not about to drink enough to get hammered, but there's no harm in a couple beers.

Rick pushes the karaoke roulette wheel toward me. "Spin."

I wait until Kai slams the next beer in front of me before shoving the karaoke roulette at him, the wheel firmly pointed on "Epic Duets."

"Tough luck, dude," I tell him. "You're going to sing with me."

He groans. "Do I have to?"

"Yep." I wink at Dan, who grins. Everyone wants to get Kai onstage, no matter how many times he tries to get out of it. "Get on the stage. I'll choose the song."

He gives a theatrical sigh, but I don't give him the chance to object as I head over to the advent pockets and pull out a popsicle stick.

"'Shallow,'" I read, though that's not what it says. It's one of his favorite songs, and if this is my last karaoke roulette for a while, I want to go out with a bang. "From *A Star Is Born*."

Kai grins, but from the way he's looking at me, he knows I fudged the answer. I set up the song track and join him onstage. The lights dim as we take the mics. The music plays, laughter ripples across the room, and lyrics scroll on the screen in front of us as we begin to sing. Our last duet together.

***

Aspen

My flight is delayed, landing in Salt Lake almost an hour after it was supposed to. The second I've got my bags, I order an Uber, heading outside into the darkness. It's not late, but night comes early in winter. A full moon crests the clouds.

Luke hasn't been replying to my last few messages. I can only hope that's because he's having a good time and not because he's second-guessing and doesn't want to have this conversation after all.

I spent the whole flight reflecting on the past few weeks. So many monumental changes in such a short time. Meeting a family I never knew I needed. Hope and healing within my immediate family. Falling for Luke, the friend and lover I've come to cherish.

My stomach is in knots. I'm three seconds away from throwing up.

The driver glances at me in the rearview mirror as we come to a complete stop, the intersection gridlocked with traffic. He's a friendly looking man in his late fifties with extremely impressive eyebrows. Any other time, I'd enjoy watching the expressive way they move.

"Are you okay?" he asks.

"Why, don't I seem okay?" Considering I'm probably green and sweaty, I deserve the way his eyebrows raise.

"If you need to be sick, the doors are unlocked."

"I'm not going to be sick." *Probably. Hopefully. Oh* God, *why isn't the traffic moving?*

"Head between your legs," he instructs, and I obey him because my anxiety is at an all-time high, and I really might vomit all over his nice, clean car. "Deep breaths."

Turns out, it really does help. I stare at a pebble next to my shoe until my eyes water.

"Have you ever had to tell someone you love them before they leave you, maybe forever?" My words are muffled, but they're no less dramatic.

There's a silence as the driver considers it. "Can't say I have."

"I don't recommend it." I suck in another deep breath. "Can you not, like . . ." There's nowhere for him to go. "Drive around them? Somehow?"

"That would be illegal, miss."

"Right. Of course." To my relief, we start moving again. "Sorry I asked. It just drives me crazy that the point of the mountain is always so damn congested." I'm muttering to myself more than talking to the driver.

He puts his foot down, sliding neatly into a small gap, and navigates the busy I-15 freeway like a pro. My heart is pounding so hard, it might just splatter across my shoes. And that tiny stone.

Luke likes me, he does, he said he loves me, and I really should not be this nervous—

"This guy must really be worth something," the driver says.

His consoling words cause my heart to lurch into my throat.

"Yeah," I say. "He is."

***

I reach the cantina in good time, considering. After tipping the driver double for his unexpected role as a therapist, I swipe a hand down my tee to dry my sweaty palms and step inside the double doors, which are attempting to hold back the music blaring inside.

Almost immediately, I know it's Luke singing. Luke *and* Kai, both onstage, giving it all they've got. Luke has his lips pressed against the mic, holding it with both hands, eyes closed, and it's like a punch to the chest. The air leaves my body.

God, I've missed him. Did he get more handsome while I was gone?

Judging by the way his hair is mussed, and by the scraping edge to his voice as he sings, this week apart has been just as hard for him as it has been for me. I'm both glad and sad.

As the music swells into the chorus, I'm drawn forward, walking toward him without looking where I'm going. I collide with a chair. It clatters to the floor and his head snaps up, eyes opening. Our gaze meets for the first time in days. If it wasn't a physical impossibility, I would think he was breathing air into my lungs. His eyes are wide, brows drawn up in surprise, dark circles underneath that shouldn't be there. His voice peters away.

His smile kickstarts my heart. All this time we've been apart, I could've sworn it wasn't beating.

After an apologetic glance at Kai, who winks at me and steps up to his mic, Luke jumps off the stage and heads straight for me.

"Luke." His name is a whisper on my lips as I take a step toward him and then freeze. I don't know how to tell him how I feel. The sensation in my chest is too big to be condensed into words anyway. I need to hold him, to take his face in my hands and kiss him until he knows, once and for all, that I want to give this a try. I want to wake up tomorrow and look in the mirror and see Luke standing behind me, knowing that's how it's going to be for the rest of our lives.

He stops just in front of me, close enough to touch but an ocean apart. "Hey," he says. Kai carries the song by himself, trying to fend off a drunken Amy, who's determined to join him onstage and help him finish out the last chorus.

"Hey."

"You made it."

"Sorry I'm late."

A smile creeps into his eyes, crinkling the corners. "Do you want to go outside?"

Good plan. We shouldn't do this here, in front of everyone, with Amy's off-key voice joining Kai's, ruining what was otherwise a very nice rendition of the song. Luke turns, heading for the doors to the alley, and I follow, leaving the noisy cantina for the alleyway where this all started just a few weeks ago.

I somehow manage not to say anything until we're in the freezing air. My breath blooms white in front of my face, and my carefully prepared speech has never been so out of reach.

"How's your mom?" he asks in the slightly awkward silence that follows. Why is this awkward? We're never awkward. Even right from the beginning, we haven't been awkward.

I just need to *say* it.

"Fine. She's in rehab now. Getting help. It's been intense, but . . ." I swallow and nod. "I'm not here to talk about that."

"No?" The smile in his eyes doesn't reach his mouth, but suddenly I'm not cold anymore. His hands cup my neck, thumbs swiping over my cheeks, and at the touch, all my breath huffs from my body. "What do you have to say, then, sweetheart? And if you're here to reject me, make it fast, because the longer you wait, the harder it'll be to walk away."

"I love you," I say, and it's like the words have been waiting inside me all this time, waiting for him, waiting for my bravery in this moment in a damp, cold alleyway. I wouldn't change a damn thing. "I'm so fucking in love with you too, Luke Simmons, and it's driving me crazy. *You* drive me crazy. I thought I was scared of a long-distance relationship, but it turns out the only thing I'm scared of is losing you."

His breath gusts out of him, and he rests his forehead against mine. I can smell the beer on his breath, but more than that, he smells like *Luke*, like pine and mountain air and something undeniably spicy and male that has my pulse thrumming.

"Say it again."

"I love you." I could spend my whole life saying it over and over again. "I love you, I love you, I love you, I—"

He cuts me off with a kiss, fingers pressing against my jaw as he devours my mouth and backs me against the wall, like he's spent the last week drowning and I am his first gulp of air. I make a noise, something needy and desperate at the back of my throat, and he groans.

"I love you," he says against my lips. His body presses me into the bricks, leg between mine, and we're so hot I feel like we should be steaming. "I've missed you. Actually, I've missed *us*." He trails kisses to the tender skin below my ear. "This week I've been out of my mind, waiting and wanting to be near you again."

"Me too. Being apart helped me realize you feel like home to me now. You're my safe haven. I've never had that before. Maybe home isn't about where I come from, it's about where I belong. And that's here with you." Words are tumbling out and I'm struggling to hold on to rational thought now that I'm here and we're together, and it feels right, feels natural, feels so freaking *amazing* that I feel like I'm going to melt into a puddle of love all across the asphalt. "I love you. Do you know I've never said it before? Not like this."

He looks at me with sparkling eyes. "Never?"

"Just you. I've been waiting my whole life for you, and I never even knew it."

"Aspen . . ." My name is a breath exhaled onto my neck, and he gathers me up in his arms, hugging me tight against his chest, so tender and so strong all at once. This is the man I want, this one right here, the one who welcomed me into his family, the one who loves me more than I could ever comprehend. The man who wraps me in his amazing bear hugs.

I tilt my head back to look at him. The darkness cloaks him in mystery, the cool-tinted neon lights coating one half of his face in dim blue, shadows marking his other side. But I like him best in the light, when I can see every tiny flaw and blemish that make up who he is. I love seeing the green and brown in his eyes, the thickness of his dark eyelashes, the soft curve of his mouth when he smiles at me. The stubble he shaves daily that leaves a shadow on his jaw by the end of the day.

I can't stop my smile. "So. Does that mean we are finally, officially dating? A *real* couple?"

"You could agree to another contract if you like." He leans closer, until his breath dances across my lips. "Aspen Shaw agrees to date Luke Simmons for real."

"Don't contracts usually have an end date?"

"I don't know." He raises an eyebrow. "Do *we*?"

"You're never going to get rid of me," I tell him, wrapping my arms around his waist. It feels perfect. "Even if I have to chain you up and keep you in my basement."

"That's an odd and slightly scary image, but more importantly, I've been to your apartment. You don't have a basement."

"Then I'll get a new one. A place in the suburbs with a picket fence."

"And two point five kids?" His nose nuzzles along the line of my jaw. "And a dog?"

"Any pet as long as it's not cats."

"You sure? I'll bring the allergy medication."

I laugh then, and it's so freeing, the stress of the last week melting away. To think I was worried that he might decide I'm not worth it after all. Luke, whose hands are splayed across my hips, holding me against him. Luke, who I can already feel is hard.

That's not love, exactly, but as far as I'm concerned, it's love adjacent.

"How long do we have until you leave?" I ask.

"I pushed my flight to Sunday morning."

It's Friday now. "So we have all of Saturday."

"I *do* need to finish packing my clothes."

I grin. "I'll help you."

"You can watch," he says firmly. "If your packing is anything like your wrapping, I don't want you touching my stuff."

"Folding is overrated."

"Remind me why I love you again?"

In answer, I pull him back for another kiss, and I lose myself in him for a while. When I surface, I've half forgotten what we were talking about. This alleyway is gross, but Horny Aspen doesn't care.

"Okay," he says when we both come up for air. "Now I remember."

"Want me to remind you again?"

His finger trails along the line of my jaw and down my throat. "How about we get out of here?" he asks, eyes heating. "My house is full of boxes and no furniture, but I hear you have a rodent-free apartment." His fingers slide their way up my shirt, across bare skin that goosebumps under his touch. "I admit I've been dying to see your bedroom."

"It's pink," I assure him.

His laugh is like the sunrise. "Of course it is."

There are more things to talk about, like the logistics and how we are going to navigate a long-distance relationship, but for now, I'm happy just to order an Uber back to my place, holding his hand the entire ride.

Chapter Thirty-Two

Luke

I spent Friday night and all day Saturday at Aspen's apartment. Her bedroom really is as pink as she promised, and it's like another little piece of knowing her has fallen into place. I didn't think it was possible to love her more than I did before, but here I am, in deeper than ever.

She tells me more about her parents, about being with her dad and what that was like for her. I tell her about growing up as the runt of the litter before puberty hit and share many of my embarrassing stories of awkward dating in high school and college.

Looking back, I realize now that the younger version of me was just trying to mold myself into who I thought I should be to be accepted by others. They didn't see the true me; they saw the person I wanted them to. The person I thought I should be. Now, Aspen sees the real me, the person I've always been, and I feel more comfortable in my skin than ever before.

Over the weekend, we swap random facts and stories, eat takeout on her couch, and watch rom-coms on Netflix.

We spend a lot of time in bed. A lot.

By the end of it, we pick up my luggage, and Aspen drives me to the airport. Most of my belongings are stored in the basement of my house—Mom and Granny helped me with the last details and gave the keys to my new renter while I spent my last hours at Aspen's place. I've already thanked them, but I've put a note in my calendar to visit them for dinner when I'm back in town.

Maybe I can take Aspen with me.

A slightly flat female voice sounds over the speakers, and Aspen follows me to security, helping me check my bags in. We haven't spoken much, but every so often, I feel her hand brush mine, or she'll reach up and kiss me on the cheek.

Our steps slow as we get closer to security and the inevitable goodbye.

Back when we were just colleagues, I used to live for seeing her working opposite me. It's going to be an adjustment not seeing her every day.

I hand her a packet of Skittles I managed to buy when she was using the bathroom. "For the journey home."

"Have I told you how much I appreciate you?"

"The thing every guy wants to hear," I say dryly.

She laughs, tipping her head back, the sound coming straight from her stomach. I've never seen her smile as much as she has the past couple days. She tilts her head, the corner of her mouth pulling into a smile. I'm certain she's going to tease me, but she says, "I love you. How's that?"

"It'll do, I suppose." I wink at her.

She makes an exaggerated waiting motion, and I laugh. "I love you too. Though that was never in doubt."

"I had a few moments when I panicked, thinking you might have given up on me."

"Yeah, well, I think the point where I might have given up on you would probably not have occurred *after* I got to experience how phenomenal the sex was."

"I know that *now*," she says, rolling her eyes, though no matter how she tries, she can't stop the smile that crosses her lips. It's magnetic, the way her joy lights everything up. "It just sucks you're leaving so soon after I figured it out."

"I'm glad you got to spend that time with your mom. You both needed it."

"I know. I don't regret going back. I just regret the way I left things with you." She reaches up to stroke my cheek. "But don't worry. I have *plenty* of ideas about how I'm going to make it up to you." Her tongue runs along her bottom lip as she looks at me suggestively, and I groan.

"I have no idea how I'm going to get through these next couple of weeks."

"Oh, don't you worry. I'll show you how," Aspen teases.

"Please don't start something we don't have time to finish."

Her eyes ignite, molten and dreamy. "I just wanted to spark your imagination, to keep you in anticipation."

"Mission accomplished."

She slides a hand down my thigh. "Is this your phone in your pocket, or are you just happy I'm here?" With a wink, she slides her fingers into my pocket and retrieves the phone.

"Careful," I say, "or I really will be 'happy.' And I don't fancy getting arrested on public indecency charges."

"Not a great look for your new job," she agrees, rising onto her tiptoes and smiling up at the phone's camera. I smile just in time, and she kisses my cheek, capturing a few photos before handing it back. "There. Something to remember me by."

"The time will fly by. At least, I hope." I pull her in closer. Her hair smells like lavender-vanilla shampoo and sunlight and *Aspen*. "I need to go so I don't miss my flight," I say into the side of her head.

"So go."

Neither of us move. It's only two weeks until we can get our next fix of each other, but as ridiculous as it seems, I'm going to miss her a crazy amount. I don't want to part ways. And neither does she.

But this opportunity is too good for me to risk missing my flight, so eventually, I step back. She reluctantly does the same.

"Crush it in San Jose," she says.

"I'll see you soon."

"I'll miss you."

"I think you know how much I'll miss you."

She nudges me with her shoulder. "Keep looking at me like that, and I'll kidnap you and take you back home with me."

"I love you, Aspen Shaw." I smile down into her beautiful, flushing face, and she takes my hand, tugging it playfully.

"Okay, that's it. I'll tell Kai you've mysteriously gone missing."

Before she can say anything too loudly that strangers might misinterpret, I lean down and kiss her. When I pull back, she holds on a second longer and whispers, "When you're on the plane, check the front pocket of your backpack."

Then, she lets me go. She watches as I walk toward security, watches me all the way through, until I have to disappear into the depths of the airport, and she finally fades from sight.

When I agreed to take the promotion, I never thought leaving would feel like this.

I never thought I would have something to come back to. Who knew so much could change in a few weeks?

While I'm waiting for the plane, I choose one of the selfies Aspen took on my phone and set it as my background. I wait until I'm in my seat, by the window looking out across the asphalt and the snow-covered mountains in the distance, before checking the outside pocket of my bag.

Red lace.

Carefully, hiding it from the person on my right, I pull out the lingerie Aspen accidentally brought to the cabin. I run my fingers along the material, trying not to smile, when I find a sticky note. *For when I come visit* is written in Aspen's scrawling handwriting. I don't know when she did this, but it makes every part of my body warm. My face splits into a wide grin.

I might be an optimist, but this feels like the beginning of forever.

Epilogue

I'm almost certain Luke has packed his entire family into this picnic basket. Any second now, I'm expecting Granny Mae to pop out with some dry wit about what we're doing on this glorious Labor Day evening.

It's not like she doesn't know. We've been planning today for *months*.

It's finally the Michael Franti concert Luke got me tickets for at Christmas, and that means I get to share today with the man I love.

And, apparently, his extended kitchen.

"What did you even pack?" I grumble as I follow him up the steep grassy hill. We're at the Deer Valley Amphitheater, where lawn seating is filling up along the steep hill. Taking in the fresh mountain air, the low setting sun that casts the world in a golden glow, and the buzz of excitement around us, I smile. It's going to be a magical night.

Luke glances back at me from where he's standing, looking like a sherpa, arms laden down with blankets and extra layers for when the temperature drops later.

Summer has seen Luke in shorts and a steady rotation of casual tees, but the advent of fall has brought back all my lumberjack fantasies in full flow. He's wearing a plaid shirt over the band tee I got him, and if we weren't in a public place . . .

"Come on," he says. "I want a good view."

"I've already got a good view. Of your *ass*."

He rolls his eyes as he turns back ahead and carries on until he finds the perfect spot, unobscured by attendees sitting in lawn chairs, that looks right into the mouth of the stage. We unpack, putting a blanket on the ground and piling the others up to one side for when we need them. Luke pulls out the food as I pour us each a glass of wine.

Long-distance dating has been going well—or as well as it can, anyway. We've taken turns traveling to each other for weekends and other stolen bits of time, although he's come to Utah more often so he can see his family, too. For my birthday, we spent Memorial Day weekend exploring San Francisco together, doing all the touristy things and creating core memories together.

As far as our relationship is concerned, we're learning from each other and growing closer every day. I adore him, more than I ever thought I could love another person. And he's the same Luke he always was, but maybe a little more confident. A little more sure of himself and of me. There's no question of that now. We've been together the better part of a year now, and that feels like a milestone in itself.

I just wish he was beside me when I wake up every morning. I wish I could kiss him good night and fall asleep snuggled on the sofa as we rewatch The Office or Friends for the hundredth time.

Recently—and by that, I mean over the last few weeks—I've been looking at job postings in San Jose. I've also considered asking Kai if it'd be possible to transfer. Leaving the girls and my city would be a blow, but it would be worth it to be where Luke is. He is my home now.

"Here," I say, extending out my glass. He's setting up what looks like a whole-ass charcuterie board. "Cheers."

He clinks his glass against mine. "Cheers to us."

"Cheers to you gifting me this concert." I blow him a kiss.

I wrap a blanket around my legs and sip on the wine as the sun dips below the horizon and the shadows lengthen. Watching time pass like this is kind of magical.

"So how's Charlie's position as Granny's barn manager going?" Luke asks. "Granny can't stop talking about it."

"Charlie either. It's *so weird*; they're basically twins, born decades apart. Two peas in a pod, you know? But she's having the best time." I smile, leaning back and looking at the evening sky. To my left, trees jut into my vision, stark and silhouetted against the pale-pink sky. Soon, navy will sweep across and darken the sky until the stars peep through.

Luke props himself on his elbow so he can look at me. "What about Annabelle? You said she was expanding or something?"

"Oh, yeah, her medical spa wing. It's almost complete, and it looks *fabulous*. She says she'll give us all treatments for free. But she's also already filling in some prepaid bookings for services, even though it won't be up and running for a few months."

"Sounds like she's crushing it."

"She *is*. And Lina's just finished a duet with Keith Urban for the soundtrack of some Western movie coming out, so I'm hoping that's going to be her big break. He's really nice, apparently." I shift to face Luke. "It's like this year has watered all our seeds, and we're blooming."

"Pando," he teases. Granny told him about that a long time ago. I've come to love the nickname, though, and his family calls me that half the time now. Luke mostly just calls me Aspen, though, like he doesn't want anything more than my name on his lips.

I lean forward to kiss him, savoring the moment. The concert starts in about fifteen minutes and the crowd is amping up, but we're lost in our little moment, caught in our bubble, and it feels like everything I've ever wanted is coming true all at once.

His phone buzzes. He sighs and kisses me again before checking it. "It's Mom," he says. "I *told* her when the concert starts."

I spear some cheese with a toothpick and pop it in my mouth with a red grape, which bursts across my tongue. "Answer it. We've got time."

He sighs again, the sound more loving than exasperated, and hits accept. I can hear Ruth start talking a mile a minute, asking if we've arrived, and if the basket is packed with enough food, and if everything is going well. While Luke catches up, I check my phone to find a message from Mom waiting for me. She's been out of rehab a couple months now and is happily living at home with Dad. Both clean. Both sober. I've flown out a few times to see them, and Mom wants to make plans to come see me this time—something she's never done before.

We're not perfect, not even close, but we're doing better than I could've ever imagined a year ago. I'm proud of how far we've come in patching our family back together. I beam up at Luke. He holds out his phone to me.

"Granny wants to speak to Pando," he says, his tone serious but a lopsided smile tugging at the corner of his mouth.

"I know what this is about." I take the phone, pressing it to my ear. "Before you say anything, you do have *other* grandchildren."

She cackles, and I do my best not to smile. Luke and I have talked about kids. We'd both like them someday, but there's no rush. Something Granny Mae doesn't seem to have gotten into her head, seeing as her catchphrase is apparently "no time like the present."

Considering we're in a very public space, I would argue that is categorically untrue.

"A matriarch can never have too many grandbabies," she says. Charlie called her "The Matriarch" once, and Granny has really taken it on board. "Enjoy your concert, honey. And don't forget—"

"Okay," Luke says loudly. "That's enough. We'll see you at the cabin later, Granny. Don't wait up." He sets his eyes on me, his grin returning in full force, though more mischievous than before.

"Luke." I point a finger at him. "What's that grin for? Because if you tell me you want babies right this instant, I'm obliged to tell you that—"

"Not yet. But I do have something to tell you." He finishes dishing up the potato salad and hands me a fork, his beam all but overflowing. "About work."

"You've been offered another promotion?"

"You guessed it. But this one comes with a great perk." He waits, just to mess with me, to draw out the tension. "I'm transferring back home!"

He doesn't even finish the sentence before I scream and throw myself into his arms, knocking the potato salad sideways, and hold his face in my hands so I can kiss him. And kiss him and kiss him and kiss him.

He's coming *home*.

This is the thing I've been dreaming of since the day he left.

"But how?" I ask as soon as I've collected myself enough to breathe normally again. "I thought advancement in the company would keep you in California longer?"

"With the merger, the company's restructuring, and I can transfer back to the Utah office, complete with a raise and promotion." He beams again, and I just *know* he's as delighted about this as I am. "And before you get carried away, there's more."

"Too late. I'm already carried away," I say with a laugh, then smooth my thumbs across his cheeks. He has such beautiful cheekbones, such gorgeous bone structure. But his eyes are my favorite feature, soft and warm and shades of brown and green that remind me of sunlit paths through an aspen grove.

Of mountain hikes and new adventures and home.

Luke is coming home.

His fingers tighten on my waist, and I give him my widest, best smile. "Tell me," I say. "I want to hear it. Every detail."

"Kai agreed to let me work remotely for the next two weeks," Luke says. "So this trip is for good. I'm here to stay."

This time, I squeal so loudly and throw my arms around his neck so violently that he tumbles backward onto the blankets, pulling me halfway on top of him. That's fine—we can stay like this forever. As long as he wants. Until the sun comes back up, or for a week, a month. He's not leaving.

He's back home for *good*.

"I hope you don't mind me crashing at your place for a while," he says between kisses.

"Mind? You can *stay*. Although . . . my apartment's crap. The lease is up at the end of next month, though, so maybe we can look for a place? Together?"

"Our place."

I replay the words in my head because they sound *so* good put together like that. *Our place.* We're going to find our place. Make it ours. Share our lives.

"I can't believe you're finally *all* mine." I press my nose into his neck and kiss the soft skin there, feeling his body respond. That's the cheat code, the instant way to get him in the mood. "Every last bit."

"I have been since I first met you."

"I can't decide if that sounds cheesy or adorably sweet."

He laughs, then sits up as the amphitheater lights go down, turning me so my back is against his chest, his arms around me. Maybe it hearkens back to sitting in his family's hot tub together, which led to our first time making love, but this is one of my favorite positions to sit in now. It's relaxing, peaceful, comforting. Wrapped in Luke's arms always feels special.

Michael Franti steps onto the stage, hands up to acknowledge the cheering, his signature upbeat energy filling the stage. The loyal fans go wild. I scream with everyone else, whooping with all my heart. He's older now, but still full of energy, bounding around the stage as the band starts playing "Life is Better With You."

I turn my head back, gazing up at Luke, and grin. Because life really, really is.

Also By

The Universe and You

Pre-order your copy now!

Charlie has met her match in Liam, the Olympic equestrian show jumper that's taken her dream job. You'll enjoy this enemies-to-lovers, opposites attract, steamy romance out in early 2024. Pre-orders available now.

Read how it all began. Aspen & Luke's adorable meet cute prequel novella is available at no cost for newsletter subscribers. Get your free copy of the book today

About the Author

Shannon Paige has been a storyteller all her life. When her three adult children flew the nest, she finally took the time to start completing some of the dozens of half-finished story ideas she's been fussing with for years. With the support of her husband, the literal boy-next-door she married decades ago, she is enjoying writing swoon-worthy storylines about perfectly imperfect people, and including a dash of heat, humor and heart into their happily ever afters. Shannon resides in the Rocky Mountains, and you can usually find her in one of two extremes; traveling the globe with her hubby or snuggled up with a book, reluctant to leave her cozy home.